The Bridge at Wilson Park

Frank Rubolino

A Detective Gianni Basso Novel

Outskirts Press, Inc.
http://www.outskirtspress.com

Paperback ISBN: 978-1-9772-0368-7

Outskirts Press and the "OP" logo are trademarks belonging to Outskirts Press, Inc.

PRINTED IN THE UNITED STATES OF AMERICA

DEDICATION

Dedicated to Sandra and Barbara for their inspiration and encouragement to complete this project.

CONTENTS

LIST OF CHARACTERS

Basso Family

Gianni Basso

Janice Turner Basso

Mario Basso

Maria Venuto Basso

Gianluca Basso

Angelina Basso

Alberto Basso

Francesco Basso

Alfredo Basso

Curto Family

Julius Curto

Eszter Abadi Curto

Robert Curto

Ronald Curto

Santiago Family

Diego Santiago

Monica Marconi Santiago

Damian DeRiso

Roberto Santiago

Barbara Santiago DeRiso

Sebastian Santiago

Central Penn Warehousing Inc. Employees

Tomás Rojas

Jose Caderas

Raphael Pino

Matias Martinez

(Carlos Martinez)

Felipe Rodriguez

Joaquin Gonzalez

Lucas Lopez

Rodrigo Sanchez

Jose Garcia

Juan Garcia

John Halbrook

(Annette Halbrook)

Susan Aspect

Jennifer Ambrose

(Gregory Ambrose)

Ruth Biantano

June Curtis

Grace Fuller

John Caravacca

I

City Employees

Jeff McIntyre	Jack Bearden
Josh Brady	Ralph O'Brian
Mary Miller	Marcus Washington
Nancy Kowalski	Bill Bixby
George Ziegler	Otto Schmidt
Gerri Allen	

Greenfield

Antonio Jackson (Speed)	DeMeritus Johnson (Yoyo)
Saul Bernstein	Joe Benjamin

Bogota

Alejandro Moreno	Hernando Gomez
Michele Sanchez	

Marines

Joseph Bennett	John Hanratty

Others

Matt Inovaca	Giuseppe Condoro
Father McGinty	Daniel Steele
Carlos Martinez	Joan McCabe

EPIGRAPH

"We are the sum total of our experiences. Those experiences – be they positive or negative – make us the person we are, at any given point in our lives. And, like a flowing river, those same experiences, and those yet to come, continue to influence and reshape the person we are, and the person we become. None of us are the same as we were yesterday, nor will be tomorrow."

B.J. Neblett

PREFACE

They say a picture is worth a thousand words. In this case, the cover photo of this book is worth as many thousand words as this book contains. When a friend sent me that picture and asked for my thoughts and reaction to it, the story you are about to read began to unfold in my mind. I immediately saw the bridge and the park it spans as a potential crime scene for murder. Encouraged to continue with and develop that initial concept, I allowed my imagination to construct a fictitious park abutting a fabricated suburb of a typical USA city. From there, the characters developed one by one in scenarios populated with people representing a cultural and ethnic mix of North Americans, South Americans, Europeans, and Middle Easterners. All of it came about because of this one picture. The story does include certain factual historic, demographic, and geographic data and was influenced at times by my life experiences.

Special thanks to Sandra Geiselman, Barbara Eaves, Bruce and Joan Boni, Linda & Perry Knezevich, Dan Molinaro, and Donn Moll for their astute insight, professional advice, and open-minded commentary on this book's content.

CHAPTER 1: THE BRIDGE

"3 a.m. Why does it always seem to happen at 3 a.m.?" Detective Gianni Basso mumbled aloud as he was jarred awake by the incessant buzzing of his cell phone. Stumbling out of bed, he began thinking of more pleasant times at Wilson Park, like the time his father took him there to fly his new kite, complete with painted warrior signs on its face. Or playing softball on the field that served as a base for all sorts of outdoor activities, including an annual dog show allowing owners to strut with their preened pets. Or swimming in the pool during the all too short summer days when life seemed to have no problems for a young boy. Or watching the parade of joggers circle the park's perimeter connected by the antique stone bridge that spanned the creek below and was the most photographed spot in the park.

Basso was reasonably tall, being slightly over six feet with jet black hair and distinguished good looks typically associated with males having a DNA sourced from the

Mediterranean region. He had maintained himself physically throughout his life, which was boding him well as he entered his fifties. After splashing his face with cold water attempting to release himself from the fog of a deep dream he was experiencing before the call, he dressed hurriedly and began the trip across town to the park to answer the call to duty. It wasn't always a tough neighborhood. It wasn't always a place that most people avoided for fear of being mugged. It wasn't always the highest crime scene area in the city. When the population consisted primarily of Italian immigrants, one could stroll the park's lanes at any time of day or evening, comfortable in knowing a casual meeting with a neighbor or friend would likely occur at some point during the route.

When Basso started working, the park was the center point of the city's social life. Picnics in the grove, bands playing at the carousal – this is how he remembered Wilson Park. But as the year's passed, he saw it all change, as inevitably all things do. He saw most of the children of the Italian immigrants grow up, go off to college, and relocate to wherever their new careers beckoned. He saw the Italian population age and be replaced with Hispanics, Asians, and Blacks. The population trended toward lower income residents, and inevitably the predatory drug pushers followed. Basso saw the police department's caseloads swell when this influx of drugs led to the predictable surge in crime.

When he approached the park, it reminded him again of happier days, only because the spinning of numerous police car halogen red and blue emergency lights simulated a carnival atmosphere, as did the long string of yellow tape cordoning off the crime scene. The extra-tall portable lighting towers brought in by the police illuminated the entire area and turned night into day.

Wilson Park is situated on roughly 500 acres of land bordering the Harrisburg suburb of Greenfield on two sides and industrial complexes on the others. A hiking/jogging trail of about three miles encircles the perimeter. The land was donated to the city in the 1930s by a wealthy steel baron who made his fortune in the early years of the twentieth century before labor unions gained significant power and before income taxes were enacted in 1913. Industry leaders amassed great wealth before these two events occurred, but the growing strength of labor unions cut into their profitability. Congress's ratification of the 16th amendment to the US Constitution permanently empowering the government to collect income taxes further constricted their riches.

Basso parked on a trail road opposite the stone bridge and climbed down the reasonably steep grade to the bottom of the ravine. "How long has she been dead," Basso asked Medical Examiner Jeff McIntyre, who was hovering over the body.

"Probably several hours," he responded looking up over the rims of his glasses. "She wasn't killed here. If you notice the grass pattern from up at the road to down here under the bridge, you see she was dragged down, probably feet first given the way her dress is pulled up above her waist."

"Any evidence of sexual assault?" Basso asked.

"No, there is no bruising on her thighs, no signs of sexual trauma or evidence of a struggle, but she did have sex within hours of being killed, from the limited examination we've already done. I'll know more once we get her back to the lab."

Basso looked at the beautiful blond corpse, as though the word beauty and death could possibly be uttered in the same sentence. She was in her late twenty's or early thirty's, was pristinely dressed in a short Saks garment too rich for this neighborhood, and she still was wearing diamond stud earrings, a thin gold Tiffany bracelet, and a solid gold Lady President Rolex watch. "Too classy to be a working girl. And we can obviously rule out robbery," Basso replied. "What are these bruises on her neck?"

McIntyre explained she had been strangled with a rough-edged cord, and she was surely dead before she was moved to this site, since there is no bleeding from the scrapes on her arms caused by being dragged down here.

"Who found the body? This is a very secluded part of the park," asked Basso.

"A patrolman who was making his regular rounds of the park. That's the one over there."

"Do we know who she is?"

"No ID was found on the body," quipped McIntyre. Just then patrolman Josh Brady approached the two.

"Detective, I found this small handbag over there in the bushes. Looks like she was a lawyer – there are several business cards in the wallet that probably are hers."

Basso read the card aloud, "Jennifer Ambrose – Attorney at Law." He knew the name well. She was the main lawyer for the head of the drug cartel that had turned this once peaceful town into a war zone.

"Did you see anything else when you spotted the body, Brady?"

"Yes, first I saw her down here as I sprayed my flash light around from my position on the bridge, and immediately thereafter, I looked up and saw a car speeding away along the trail up there. It did not have its lights on, so I was unable to get a plate number or even the color of the vehicle."

"Well, looks like I've got my work cut out for me. This is not going to be much fun starting the investigation with a notorious Colombian crime boss who is sarcastically said to be made of Teflon. Despite all our efforts over the years, no charges have ever been able to stick."

CHAPTER 2: THE DETECTIVES

Gianni Basso returned to his car and started back to the station in downtown Harrisburg. As a 25-year veteran of the police force, he was well accustomed to these emergency calls in the middle of the night. In fact, they played a big role in his current marital position – his ex-wife found it hard to adjust to his erratic hours, and she found it difficult accepting the uncertainty of his surviving such a dangerous job. But Basso was used to the exposure a risky job entails. Right out of high school, he joined the Navy, working himself up to a skilled position as a Navy SEAL. And more than once, his life was in jeopardy, but he seemed to have nine of them. He dodged bullets in far-off lands, extracted himself from dangerous and delicate situations, and was the go-to guy for tough assignments involving stealth and its associated danger. Executing covert assignments seemed to be his forte.

On one mission in 1986, for which he was forbidden to discuss with anyone, including any family member, Basso and a team of five other Navy SEALs were dropped from a helicopter into the Khuzestan Province near the Iran-Iraq border. Both countries had been at war since 1980 when Iraq tried to annex this oil-rich province against Iran's resistance. The border dispute had been going on for years. There was growing tension between the United States and Iran, resulting in the USA siding with Iraq together with the Soviet Union, and most Arab nations. This left Iran without any outside support. The SEAL assignment was to destroy a strategically located ammunition depot Iran maintained in the area. They made their way to their assigned destination under concealment of darkness, being out of communication with anyone at their base. They knew if captured, they would surely be subjected to brutal torture and probably executed as a political show to the world to deter anyone from trying to infiltrate their land. Iran was notorious for mistreating prisoners of war in the most inhumane ways. Each member of the team carried a substantial quantity of explosives, but Basso was the leader of the group and self-elected person to set the first charges while the others either maintained a covering position or planted explosives in less-critical sections. The mission came off successfully, the depot was destroyed in a blaze that lit up the night sky, and the SEAL team made their way to the rendezvous point where they were airlifted back to the base. Although tensions persisted for some time, the United Nations eventually brokered a ceasefire between Iraq and Iran in 1988 with no borders being altered by the conflict.

After six years in the Navy, he returned to his home state of Pennsylvania and attended Pennsylvania State University in University Park under the GI Bill, earning a degree in sociology. It was at Penn State that he met Janice Turner, an Anglo-Saxon Protestant with a cultural background completely different from his Italian Catholic upbringing. But their innate sex drives and a confirmation that opposites do truly attract caused both to be drawn to each other. They married in his senior year, and after graduation, moved back to Basso's suburban hometown just outside of Harrisburg.

Harrisburg is the state capital, but it is not a large city. It ranks ninth in size compared to all Pennsylvania cities with about 50,000 people. However, the collective Harrisburg-Lebanon-York area has about a million and a quarter people, making it the third most populous area in the state. It sits about 107 miles west of Philadelphia. Arguably Harrisburg's most defining geographic characteristic is its strategic placement along the eastern bank of the Susquehanna River. The road and walkway running parallel to the river as it flows past the city offer innumerable vistas to ponder the distinct natural beauty. The governor's mansion overlooks this grand waterway. The river's depth is deceptive, however; the water is remarkably shallow at points, causing residents to suggest in jest that the river could freeze solidly during the depths of winter.

During the 19th century, Harrisburg was a heavily industrialized city, but today most of the workforce are either government or military personnel. Its contributions to American history center around its role in the western migration of the colonial population, as a training center for tens of thousands of new recruits during the American Civil War, and as a key player in the industrial revolution.

Basso's return to Harrisburg caused him to realize he wanted more from life than what an undergraduate degree provided, so he accepted a job as a security guard and enrolled in a night-school graduate program that the University of Pennsylvania in Philadelphia offered at their satellite campus in Harrisburg. Juggling a full-time job and a heavy class load was a challenge, but Basso persevered and graduated with a degree in criminology, which was a natural threshold for entry into his first significant non-military job as a police officer on the Harrisburg force. Harrisburg's police bureau has about 130 officers on its roles.

Basso attended the rigorous Police Academy and climbed up the ladder of the force, starting as a beat policeman and advancing up several levels before sitting for the detective's examination, which he passed easily. Both college degrees played a large role in his easy assimilation into the rank of police detective. He was now a veteran police officer with many years of distinguished service.

From the car, he called his partner, Assistant Detective Julius Curto, who was just rising and getting ready to go to work. Curto and Basso had similar backgrounds as first-generation Americans. Basso's father Mario emigrated to the USA from Potenza in southern Italy, while Curto's family came from Sulmona, Italy near the Adriatic Sea. Their parents were pursuing the American dream, sacrificing everything so their children would have a better life than they experienced in Italy.

"Get over to the medical examiner's office right away. We have a hot one on our hands. Diego Santiago's chief legal counsel Jennifer Ambrose has been murdered, and I want to know everything about her. Find out from them what she ate for dinner. Maybe we can get a clue as to where she dined last night. And check her credit card receipts for the last months. I want to know her spending habits. And don't forget to print out the LUDs for the last month on her cell phone, office phone, and home phone. I want to know who she has been talking with in the last few weeks."

Curto had been on the force about nine years, having transferred to homicide after spending several years as an undercover police officer trying to penetrate the local drug cartel. He joined the force after a tour of duty in the US Marines. He met and married his wife Eszter Abadi while in Iraq, and she relocated back to the states with him after his tour of duty was over. Unlike Basso, he had two children, and another was on the way.

"I'll get right on it. We have been trying to get that bastard for a long time, so maybe this thing will lead to something. See you later in the day at the station."

Basso arrived at the station just as the night shift was leaving and the day shift checking in for duty. He picked up a cup of coffee in the lunch room before proceeding to his second-floor office up the wide wooden stairs facing the front doors. The precinct building was built in 1940, and the red brick structure with creaky floor boards and leaking roof showed all the signs of its age. His desk was piled high with reports on the dozen or so cases he was juggling, but since high-profile murders operated on a last in–first out basis, he knew this Ambrose case was going to take precedence, and he didn't need his captain, Ralph O'Brian, to tell him so. He called out to his administrative assistant Gerri Allen to bring in the complete file on Diego Santiago.

Allen remarked, "What's up, Gene?" using the Americanization of his first name, although John technically is the accurate English translation for Gianni. Nevertheless, Basso found the change beneficial to him in defraying the stigma of being an immigrant's son and actually liked the sound of it.

"We have a new homicide to add to the backlog. Someone killed attorney Jennifer Ambrose, who was legal counsel for Santiago, and dumped her body under the bridge in Wilson Park. I have Julius running down some data at the medical examiner's office, and I will need you to compile as much information as you can about her and the work she was doing for Santiago. I know attorney-client privilege survives the death of the client, but I do not know what can be made available to the police when the lawyer is murdered."

Allen did her best, as she always did, at acting extremely professional in the office to avoid any suspicion of her ongoing affair with Basso, an association strictly forbidden by departmental policy. "We have a massive amount of data on him, but I am not sure how much there is on his lawyers. I'll look into it right now."

Basso watched Allen's graceful movement as she exited his office, but he also went out of his way to avoid any suggestion of impropriety when it came to her. He sank back in his chair and pondered his options for initiating the investigation, starting probably with Ambrose's ex-husband and any known romantic associations she might have had, either before or after her divorce.

CHAPTER 3: THE MORGUE

Julius Curto never could get used to the aroma of death that hovered over the medical examiner's lab like the fog trying to penetrate the atmosphere while competing with the early morning sunrise for stage rights. He had seen enough death in the military and on this job to last a lifetime, and although it no longer bothered him, it was something with which he never became fully comfortable. He made his way down the long corridor to Lab A where he presumed correctly he would find Jeff McIntyre and the body of Jennifer Ambrose.

"What have you learned so far, Jeff?" he asked, trying to be nonchalant in a situation that would make most people uncomfortable.

McIntyre was hovering over the body decked in a white gown, rubber gloves, and a surgical face mask. He put down a cutting instrument to respond. "Her ex-husband has already been in to confirm the identity of the body. As I already told your partner, she was strangled with a rough-edged cord. Looks like death was reasonably prompt soon after the attack, so that suggests the killer was very strong or as a minimum had very strong hands and arms. It certainly suggests a male but does not rule out all women. I also told Gene she had sex shortly before she was killed, but what I have just now discovered is she was pregnant, probably in the early stages, since she shows no outward evidence of it. I'll pinpoint that more precisely later."

"What about her stomach contents?" interrupted Curto.

"Death came soon after eating, so we have definitive evidence of pasta, artichokes, and several other ingredients associated with an Italian meal. She was not inebriated, but she did consume a moderate amount of red wine, which from my tests point to an Italian varietal. Given that women of this class are not likely to cook at home, it is not a big reach to say she had dinner at an Italian restaurant, probably an upscale one if she stayed consistent with her station in life."

"Are there any other bruises on her other than from the neck cord?"

"No, none other than the body scratches I attribute to being moved from the place of death to under the park bridge. She has no other contusions and shows no evidence of scratching her assailant or putting up much of a struggle. From that, I surmise it was not a standard mugging. She probably knew her attacker and was off-guard when it occurred. There is, however, something unusual about the fibers of her dress. Mingled with those of the expensive material of her clothing were other strands of a cheaper variety one would not likely see in a Saks Fifth Avenue piece. This lady reeked of expensive taste, and that fiber is inconsistent with such a style."

"When do you think we can have your full written report, Jeff?"

"I should have it fully documented in a couple of days. I'll have it sent over to you as soon as it's ready."

Curto left the lab with a lot of facts and a bit of conjecture but with enough preliminary data for him and Basso to formulate a plan of attack. He enjoyed working with the detective, whom he respected for his knowledge, confidence, and professional investigative manner. Curto was assimilating many of Basso's qualities into his operating methods, aspiring to reach that level on the force in what would be the shortest time anyone had achieved full detective status. He was considered a wonder boy by his peers, having parlayed a strong favorable record as an undercover policeman into a starting level position with the detective bureau, and specifically the homicide sector, which was considered the glamor segment of the force and a sure sign of upward mobility. Curto did worry, however, about how his marriage would play out with his bosses, since being married to a Middle Eastern woman in this post 9-11 era was not the best profile to ensure fast movement up the civil service ladder. In his undercover role, it never was an issue, since he was almost always out of the office fold and away from the politics. But now he showed a higher profile daily, and his marital status did occasionally cause him to wonder.

Still, he was happy with his marriage to Eszter and never thought twice about wanting to bring her back with him to America after his Iraq tour. He received special permission from the marines to marry while still in Iraq, which was not always an easy approval to secure. She had provided him with two sons, and they were expecting a girl this time. Through having saved his Marine signup bonus, he was able to afford a starter home in Camp Hill across the Susquehanna River from Harrisburg. Their first born arrived only a few months after getting back home. Curto had already asked Basso if he would be the godfather for the new baby girl, but he and his wife had not yet picked the godmother. To all outside appearances, Curto had adjusted well to his reentry into civilian life and into the role of being a husband.

Although his home in Camp Hill is closer to Philadelphia than Pittsburgh, Curto adopted the Pittsburgh Steelers as his favorite National Football League team. He always had been a very competitive person. The physicality of the game intrigued him, and the team's long history of being a winner, including a record six Super Bowl championships, matched the way he tackled assignments. Winning was important to him. This same physicality showed in the way he participated in sports as well. Curto was a very aggressive squash player. Dominating an opponent was a driving force for him on the court.

Socially, Curto always had an easy time with women, based on his outgoing personality and his devastatingly good looks. He broke his share of hearts as a young man, and many were puzzled by his choice of a foreign-born wife, although Eszter was by all accounts a beautiful woman with a bronze skin tone and dark, penetrating eyes. She spoke three languages fluently and had an intelligence level far superior to most of the women Curto ever dated. They made quite a handsome couple when seen together.

He left the medical examiner's building and headed across town to his precinct, stopping off to get an early lunch and to call Eszter, but her phone rang six times and then went to voice mail. Puzzled, he finished his lunch and headed for the station.

CHAPTER 4: THE PRECINCT

As Basso began formulating the investigative path he and Curto would take, his mind slipped back to three years ago when Janice told him she could no longer tolerate the tension his job created in her. The finality of her statement caught Basso by surprise; he knew for some time she was not happy with the job he did, but he never suspected she would actually make up her mind to leave him. Basso tried desperately to dissuade her from leaving, since he was very much in love with her. He made an impassioned plea to her to reconsider.

"I know you are unhappy with our lifestyle. I love the work I do, but I don't want to lose you. Think about the years when we were happy together. I know we can recapture that if only we put forth the effort."

All this was to no avail; Janice Basso was determined to escape the life of a police officer's wife, and nothing he could say was going to change her mind. The divorce was swift and uncomplicated, given they had no children, and she made more money than he did. He was given the house in the settlement, since Janice planned to leave the city. It took a while for him to accept it, but he did finally come to the realization that the infallible cure for a broken heart was time and distance – and her leaving town provided the means for him to recover, albeit very slowly.

It was some time before he could bring himself to get back into circulation. After all, he thought, he was not a young man anymore, and the idea of again going through the entire courting process turned him off. So, he was quite surprised at himself when he accepted an invitation from Allen to have a drink after work. She was a dozen years younger than he and had been divorced for several years before she joined the force. Over cocktails, they talked about many things, mainly cases that were ongoing, but gradually the conversation got off the business theme and into more personal subjects. He told her about his passion for free, unstructured jazz music, and she discussed how she appreciated classical music. This difference in musical tastes was not a deal breaker, and the evening ended up back at her apartment, again surprising Basso at the swift pace this liaison had taken. He was a little hesitant to proceed down this slippery slope, but the passion in both had been building up all night, and neither could resist the temptation. Since then, they saw each other on a regular basis, but never in public where they could be seen by anyone on the force. The refreshing part of the relationship was she was part of what he did for a living, and he did not have to justify himself to her.

He snapped back to reality quickly when she brought in a file they had on Santiago that also contained information on Ambrose.

"This is only a small part of Santiago's file, but this one does contain some data on surveillance we did that included a meeting with Ambrose."

Long ago, they had gotten a warrant to tap Santiago's phones and film his actions outside the building he called his office. What was divulged in this specific surveillance tape was information that Ambrose was involved with someone in Santiago's organization.

"Did any names get mentioned about the person she was seeing?"

"No, they were very cautious about getting specific. It is quite possible they knew about the surveillance warrant and acted accordingly."

"Anything else of interest in this particular file?"

"No," she replied, "Other than that Santiago was not very happy about her affair and felt it had the potential to compromise her position with his organization."

"Give me a list of every known member of the Santiago gang, along with any rap sheet we have on them. That should be a good starting point into this crime. Has Curto gotten back from his visit to McIntyre's lab?"

"I'll check and send him right in if he is here," Allen said as she left his office.

Curto came in and sat down to tell everything he had learned from his morning visit, including the big surprise that Ambrose was pregnant. This really piqued Basso's interest after what he had just learned from Allen and the tape about Ambrose's involvement with a member of Santiago's organization.

"Why would a classy dame like Ambrose get mixed up with an associate of Santiago, when she was intimately familiar with all the dirt attributed to every one of them?" Basso asked somewhat rhetorically.

"Who can explain the actions of any woman," quipped Curto. He felt he never could really understand the female sex despite all the entanglements he had survived over the years. Allen brought in the list of Santiago gang members, which numbered ten. All had criminal records that included significant prison time, and some had gone this route on more than one occasion.

Allen volunteered another finding she had just learned. "The police found a late model Jaguar sedan parked in a public garage. The garage attendant knew Jennifer Ambrose as a frequent customer at that location. When he saw the news of her death, he called the police. The car was impounded and thoroughly swept for anything that would explain why she left it there. All their tests came up negative."

"Interesting, Gerri. Wonder why she parked it there. It suggests she left that area with someone else or was abducted in that area. I would like to split up this Santiago list with you, Julius, but it is best I do that alone. I also want to interview Ambrose's ex-husband. He could possibly have a clue as to whom she might have been seeing. We must learn who had dinner with her last night and what time it ended. Gerri, get me the address of Ambrose's ex. I think Julius and I should pay him a visit as soon as possible."

Basso had Allen call the dental offices of Gregory Ambrose and learned he was out of the office for a few days, so the interview would have to wait.

The working relationship between Basso and Curto was strong from the start, but their personal relationship was firmly cemented three years ago. Curto had been with the homicide division about a year following his stint as an undercover policeman. He and Basso were on the job interviewing a suspect in a child molestation/murder case.

The man had a criminal record, having been convicted many years ago of molesting a four-year-old boy, so his name automatically popped up on the department's database. The man was out of prison for about a month. He was currently on parole and was being monitored regularly. The city had seen a rash of child-related crimes at that time, causing school grounds and playgrounds to be guarded not only by police officers but by neighborhood watch groups as well.

While talking to the man, Basso received a call from headquarters telling both to return to the station immediately. Puzzled by the call, they abandoned their current person of interest and headed to the station. "Wonder what it could be, Gene."

"We'll learn soon enough." They reported in to Captain Ralph O'Brian with a tinge of anxiety. O'Brian asked both to sit down, thereupon telling them that Curto's younger son Ronald, who was four years old at that time, was missing. Eszter Curto had frantically called the police station, asking to speak to her husband, and when told he was on assignment, she spoke directly to O'Brian.

Eszter relayed she had gone to the daycare center to pick up the boy, only to be told he had already been collected by his father. Eszter knew that could not be possible, since her husband routinely told her where he could be reached, and this day, he said he would be miles away investigating a case with Basso. Besides, he had never picked up either of his sons; his job schedule simply would not allow it. Thus, the people in charge at the day care center did not know him and released the boy to an impersonator.

Curto was in a state of shock. He saw this type of crime regularly but never dreamed it would ever involve a family member. The first thing O'Brian said was Curto would not be assigned to the case. He was put on desk duty temporarily to protect him from doing anything rash as well as to avoid any negative impact on the investigation. Personal involvement in a case was not acceptable. Basso mentioned that the FBI had to be called, and he wanted to work with them, since he was familiar with the school area and the family and could be of assistance.

Curto demanded he be included, but O'Brian overrode his objection. It would also violate departmental policy were he to participate. While O'Brian was contacting the FBI, Basso went right to work. He went back to the database of known sex offenders, since he surmised this was not a kidnapping for ransom. Everybody knows what police officers earn. Basso spent the entire evening combing through the on-line files. The man they were questioning when O'Brian's call came was automatically eliminated from the list. Basso isolated three names he judged could possibly be suspects. All had similar histories, and all were out of prison with addresses in the area, but one name stood out. While reviewing the case details, this man had been in the Marines in the same unit and at the same time as Curto. He read that Curto was the arresting officer and testified at the man's court-martial. The man was found guilty in the military court and in a state court. Being tried in both courts is permitted by law. Thus, the records were readily available to Basso. The man served seven years in prison and was recently released on probation.

Feeling this was too much of a coincidence, Basso immediately contacted the FBI, gave them the information, and within hours they conducted a raid on the man's home. Basso was permitted to accompany them, and they were successful in rescuing Ronald Curto. The perpetrator was arrested on the charge of kidnapping. He wanted revenge for going to prison based on Curto's testimony. Ronald was not hurt, but he was in an extreme emotional state, continually crying out for his mother and father.

Curto pledged eternal gratitude to Basso, whose dogged detective work resolved a very bad situation promptly before any harm came to his son. After that, the bond between the two men grew substantially.

CHAPTER 5: THE ORIGINS

Diego Santiago came to the United States with his parents when he was twelve years old. His father etched out a meager existence as a janitor in the apartment building where they lived in the Hispanic sector of the city. The family was fleeing political oppression in Colombia, and their entry to the US was uncontested under those grounds. They chose the northeast sector of the country, thinking this would give them an added buffer to the evils of their home country. Santiago learned English very quickly, although that could not be said for his parents, who struggled with the changes coming to America brought. But by living among other Spanish speaking immigrants in the district, they could manage the daily demands of a city so remote from their own. Santiago did well at school, but he realized very early that success for immigrants in this country was a long tedious process of overcoming the bias that permeated the entire social environment. He was determined not to fall into the rut his father was forced to endure. Enslaved by someone else at a minimum wage job was not his idea of the American dream.

So, in his early teens when he was approached by a well-dressed, stylish man who asked him in Spanish if he would like to make $100, Santiago jumped at the chance to earn quickly what took his father several days to earn. The job seemed simple enough; all he had to do was deliver a small packet to a neighborhood business man and return with a package from the man. He did not question what was in either bundle, knowing full well the transaction had to be illicit if he was being offered such a large sum for doing virtually nothing. Santiago also was fully aware of the underground economy that existed in the neighborhood just like what he knew sustained the economy in the town in which he was born in Colombia.

The transaction went down smoothly without incident, and the well-dressed stylish man was pleased with having found a runner who seemed to be street smart and did not ask any questions. Santiago continued to act as the middleman between what he soon confirmed were cocaine and heroin sales transactions. The product was sourced somehow from the man's contacts in Colombia and distributed throughout the neighborhood by young boys like himself. He continued working for the well-dressed stylish man throughout his high school years, gradually building up a substantial reservoir of ready cash. Over these teen years, he learned how the drugs were smuggled into the country hidden in carloads of foodstuffs destined for area grocers. It came through the Port of Philadelphia, via the ship channel in the Delaware River that led to the Atlantic Ocean. He learned payment for these shipments occurred through local bank deposits that were then transferred to a bank in the Bahamas, then to a bank in the Cayman Islands, then to a bank in Bogota, with each transfer always in a different amount that did not correspond with the receipt. He learned the shipper in Colombia was Alejandro Moreno, one of the most powerful and notorious drug lords in South America. And he learned that the profits for the stateside part of this enterprise were enormous. But as often happens when people realize large gains from little effort in a short period of time, the desire for more caused Santiago to rethink his position. He had built up a network of his own during these years for the distribution end of the business, and he knew all the contacts, finance people, and other links in the chain that composed this overly lucrative business.

So systematically, he initiated a series of takeover moves to allow him to control the entire stateside part of the business. The well-dressed stylish man mysteriously disappeared one evening, and Santiago announced to the man's local superior that he was taking over his franchise. In a year or so, the same tactic was used to insert himself up a level, all the while growing more powerful and more ruthless and more feared. Eventually, the entire chain on the East Coast was replaced by Santiago's organization. He sat as the kingpin of the whole operation, generating millions of dollars of profits locally and laundering millions of dollars back to Colombia.

His enterprise, registered under the name Central Penn Warehousing, Inc., was now equal to a Fortune 500 company, complete with a professional group of business analysts, marketing experts, accountants, administrative professionals, and a staff of lawyers, plus the necessary enforcement thugs who were required to manage such a large underground network of workers. There were two distinct sectors of the business: one that operated as an administrative and logistic arm for the legitimate business, and the other as an enforcement arm for the illegal portion, which included processing, distribution, and collection activities.

Santiago's empire in the early years when his drug business was in the fledgling stages was complemented by a vast gambling network. He ran the city's largest numbers racket. This form of betting had been entrenched in the state's society for many decades and consisted of a person betting on what three numbers would 'hit' determined by the numbers of the winning horses in selected races at three different national racetracks. Eventually, a second game less likely to be fixed based on the ending three numerals of the closing value of stocks on Wall Street was the determinant for winning. The winner could collect $700 on a $1 bet, or a lesser amount if the numbers were correct but not in the exact order. This sideline from the drug business was a huge money maker until 1971 when the state legalized the game by instituting the lottery program. Santiago's numbers racket maintained its profitability for a while thereafter, since the state only paid $600 for a $1 winning bet, plus winnings from the legitimate lottery were taxable by the IRS. But as the state became more creative with betting alternatives and introduced new games, gigantic purses proliferated. Soon, the numbers racket became less popular and less profitable. Santiago finally decided to concentrate only on drug trafficking.

Soon after the takeover, he made a trip to Colombia to meet the man responsible for supplying the product to his expanded business. He was able to get a meeting with Alejandro Moreno, which required considerable clandestine negotiating to arrange. Moreno, though, was actually anxious to meet the young man who was now dominating the East Coast USA market and who had enhanced his profits threefold over that being realized from the previous administration. Moreno was extremely impressed with the young Santiago, and the meeting went exceedingly well as they plotted out a strategy for even greater expansion. This trip cemented Santiago's position as the czar of the USA East Coast syndicate and a prime link in the Moreno cartel.

Santiago was in his plush office in the warehouse district of Harrisburg where Central Penn Warehousing, Inc was headquartered. The facility also served as a staging, processing, and packaging area for much of the product coming from Philadelphia. His top lieutenant, Tomás Rojas, burst into his office gusting with alarm, saying "Diego, I just learned Jennifer Ambrose was murdered last night. This is a very large blow to our organization; she was the lynchpin of our legal staff that buffered us from those apes who keep trying to interrupt our business."

"Yes, I heard," Santiago answered. "But I do not smell the disaster you seem to anticipate. No one, and I repeat no one in an organization is indispensable. Yes, she knew all the secrets of our business, but her death in no way puts anything in jeopardy. Assemble the staff. I want to talk with all your local people to learn what they know about this situation."

Ambrose had been Santiago's chief legal counsel for several years. She first represented one of his underlings in a criminal charge that seemed destined to result in conviction, but she used her skills to secure an acquittal through introducing a defense that attacked more than it defended, and she also brought into question the methods used by the District Attorney's office to gather evidence. Her credentials as a Princeton Law graduate were impressive, and Santiago immediately took a liking to her. Over the years, she or members of her growing staff defended numerous henchmen of the Santiago gang, both locally and organization-wide, including Santiago himself, and in each case, she used her courtroom skills and knowledge of the law to accrue rapid acquittals.

Of course, being Diego Santiago's chief legal counsel was a lucrative proposition for Ambrose, and she embraced an upscale lifestyle complete with all the amenities money could offer. Her marriage to Gregory Ambrose had been a disaster from the start, but she kept her married name after the divorce because of the goodwill the name Ambrose carried in legal circles due to her reputation as a successful litigator. Her staff was actively working on three separate charges brought against members of the Santiago organization, and Ambrose was always hands-on with each case to ensure the perfect record she had amassed over the years remained intact.

Rojas assembled the nine other members of his local enforcement staff in Santiago's elegant board room, which had hosted many prominent political and business dignitaries for discussions with Santiago. Rojas picked each of the men personally, judging them to be loyal and trustworthy, and although all of them had prison records, they were consummate professionals who pledged allegiance to him and the Santiago organization.

"This Ambrose killing is a very sensitive matter. You are probably all going to be questioned by the police. I want you to say as little as possible to them without coming across

THE BRIDGE AT WILSON PARK

as hiding something or failing to cooperate. Get a handle on where each one of you were last night and establish a solid alibi that can be corroborated. I want to minimize the amount of snooping those guys do around here, and I don't want the blood thirsty media having a feeding frenzy over speculation about our organization's involvement."

The meeting broke up quickly, and Santiago again admonished Rojas to keep those guys in line or else. Rojas knew exactly what 'or else' meant, since Santiago had a reputation for extreme brutality that was frequently unleashed when he lost his temper. His Jekyll and Hyde personality allowed Santiago to be the consummate business man or the vicious aggressor, depending on the situation or circumstances.

CHAPTER 6: THE ALLIANCE

Tomás Rojas earned his top position with Santiago the hard way. Like so many other immigrants from South America, Rojas had to fight for everything he attained. He was born in Venezuela and worked in the oilfields during his teens. Wages were minimal and inflation rampant, making it difficult for most working-class people to advance above the poverty level. Envisioning a much better life in the USA, he drove his dilapidated car through Central America into Mexico. Rojas crossed the border from Mexico into the United States without being detected. Border security was almost non-existent to any street-smart immigrant wanting to make the crossing.

He secured menial jobs to make ends meet and gradually worked his way north, hoping to find more opportunities on the East Coast. Rojas joined a group of workers as a crop picker, being paid a piece rate per bucket or bag of fruit or vegetables, eventually ending up in the Garden State of New Jersey. It was backbreaking work and the wages were miniscule, but he used the job as an opportunity to make his way north. When the harvest season was over in New Jersey, he moved on to Pennsylvania and worked in a steel mill in the town of Bethlehem. Wages were considerably better than crop picking, but the work was just as arduous. It was during this period he met Diego Santiago, who was just getting a foothold on the drug business he would eventually rule nearly exclusively. Rojas was having a beer in a local bar one evening when he met Santiago by chance. He heard men speaking in Spanish, which drew him into the conversation. They talked about life back in their respective South American countries and continued to drink. Santiago took a liking to Rojas, who appeared to be the type of man he could use in his quest to dethrone the current lord of the drug kingdom.

As the evening progressed, the group of five men drank increasingly more beer, and the inevitable fighting began, first as a simple argument over some sports statistic, and then into a more physical brawl. Santiago and Rojas were paired against the three others. The two placed themselves back to back and fought off their aggressors until one picked up a cue ball from a nearby pool table and slammed it into Santiago. Stunned by the blow, his immediate reaction was to pull a knife from his belt and slash at the man, cutting him severely in the stomach. Rojas picked up the fallen knife from the floor and jumped on the man and continued to beat him with one fist while pointing the knife at him. The rumpus was loud and disorderly and attracted two policemen who were walking their beat. When they arrived, they pulled Rojas off the wounded man and wrestled him to the ground. Without questioning anyone else, Rojas was arrested on the spot and accused of attempted murder. The knife wound was not fatal to the man who recovered in a few days at the local hospital.

Feeling a sense of honor and loyalty toward Santiago, Rojas never told the police he was not the knife wielder. Santiago was overwhelmed by the actions of this man who sacrificed himself for him – a man he only met that day. Rojas was convicted of the assault and sentenced to three years in prison. Apparently, the victim was angrier at Rojas than Santiago, so he testified that Rojas did the stabbing. Rojas was sent to Western Penitentiary on the north side of the Ohio River just a few miles downstream from downtown Pittsburgh.

This prison has a long history starting in 1826 when the original structure was built. It was used to imprison Confederate troops in 1863 during the Civil War. Conditions in the prison were not horrible, but before the men were transferred to another facility in New Jersey, eight of them died. Following the Civil War, it was classified as a maximum-security facility. By the time Rojas was an inmate, the prison had been downgraded to house low and medium security inmates. Drug offenders made up most of the prison population. More recently, Western Penitentiary was used as a detention center in 2009 to process protesters arrested at the

G-20 summit, which was held in Pittsburgh. This economic conference of heads of state was disrupted by picketers protesting issues on peace, the environment, labor, and social injustice.

Rojas was assigned to laundry duty in prison, a soft position coveted by many. He never asked why he was given this favorable treatment, but he did suspect Santiago had something to do with it. Even though Santiago was just starting to grow his empire, he realized that cultivating friends in influential positions would pay dividends. A phone call to a politician on his payroll was all it took for Rojas to get the job. Rojas was a loner in prison. He did not align himself with any faction, and for the most part, the others did not hassle him. They knew if a newcomer could get a comfortable job, he must have connections to important people.

He did, however, run into some difficulties in the initial days of his term. Since the prison housed a large population of drug offenders, it fostered gangs that had roots in the violent neighborhoods of Central America, Mexico, and California. Two of the most vicious were Mara Salvatrucha (MS-13) and the 18th Street Gang (Barrio 18). Their span of influence stretched from Central America to Canada, and their illicit activities included selling drugs, human trafficking, kidnapping, money laundering, and contract killings. These two gangs are deep-seated enemies, having killed countless of each other over the years in all-out warfare for territorial control. Law enforcement administrators thought arresting the leaders of these gangs would cause their demise, but it simply transferred their base of operation to United States prisons.

Western Penitentiary hosted cells of both gangs, and the vicious rivalry that existed on the outside continued on the inside. It was not a rarity to find a member of one or the other slashed with a shiv created from some metal object despite the regular prison searches to eradicate these weapons. As a newcomer, Rojas was expected to join a gang, and both MS-13 and Barrio 18 recruited him heavily. If he spoke with one gang member in the yard during their outdoor activity time, the other group challenged him. The two organizations were in a tug-of-war over control of him, and Rojas was the rope being pulled in opposite directions. Both groups realized he knew powerful people on the outside, so having him as an ally could be extremely beneficial.

Rojas decided he had to take aggressive action against both groups, since his desire was to do his time and not get involved in prison warfare. Both gangs had distribution networks selling cigarettes to inmates, so rights to this activity were a point of contention between them. On one occasion, he was seen buying cigarettes from an MS-13 member. That evening in the communal lavatory, a Barrio 18 gang member accosted him. Little did the aggressor know that Rojas was capable of being as vicious as any of them. He not only defended himself, he brutally beat the man and left him unconscious under the running showers that permitted the man's spilled blood to wash slowly down the drain in a constant stream. The prison guards were not able to connect Rojas or anyone else with this incident, so nobody was punished. All the inmates, of course, knew what happened and who was responsible.

MS-13 took this as a sign Rojas was on their side, but just to show they were mistaken, a few nights later, he became the aggressor and repeated the same violent act on one of their men. At this point, both groups received the message loudly and clearly that Rojas was nobody to be taken lightly, particularly since they did not want whomever was supporting him to retaliate in any way. From that point on, he was left alone to serve his time without being hassled by anyone.

Rojas kept to himself thereafter and stayed out of trouble. He was released from prison early. The time in prison turned out to be helpful to Rojas in one aspect, though. It gave him a source for recruiting henchmen later when he became the right-hand enforcer for Santiago. Over the years, Rojas recruited several Western Penitentiary released prisoners whom he met there to work under him at the warehouse.

He returned to central Pennsylvania, since the only people he knew in the USA were living there. Rojas looked up

Santiago, hoping he could find work for him to satisfy his parole requirements. Santiago was overjoyed to see him. He had kept in touch with him while in prison and sent care packages regularly. By this time, Santiago had made several takeover moves in his growing drug business and knew he could use a man like Rojas. This was the period when Santiago opened Central Penn Warehousing as a shield for his illegal activities. The most important character trait a man could have, in Santiago's mind, was loyalty, and Rojas displayed this characteristic beyond what would ever be expected of a man.

Rojas and Santiago became a team. As the drug business grew and Santiago's stranglehold on the business tightened, he asked Rojas to build a staff of trusted men who would be the foot soldiers in monitoring his business. Santiago approached the Pennsylvania Board of Probation and Parole and suggested a partnership for rehabilitating released prisoners. The program was a great success and both parties benefited from the arrangement.

Eventually, Rojas's gang grew to nine or ten men who became the enforcement arm for Santiago's business. In the company's Human Resources records, they were designated as hourly-paid fork lift drivers, stacking hands, truck drivers, and other manual labor jobs typical of a public warehouse. Of course, they rarely worked at those jobs. Instead, their work consisted of receiving, processing, packaging, and distributing the drugs. Collection for the sale of drugs was also their responsibility, and this phase often required more muscle than brains.

CHAPTER 7: THE PARK

B asso asked Allen to get in touch with patrolman Josh Brady and have him meet him at Wilson Park in about an hour. He wanted to go over the crime scene in daylight while it was still closed off to the public.

Wilson Park was named after the 28th US president, Woodrow Wilson, who served during World War I. After the war, Wilson became a strong proponent of the League of Nations, the forerunner to the United Nations. But the organization never came to fruition, since the USA did not endorse the concept. Wilson's Democratic party was unable to get the support of the opposition Republican party, mirroring a pattern of conflict between the two political groups that has reoccurred throughout the history of the USA. Without USA involvement, the League of Nations concept died.

The park was built in the mid-1930s by the Civilian Conservation Corps (CCC), a government agency formed by Franklin Delano Roosevelt, the 32nd USA president, to provide work country-wide for hundreds of thousands of unemployed young male adults who were seriously impacted by the Great Depression. It all started when the US stock market experienced a serious decline on September 4, 1929. After that, the situation worsened, and on October 29, 1929, commonly known as Black Tuesday, the market dramatically crashed. Nearly everybody who had investments in the stock market suffered severe losses, causing the suicide rate in the ensuing weeks to increase dramatically. The impact was felt worldwide, and the economies of other industrialized nations followed suit. The USA saw a 15 percent decline in the Gross Domestic Product, and during the 1930s, unemployment rose to over 25 percent, an increase of 600 percent over previous levels. As more people hoarded their money by withdrawing from the market and from banks, which also experienced failures, the decline in the money supply had a further negative impact and continued to fuel the depression.

Italy was not immune to the drastic collapse of the world's economic foundation. After the 1929 stock market crash in the USA, the effects touched most countries. Italy, however, was fortunate that under the regime of Benito Mussolini, economic policies had been implemented in the 1920s that somewhat buffered the impact. But after 1929, it still had a serious effect both in the industrialized north of the country and the agrarian south.

Basso's father, Mario Basso, was born during the worst period of this depression in 1934 in a small village near Potenza in southern Italy. Gianni's paternal grandparents, Gianluca and Angelina Basso, had been farmers and managed a small herd of Mediterranean water buffalo. These animals were introduced into Italy during Roman times or possibly earlier during barbarian invasions of the peninsula. Their milk was highly prized for making mozzarella cheese. Gianluca lost his farm when he was unable to make mortgage payments to the bank, and the family struggled throughout the 1930s as he tried to eke out a meager existence. World War II began in the late 1930s in Europe, and Italy entered the fight in 1940, initially as part of the axis power but eventually changing sides to support the allies. The economy began to recover somewhat, but Italy was war-torn during the first half of the 1940s. The repercussions from changing sides caused it to be occupied by the superior German forces before becoming a battleground as the allies invaded from the south after subduing the Germans in North Africa.

The US army eventually liberated Italy from the stranglehold of the occupying Nazis, starting in Anzio at the tip of the boot in early 1944, working its way up the peninsula, and eventually moving into France. But the impact of the depression followed by the war left its scars and financial hardships, so in 1946 Gianluca decided to send 12-year-old Mario to the USA where he surmised a better life could be realized. Gianluca had a brother living in Scranton,

Pennsylvania working for the Delaware Lackawanna Railroad, so Mario Basso made the trip alone, entering the USA though Ellis Island, and finding his way by train to Scranton. He had no passport or other documents, but he gained admission as a refugee from war-torn Europe. President Harry S. Truman issued a directive in 1946 allocating half the European immigration quota to refugee admissions.

Mario found work on the railroad with his uncle, initially as a water boy supporting the gandy dancers, who were the section hands who laid and maintained the tracks. Eventually he became a skilled machinist making bushings in the railroad's factory near Harrisburg. In 1956, Mario met and married Maria Venuto, also an Italian immigrant from the southern region, and in 1964, Gianni was born as their second child.

Throughout the USA, however, the results of the CCC's construction efforts are still available to the country, including roads, bridges, dams, parks, and other infrastructure facilities, with Wilson Park being a prime example of these efforts. Living in campsites struck near each construction project, these young men created structures that have endured the test of time. The beautiful stone bridge in the park is just one example of the contributions the CCC made.

Officer Brady was already there to greet them when Basso and Curto arrived. A police officer assigned to guard the site until the crime scene designation was removed was also present. The four began a tour of the entire area.

"Do we have any details of the tire tracks of the car you saw that might help us identify the vehicle used to transport the body here?"

Brady replied they were able to identify the tire tread, but it was a commonly used variety and would not really be helpful in advancing the investigation. "We can ascertain, however, it was a passenger car and not a truck. There appears to be only one set of footprints other than her drag marks leading from where the car stopped to the point where the body was pulled down the steep grade and placed under the bridge. Ambrose was not a large woman, so the movement could certainly have been handled by one person. But again, the footprints are of such a common sole style that it makes the possibilities too extensive to be of much help."

"That's fine, Josh. Although we don't know if others were involved in the killing, as least we know the disposal was most likely carried out by one person. Let's do a walk-through as to how it possibly could have gone down."

They began at the site where Brady had seen the car and proceeded retracing the path taken by the driver. The route down the steep grade to under the bridge was followed until they reached the gulley at the bottom where the body was found.

"How do you suppose her handbag ended up in the bushes over there?"

Brady could only surmise that the killer or person driving the car threw it away from the body.

Basso added, "He or she did not go to great lengths to conceal it. You seemed to have found it fairly quickly. It almost makes me think the killer wanted her identity to be known fast."

"You could be right, Gene" interjected Curto. "Given her association with Santiago, it could be the killer wanted to shine light on him. But possibly one of his gang members has gone rogue and wanted to pin it on Santiago. We should make investigating those guys a priority."

Basso agreed that considering each of them was important. As he stepped backward, however, he heard a crunch under his foot, and looking down, he realized he had stepped on a piece of metal. It appeared to be a small fragment of a jeweled belt, most likely a woman's belt. "Was she wearing a belt when you found her?"

Brady said she did have a studded belt on her waist when he found her, but it was not fully intact.

"This piece seems to have blood on it. Get it to the lab and see if it matches the blood of Ambrose. This could help in establishing more precisely the time of death, since her blood had not coagulated at this point."

"What's your spin on this whole thing, Julius?"

"Well, a woman in her profession is surely to have a lot of enemies. My thought is she pissed off one of Santiago's gang members, maybe with her approach to a legal defense or maybe in some other way. There could be a motive in there somewhere."

"You might have something there, Julius. Get over to the district attorney's office and see how many cases are pending on which Ambrose or a member of her staff are listed as the defense counsel."

CHAPTER 8: THE DATE

That evening, Basso had a date scheduled with Allen. They took separate cars. Allen parked in an all-night diner's lot outside of town, and they proceeded in Basso's car. He planned the evening thoughtfully. They drove the moderate distance to Philadelphia to avoid local scrutiny, leaving in early evening to have dinner at a small French restaurant. Their relationship continued to blossom even though they knew they were playing with fire by ignoring departmental policy. But the attraction was too great for either of them to suggest ending the relationship. They enjoyed an intimate French dinner where Basso succumbed to the waiter's suggestion by ordering a 2011 Chambolle-Musigny, a delightful Burgundy principally made from the pinot noir grape. His preference normally leaned toward wines from Italy, but this night he matched the wine to the cuisine. Basso and Allen went on foot to the Living Room, a small jazz club in an artsy/craftsy neighborhood. It featured relatively unknown artists who were stretching the boundaries of improvised music while also applying the same free thought process to the construction of composed music.

"I am gradually getting to hear what you hear in this music, Gene." It has taken a while, but I now appreciate the creativity that goes into instantly composing a piece on stage, especially when these highly talented artists may not have ever played together before."

"That is the beauty of this music, Gerri. Artists have the freedom to create without being constrained by the rules musicians were forced to endure in the past. They also have the additional burden of having to cast off the rules imposed on them by college music educators. Since they all have this same mindset, they can instantly communicate without having had prior exposure to each other. I am thankful that this style of freedom has survived since the early 1960s when music pioneers like Cecil Taylor, Ornette Coleman, and John Coltrane turned the jazz world upside down with their atonal sounds. Even so, as you can see by looking around, it does not draw large audiences, but the ones it does draw are fully dedicated."

Music was another major difference that contributed to the barrier between his ex-wife and him. She had absolutely no tolerance for it, calling it screechy noise, and she failed to see any inherent beauty in freeform playing. But Allen had not displayed this negativity and was open to hearing what obviously was a passion for him. She was rewarded for this effort by not only endearing herself to him, but by broadening her own appreciation of art in its most exploratory form.

During the musicians' break, they talked about many things, for it was quite easy for them to sustain an endless flow of conversation about most any subject. In previous conversations, he learned she had married her high school sweetheart as soon as they graduated. Although everything prior to that had signaled a solid marriage would ensue, given their popularity and label as an ideal couple, it did not turn out that way. Her ex proved to be the jealous type, for which he had absolutely no basis, but it did not stop his suspicions. They had a son born only five months after the wedding whom they named Dominick, and both felt highly restricted by having to take on the role of parent without having experienced the freedom of adulthood beforehand.

This contributed to his feeling of insecurity, leading to his becoming an abusive husband. Allen tolerated it for several years, as so many abused women do, but after a particularly vicious and unwarranted attack on her, she decided to leave him. Taking her son in the middle of the night and two small suitcases, she caught a bus and headed east and never looked back. She assumed her maiden name, and her husband was not able to find her. After years of separation, she filed for a no-fault divorce. They were never able to locate her husband, and since virtually no property was involved, she was officially declared a free woman.

"Where is our relationship going, Gene? Can we sustain this clandestine arrangement indefinitely? I think at some point we are going to have to decide to go public, even if it means I must quit my job. Dominick is now in his first year at the community college, and soon he will be on his own."

"It most definitely will mean you have to leave the department, Gerri. Are you prepared for that? You have been so happy and comfortable with your role on my staff."

"I am absolutely prepared for that. If we can be together without sneaking around corners, that would be wonderful."

"Well, I am ready as well, but can we wait until we get through this Ambrose mess. I am going to need your expertise to get to the bottom of this murder. This crime has gotten too high a profile with the brass and with the press, so I believe it is imperative we solve it quickly. What you suggest sounds like just the motivation we need to push this case to its conclusion."

The musicians were making their way back to the bandstand, which curtailed the conversation. This music required disciplined listening with no outside distractions. Gene was friends with two in the band, and they both stopped by to say hello and thank them for coming out. These musicians were quite accustomed to playing to a half-filled or less room, so they were always most appreciative when customers returned to hear them.

They left the club after the second set to make the hour and a half drive back home. They were both off duty the next day, allowing the trip to be unrushed. This time, the discussions centered on how to proceed with the case.

The next morning, Basso visited his mother, Maria Basso. She had been coping reasonably well since the death of his father Mario a year ago, but every so often, she would slip back into a depressive mood. His parents had celebrated their 57th wedding anniversary about a week before he died. Italian families tend to be clannish. She had numerous relatives from her Venuto side of the family to comfort her, but somehow, she did not seem to adjust well after his death. Still living were two of her sisters and their husbands, who had seven children between them, and from Mario's side, one brother Alfredo and his wife were still alive. Alfredo had come to America about two years after Mario, and of course, he settled in the same suburb as his brother. Gianni's two brothers were also frequent visitors of his mother at the family home where all the children lived out their childhood. His mother remained in the house after his father's death against the urging of all the family members to move to a smaller place, but she steadfastly refused, claiming this house would be the last house in which she would ever live.

Gianni Basso was a middle child, but all three siblings benefited from the demands of his parents to go to college. There was no discussion, no negotiating; they had to advance their education. And there was no discussion about the cost either; Mario and Maria had saved for years with the express purpose of giving the boys a higher education. This concept appears to be most prevalent with first or second-generation Italians in America, who gain a better life through the sacrifices of their parents.

His older brother Francesco earned a degree in Political Science and became very involved in the politics of the city. He was the campaign manager for Mayor Bill Bixby in both of his elected terms. His younger brother Alberto was an accounting major who became a CPA and started a private practice. But his business did not do well with a limited client base, so he closed it and took a job with the Internal Revenue Service. Although originally disappointed that Gianni joined the Navy after high school, they were overjoyed when he pursued a higher education after being discharged.

Maria Basso, however, still maintained all the traditions the family enjoyed while his father was alive. It was not unusual for her to prepare a lavish Italian feast for Christmas, Easter, and many of the other major holidays. All family members on both sides were required to be present. Maria was the oldest of her generation and accepted the honor of matriarch with pleasure. Maintaining these traditions was the glue that held the family together, even though they all had separate careers and separate lives.

Gianni was the first to marry a woman who was not of Italian descent. Still, Janice was welcomed wholeheartedly into the family and most warmly by his mother. It was very difficult for him three years ago to tell her they were getting divorced. To Maria, things like that don't happen to her children.

As always, she insisted he have something to eat on this and every visit. They sat at the kitchen table talking, and his mother brought up the subject of the Jennifer Ambrose killing. "Son, I read about that beautiful woman being murdered, and the article mentioned you were responsible for learning who killed her. It made me very proud to see your name in the newspaper."

"Thanks, Mom, but at this point, I have nothing for which to be proud. We have a few clues and a lot of people to interview, but we have learned nothing so far that would reveal anything conclusive about who did it. The case is being managed in the newspapers because the woman was a big-time lawyer who worked for a very powerful man in this city. It is getting a lot of press, and I am getting a lot of abusive criticism. Mayor Bixby, the chief of police, my boss, and the media are putting a lot of pressure on me to get some quick results, but so far, we have not made much progress. But I have a great team in Julius Curto and Gerri Allen, plus all the support staff of the bureau, so I am certain it will all work out just fine."

"You will just have to speak to Francesco to make him tell the mayor to stop pressuring you."

"Mom, that's not how it works."

"Tell me about this woman you are seeing, Gianni. Is she a nice girl? I still can't accept that you and Janice are not together."

"Yes, Mom, I know you would like her. We need to be careful because we both work for the city, and it frowns on dating within the office. But she is very supportive of me and my job, which is something I could never say about Janice. Maybe when we get this murder case behind us, I'll bring her over for some of your lasagna."

While Basso was talking with his mother, his brother Alberto came by. Maria was so pleased to see two of her sons on the same day. Alberto kissed his mother and said, "Gianni, great to see you again. I have been reading a lot about you in the paper. You certainly have a high profile in this town."

"Too high, Alberto. I was just telling Mom about the pressure a thing like this can put on a person. How are things at the IRS?"

"Well, I may be breaking protocol by telling you this, but it might not only interest you, it might influence your current case. I have been assigned as lead investigator to an important audit of none other than Diego Santiago. His business tax filings did not raise any red flags, but his personal taxes are what caused us to undertake an audit. When you look at his total compensation as president of his company, plus all his other outside income, it is substantial compared to the average citizen. But when you compare that against his lifestyle and spending habits, the two pieces do not match. We have undertaken an alternate auditing method often used in these situations called a net worth determination. If a taxpayer's net worth at a starting point plus what he claimed to have earned during the period, less expenses that are not deductible, do not balance with his net worth at the end of the period, there is a presumption of unreported taxable income. Santiago has an excellent tax accountant, but when we apply the formula to his formidable holdings, it leaves a huge hole in his calculations. We are in the tedious process of looking at his entire financial picture, and the fallout could support your contention that this additional unreported income is coming from illicit activities."

"Wow, Alberto, that is astounding. Reminds me of the way the government was finally able to put Al Capone in jail in 1931. Despite living a life of crime, his conviction was based on tax evasion. Does that mean you and I are going to be in competition to see which one of us can convict him first?"

Maria butted into the conversation. "Sit down, Alberto, and have something to eat. You two talk about business later."

CHAPTER 9: THE EX-HUSBAND

Basso scheduled a meeting with Gregory Ambrose, D.D.S. through the dentist's receptionist. He had a very successful practice that employed two other dentists, three dental hygienists, and the receptionist, all at his one location in the downtown section of the city. He and Curto sat in the waiting room for a short time, scanning the educational credentials the doctor so proudly displayed. They were called into his office shortly after arriving.

"Thank you, Doctor, for seeing us. I am Detective Basso, and this is Assistant Detective Curto. I know you are a very busy man based on all those people in the waiting room."

"Not a problem, Detective. I know why you are here, and I want to help in any way possible. This is a tragic thing that's happened to Jennifer. I still can't believe it, but as I told her many times, she was playing with fire by representing a man like Santiago."

"How long have you been divorced, Doctor?"

"We separated four or five years ago and formally divorced three years ago."

"Was the parting amicable?"

"As amicable as any divorce can be. We got along well while we were together, but Jennifer is, was, such an ambitious person that her career took precedent over our marriage. She never wanted to have any children, and I did. She was such a determined person, and it was hard to convince her otherwise."

"Can you tell me if she was seeing anyone romantically since your divorce?"

"Jennifer was a very private person, even with me. I guess that goes with the territory of being a lawyer. She was in the fast lane with that job of hers, and I suspected she was involved with someone, but I never knew who that might be."

"What gave you that impression?"

"It was very hard to get in touch with her in the evenings. Numerous times I tried to contact her about certain administrative matters, but she almost always was unavailable after business hours. I found it was easier to contact her during the day at her office, although that also was not an easy thing, given her heavy work load."

"Did you ever have a feeling she might be involved with Santiago or someone in his organization?"

"There were rumors to that effect, but I never heard of anything that would substantiate it. I wrote it off as simply gossip. I would find it hard to believe it was Santiago himself, given their age difference, so I surmised it was someone within his organization."

"Were you surprised to know she was pregnant?"

"I found it hard to believe when I read that in the paper. As I mentioned, she never wanted children, and she was a strong advocate of a woman's right to control her own body."

"What about the financial aspects of the divorce? How did that work out?"

"Jennifer and I did very well in our respective professions, so there really was not a need for either of us to bring finances into the equation. She had her money and I had mine, so when we parted, it was fairly clean financially. She took the house, which she owned prior to our marriage, so that was the only real property in the settlement. We had separate bank accounts during the marriage, so that presented no problem either. Since no children were involved, the whole matter went very smoothly."

"Sorry to ask this, but did she ever have an affair while you were married?"

"Not to my knowledge. If she did, she was infinitely discreet."

"Can you think of anyone who would have wanted her dead?"

"No, she was a very likable person despite her determined nature, which she used to good advantage in court. She had a type A personality and she seemed to have everything – intelligence, education, great looks and body, high paying job, tremendous confidence – all the tools for success, and she certainly achieved that without question."

"Who is making the funeral arrangements?

"I would have to think that would be handled by someone in Santiago's organization. We had no other family members in town. Both our parents died while we were still married, so basically, one could say that all she had in terms of family was her job. Even when we lived together, we had a different circle of friends, hers almost exclusively business related."

"We have to ask this question, Doctor. Where were you on the night Jennifer was killed?"

"That's an easy one. I was in Pittsburgh at a dental convention. Stayed at the Sheraton at Station Square. Would you like to see my hotel bill?"

"That won't be necessary. Well, that should do it for now. Thank you again Doctor for seeing us. Even though you have not been together for quite a while, I am sure this is a difficult time for you."

"You are both welcome. If I can be of any more help, please do not hesitate to contact me."

Curto and Basso left the dental office and headed back to the precinct. "What do you think of him, Julius. He did not seem terribly broken up by it, but then again, they broke it off quite a while ago."

"My guess is the marriage was more of a financial merger than a blending of lovebirds. That would explain his somewhat aloof attitude toward her death. It was more a marriage of convenience between two professionals than a union of love."

"You are probably right. Nothing we heard would make us put him on a prime suspect list, but I am not exonerating him just yet."

"He does not seem to have a motive," Curto added, "neither finances nor jealousy, but one never knows about people that cool."

"We really did not advance the investigation much through this interview. I was hoping to get a lead on who might have been involved with her. We might learn about that if we talk with the other people on her legal staff. I understand two of the three other lawyers are also women, and she had a female paralegal on her staff as well. If a woman is going to confide in anybody about her relationship with a man, it would likely be another woman. And who better than the women with whom she worked. I'll set up a meeting with them at their warehouse office. First, tell me what you learned about the cases they were currently handling for Santiago's organization. "

CHAPTER 10: THE CASES

On the way back to the precinct after the interview with Gregory Ambrose, Curto briefed Basso on what he learned earlier by reviewing the pending court cases.

His trip to the district attorney's office had been enlightening. He used his boyish charm and good looks to gain access to the three open cases involving Santiago's organization members. "It really would make me look good with the boss," Curto pleaded to Mary Miller, the receptionist on duty in the DA's office. Although she realized she might be breaking some rules, she knew Curto for a while and was quite enamored with him. Curto always used these situations to his best advantage; he explained that all he wanted to know was the name of the defendants and who were the lawyers representing them on any of those cases – knowledge that was a matter of public record. In her trustworthy way, Mary Miller gave him access to the stacks having all the public and confidential information on open cases. Left alone, he quickly isolated the documents he needed.

The first file he found was for Jose Caderas, a convicted felon who had done two tours of duty courtesy of the Pennsylvania prison system. Caderas was one of the first people Tomás Rojas recruited for his enforcement organization. This time, Caderas was being charged with assault and attempted murder. He had not actually intended to murder his victim; the man he assaulted had reneged on paying a large narcotics debt, and such behavior could not be tolerated if they were going to continue ruling the city. His lawyer was John Halbrook, a young man who had been on Ambrose's law staff for about two years. He had an Ivy League law degree and came highly recommended by a close associate of Santiago. From what Curto could see, there was nothing unusual about the case. His judgment told him the evidence was very flimsy and most likely, Halbrook would have an easy time in getting the case thrown out. Curto seriously doubted the victim would ever be willing to testify in court, so most likely the case would be dismissed.

Information in the second file he located appeared to be more serious. Raphael Pino was being accused of possession and sale of a substantial quantity of illegal drugs. He was arrested during a sting by the police who had set up an elaborate scheme to trick Pino into making a narcotics sale to an undercover policeman, known in law enforcement parlance as a 'controlled buy'. A sales deal like this would obviously have been blessed by the top of the organization, so the exposure to Santiago was significant. Curto was very familiar with this type of police exercise, having spent his early years on the force in just this type of work. Pino had only one conviction on his rap sheet, which Curto thought could be used favorably by his lawyer, Susan Aspect, to good advantage. Aspect had been on Ambrose's law staff since Ambrose took over the legal affairs of Santiago, so she was a seasoned veteran in these matters. Although her law degree from Villanova University was not quite as auspicious as those of the Ivy Leaguers, she had a solid record of accomplishment on the job to compensate for not having the pedigree others on the staff had. This case, however, troubled Curto, since he knew how easy it was for a defendant to beat charges like this by using the law against the police. Asserting his rights had been violated by the sting was a natural defense, but Aspect had not filed the court motions to have that evidence thrown out of court. And without that proof, the State had no case. He promised himself to look into this further and went on to the next case.

Matias Martinez was facing similar charges to Jose Caderas. Muscle was the stock in trade for this man; he had a reputation for severely punishing those who went against their rules. In this case, however, the victim was not a drug user or drug middleman; he was a member of a rival gang trying to make inroads into Santiago's territory. Curto believed anyone who would try such a thing would have to be either stupid or crazy, since Santiago had a stranglehold on the drug business all over the Eastern seaboard. Martinez was told to send a message to the interlopers, and he showed no mercy in doing so. His lawyer was Ruth Biantano, a feel-good story in the Italian community; she had risen above a poverty-plagued childhood to work her way through college, and then law school. Her ambition and determination had impressed Ambrose, so she went against the grain and hired her. Based on her accomplishments to date, Ambrose did not make a mistake. Given both the accuser and the accused in her case were known thugs, Curto believed Biantano would prevail in any ensuing litigation.

Curto tried to put all these cases into perspective and speculate on how any of this could possibly have anything to do with the Ambrose killing. Jose Caderas and Matias Martinez did not appear to be having any problems with their defense, but in his opinion, the same thing could not be said of Raphael Pino. He knew from experience that entrapment was a perfect defense if the police did not follow all the rules. An entrapment defense could be introduced if the police resorted to threats, harassment, or even flattery to induce defendants to commit a crime, and a good lawyer could almost always attack on that basis. Yet there was no indication in the files that this defense was offered. He mused, *"Was his lawyer Susan Aspect playing some sort of dangerous game? Was she deliberately trying to sabotage the case? Why wasn't she exploring this defense? What could be a possible motive for such action?"* All these questions rattled around Curto's brain as he replaced all the files. He speculated that Aspect would not be making this decision on her own, so if Ambrose was pulling the strings, could it be that the organization wanted Pino out of the way. And what better way than to let the legal system do it. If Pino realized what was going on, Curto saw how he would be a prime suspect for this murder. On the way out, he made sure to thank Mary Miller again, making a leading comment about owing her a lunch. Curto knew Miller would jump at such a chance, but for now, he had no intention of following through with the invitation.

Curto made a special effort to relay his concerns to Basso on the Pino/Aspect circumstances and suggested Pino should be high on the list of those they were going to interview next.

In any contacts with Santiago or his staff, Basso thought it best that Curto not be included, even though his disguise as an undercover policeman had changed his looks drastically. His undercover identity years ago had never been divulged, so as far as anyone knew, Julius Curto was a different person.

CHAPTER 11: THE LAWYERS

As a professional courtesy to Diego Santiago, Basso phoned ahead to let him know he wanted to speak to the other lawyers on Ambrose's staff. Santiago said he was more than happy to cooperate, since he wanted to minimize the impact of this investigation on his organization. Basso arrived at the warehouse office, which for all intents and purposes looked to be a normal two-story warehousing business operation with offices included around the perimeter of the second level. Santiago went to great lengths to disguise the location from its prime purpose as a staging area for incoming drugs and as the location of a processing room where pure cocaine and heroin were cut or mixed with impurities to alter the intensity and expand the profitability. The building's cover was a public warehouse where various businesses temporarily stored their goods, paying a fee to move the goods in, move the goods out, plus a monthly storage fee.

Central Penn Warehousing Inc., Santiago's company in the northwest sector of the city along the Susquehanna River, provided the trucks, pick-up and return delivery service, fork lifts, pallets, and labor for this storage operation. It included a main storage area of 20,000 square feet dotted with aisles of racks and bins, six truck bays, and a railroad siding ramp for incoming and outgoing shipments. They also provided value-added services such as bundling, assembly, packaging, and labeling. On its own, Central Penn Warehousing Inc. was a viable business enterprise that serviced many of the companies in central and eastern Pennsylvania needing additional storage space on a temporary basis.

Basso decided to meet initially with the three lawyers as a group, and to schedule private meetings as he judged necessary. John Halbrook, Susan Aspect, and Ruth Biantano came into the conference room where Basso was already waiting.

After introductions, Basso said, "I am sure you are all very saddened over the death of your boss, just as we are. Was she in the office on the day before the body was found in Wilson Park."

"Yes, I am sure she was," Halbrook remarked. I saw her on several occasions that morning."

"I had a meeting with her that day in the early afternoon," interjected Biantano," but she cut it short to keep an appointment she had outside the building."

"Did you notice anything unusual about her behavior? Did she seem troubled or overly concerned about anything?"

"No, nothing other than the usual concern about how our cases were going," added Aspect.

"Can you tell me anything about those cases?"

"I'm sorry, but you know that would be a breach of confidentiality if we discussed anything about those," Halbrook said.

"I understand that, and I certainly would not want you to breach any confidentiality. I am just trying to get a handle on who might have had a motive to kill her, and I thought your case load might give us an insight into that."

Aspect spoke up first. "To my knowledge, all the cases we have open are fairly routine, and none of them directly involved Jennifer. She oversaw our activity, but she gave us a free reign to do our job."

"Did she handle any cases on her own of which you three would not be aware?"

All three shook their heads no. They explained that Ambrose was an excellent attorney, but the case load nearly always became their responsibility. They explained her role had evolved into that of an administrator.

"Strictly for the record, can each of you tell me where you were the evening of the murder?" Halbrook said he had dinner with his wife at a local restaurant, Aspect was tending to her sick mother at a nursing home, and Biantano claimed to have gone to a movie with some friends. Basso took notes of all these remarks for confirmation later.

Basso decided to hold the question of Ambrose's private life until the separate meetings, thinking one of them would be more willing to share thoughts privately rather than in a group. He thanked them for attending but asked if he could speak to each of them alone. John Halbrook led it off.

"Mr. Halbrook, what can you tell me about Jennifer Ambrose's social life?"

"I am afraid very little. She was a very private person who to my knowledge did not mix business with pleasure."

"Did you ever see anyone visit her in her office who to your knowledge was not a client?"

"Again, no. Her office is on the other side of the building, so none of us would be likely to see who came or went there."

"What was your relationship with her like? Did you have any problem reporting to a woman?"

"None whatsoever. Jennifer was extremely professional, and she had my respect both as a lawyer and as a boss. And I believe she respected me for my work. My progress reviews were always favorable."

"Thank you, Mr. Halbrook. Could you please send in Ms. Aspect?"

Susan Aspect came in, sat down, and exhibited a slight bit of nervousness.

"How long have you and Ms. Ambrose been associated?"

"I was the first attorney she hired after she saw a need to enlarge the staff, so I have been with her from the beginning."

"Then you probably know her quite well. Did Ms. Ambrose ever confide in you about her social life? To your knowledge, did she have a steady boyfriend? Did she date frequently?"

"Jennifer always tried to keep her personal life private."

"But surely being as close to her as you were, she would have told you something about who she was seeing. I can't imagine you two never discussed things of a personal nature."

"A couple years ago, she was seeing a lawyer named Daniel Steele, but to my knowledge, that relationship stopped quickly after it began. He took a job in Europe with an international firm, and she never spoke of him once he moved overseas."

"Ambrose was a beautiful woman in the prime of her life. I find it hard to believe she was not involved with someone. Are you sure she did not confide in you about this?"

"I am sure. If she were seeing someone, I believe I would know about it."

"Well, thank you for your directness. One last question. Was she heavily involved in your cases? Did the two of you share input into how to structure your defense?"

"Jennifer allowed each of us to plot our own course of action. And we respected her for that."

"Thank you, Ms. Aspect. Could you please ask Ms. Biantano to come in?"

Ruth Biantano returned, and Basso immediately noticed she was a bit defensive. He started off with the standard question to put her at ease. "As a woman, did Ms. Ambrose confide in you about her social life?"

"I was not that well into her confidences, but from everything I have observed, she was dating someone on a regular basis. I have no idea who that might be, but possibly it was someone in our organization. We have a large company with many employees, so it would not surprise me if she had a relationship with one of them."

Basso realized that Biantano would not be the one in whom Ambrose confided, so he dismissed her and left the office and headed back to the precinct.

Before leaving, Basso set up an appointment with Santiago through his administrative assistant, Grace Fuller. She put him on his calendar for the coming Tuesday. Basso decided to skip for now speaking with the paralegal, since she had only been employed in the previous month and was not likely to know anything about Ambrose's personal life.

When Basso briefed Curto on his meetings with the lawyers, Curto said, "I think Aspect is holding back on us, Gene."

"I agree. If Biantano could notice something, and she obviously was not as close to Ambrose, then Aspect surely should have been aware of more than she leads us to believe. Plus, she insisted she had the authority to act independently on all her cases, yet we know that Ambrose was very much a hands-on boss. We need to dig into that more."

CHAPTER 12: THE INTERVIEW

Sitting at his office desk, Basso decided to phone McIntyre about the status of the full autopsy report and about the belt fragment. McIntyre promised to have the report to him in the morning. He did, however, have a startling revelation about the belt fragment. The blood was not Ambrose's. He therefore did some further checking on the body and discovered she had remnants of the same blood type in her mouth. This could suggest she did put up a fight after all and had bitten the assailant while he was in the process of strangling her. The killer must have brushed his bloody finger against her belt.

"Can you match it to anything?"

"I can tell you only that it is AB positive, which occurs in only six percent of people on earth. O positive is the blood type of 39 percent of all humans, followed by A positive at 27 percent and B positive at 22 percent. Negative blood types make up the balance. But it definitely is not Ambrose's blood. She is O positive."

"What about those thread strands you found on her dress?"

"They are from a very inexpensive suit or jacket. Guessing again, but I'd bet they belong to the assailant."

Basso mulled over the thread strand findings in his mind. "Ambrose was found wearing a very expensive designer dress, yet what McIntyre found was from a garment much less expensive. Was she actually involved with someone of a lower class than her obvious level?" He called Curto into his office.

"Julius, what have you learned from her credit card report?"

"She used it quite frequently, so I concentrated first on the day of the killing. There are no charges at any restaurant on that day, which would indicate she was not the one paying the bill. I made the rounds already of all the upscale Italian restaurants in the area, and nobody recognized her photo."

"Well, that certainly does not fit with what McIntyre told us. All the stomach contents suggested an Italian restaurant. Check other restaurants in the area to see if they carry an Italian menu in addition to their standard fare." Curto agreed and put it on his to-do list.

The following Tuesday, Basso went to the scheduled meeting with Santiago at the warehouse. Basso considered this interview critical, but he also knew he had to tread lightly. Although it was common knowledge within the police force that Santiago was heavily involved in illicit drug trafficking, Basso was investigating a murder and did not want to mix the two crimes. Santiago greeted him and ushered him into his office. He was dressed impeccably, as always, this time in a dark blue Kiton suit, light blue Ballistoni shirt, striped Ermenegildo Zegna tie, and Berluti shoes. Basso did not know the brands, but he correctly guessed that this outfit had to cost in the mid five-figure range. *"Life was good in the fast lane,"* he mused to himself.

"I assume you found all the lawyers cooperative when you spoke to them last week?"

"Yes, they certainly were. It was very helpful. I do have just a few questions for you. First, just to get it out of the way, where were you on the night Ambrose was killed?"

"That night, I had a business meeting in Pittsburgh with a company we are talking to about a possible acquisition. They are in the similar warehousing business as we are, and acquiring them could be beneficial to both firms. I insist you keep this information to yourselves, since we are both publicly traded companies. Any leaking of this information would be considered insider information. I am telling you only because it is necessary for you to know where I was that night."

"I assure you Mr. Santiago, you have my confidence on this matter. I am sure you have a way to corroborate this, don't you?"

"Certainly. If you would look at the E-ZPass toll charges available from the Pennsylvania Turnpike Commission, which I know you have access to, you will find that I drove my car there that morning and did not return to Harrisburg until well after midnight. Further, I have a credit card receipt for lunch where I entertained the president of the company. My administrative assistant, Mrs. Fuller, can provide that to you on the way out."

"Thank you. I am sure that will check out. I have a question on the employees you have in your organization. Reviewing prior and current court cases indicates that several of your people have been arrested and charged with felonies. Can you explain your hiring practices?"

"I am always saddened when one of our employees gets into trouble. But if you look at our employment statistics, you will see that we work very closely with the Pennsylvania Board of Probation and Parole to give job opportunities to men who have served their time and are ready to be rehabilitated. I am proud of this tradition we have established of being a good citizen in helping these people get a fresh start in life. For the most part, the program has been very successful, but every so often, someone slips back into old habits. I offer my legal staff to them free of charge to get them back in the fold and on the right track."

"Did Jennifer Ambrose oversee all these cases? Does she get directly involved or does she leave the planning to her legal staff?"

"I had total confidence in Jennifer to handle all these matters discreetly and professionally. Although she has three lawyers on her staff, she was intimately involved in the details. That was the work ethic she embraced, since she was ultimately responsible for the results."

"That is interesting, since Susan Aspect told me she was able to make all the decisions on her cases with little direction from Ambrose. The case she is currently working on involves Raphael Pino. Is there any reason she would make such a contradictory statement?"

"I have no idea, but I will speak with her about it."

It was difficult for Basso to hold this type of interview when he knew he should be attacking Santiago more aggressively, maybe even interrogating him. But he kept reminding himself it was a homicide, and he was not investigating a drug case. "One last request. While I am here, could I please speak with Tomás Rojas?"

"Certainly." Buzzing Mrs. Fuller, he asked her to send Rojas to the conference room to meet with Basso.

CHAPTER 12: THE INTERVIEW

Basso thanked him for his time, picked up the credit card information from Mrs. Fuller, and was escorted to the conference room to meet Tomás Rojas.

"Mr. Rojas, I just have a few questions about the murder of Jennifer Ambrose. Can you please tell me where you were on the night she was killed?"

"Well, all the guys generally play poker once a week in the lunchroom, and I usually participate. But on that night, which was our poker night, I had business in Philadelphia, so I could not play."

"Can anyone vouch for you?"

"Yes, I can give you the names of the people I was with. Would you like to write them down?"

Basso listed Rojas's alibi names. "Did you know Ms. Ambrose well?"

"No, only to the extent she interacted with any of my staff in a legal capacity."

"What is your role here at the warehouse?"

"I am the foreman of the men who operate the forklifts, unload and stock the customers' products, and drive the trucks, as well as all the other hourly-paid employees. They all report to me."

"Did she ever act on your behalf in any legal matters?

"No, I have had no problems with the law since serving my time at that Pittsburgh penitentiary. Never want to be confined like that again, so I have learned to control myself. My crime was an emotional reaction to the situation, and I know now it was wrong to allow myself to get out of control"

"Your altar boy persona does not ring true to me. You oversee all the parolees on the payroll, yet they consistently get into trouble. Most of them seem to be men who take orders rather than give them, so it would seem to a reasonable man that they were acting on someone else's orders. Since they work for you, the conclusion is obvious to me. I do not think you are as lily white as you suggest."

"Look Basso. I told you I have a clean record, and I do not support any of the actions of those guys, nor am I responsible for how they act. They are grown men, and they act accordingly. Get off my back."

"Mr. Rojas, I thought you said you were in control of your emotions. You just went off on me with very little provocation."

"I thought you were investigating a murder. You are a homicide cop. Why are you questioning me about those phony assault charges?"

"Because I can't rule out you or anyone of those guys as the perp in this case. She could have been killed on orders – maybe yours or maybe your boss's."

"Do you have one shred of evidence to suggest any of my people were involved in that killing? If not, I suggest you change your line of questioning or leave this building."

Basso was the one now with a short fuse. He stood up and reached across the table and grabbed Rojas by his shirt collar, which lifted him out of his seat. Holding him in that position, Basso said in an overly loud voice, "It seems you only know how to respond to physicality, so if you don't change your tone with me, I am going to get very angry. Do you understand?"

At that point, Mrs. Fuller entered the room. "What is all this commotion? Everyone on this floor can hear you two."

Basso released his grip on Rojas and forcibly shoved him back in his chair. "Sorry, Mrs. Fuller, but the people who work on the lower level do not seem to have the manners of those on this floor."

"You don't seem to either, Mr. Basso."

Basso accepted the rebuke and said to Rojas, "I have no other questions now. I may want to talk to you again, so don't leave town."

"I'm not going anywhere. Next time come with a subpoena."

As he was leaving, Basso saw a well-dressed man in his late 40s or early 50s in the hallway. Remembering that the Ambrose affair was most likely with a member of the firm, he returned to Mrs. Fuller and asked for his name.

"That is Mr. DeRiso, Mr. Damian DeRiso. He is Mr. Santiago's son-in-law. He heads up our marketing department."

"Does his wife work here also?"

"No, she is an accountant for a national CPA firm downtown."

Basso made a mental note to learn the names of all the men in the organization who could possibly qualify as Ambrose's lover. In the car, he phoned Curto to bring him up to date. Curto was annoyed at hearing that Basso had to sit there and politely listen to Santiago, a man he had spent many years of his career trying to put in jail. But he was pleased to know that he roughed up Rojas.

"You'll just have to be patient, Julius. We have a murder to solve, and with any luck, the fallout will also accomplish what you want."

CHAPTER 13: THE MARRIAGE

Diego Santiago married when he was in his mid-20s to a woman born in Italy but who had been in the USA since she was a very small child. Her parents emigrated from their home in southern Italy like the way Basso's and Curto's family came to America, arriving in the same post-World War II time frame. Santiago met Monica Marconi at a dance sponsored by the local chapter of the Order Sons and Daughters of Italy in America (OSDIA), an organization founded in 1905 in New York City dedicated to providing a system of support to Italian immigrants in achieving citizenship. The organization also served as a provider of health care benefits, classes in the English language, educational support, and other social welfare programs designed to make the assimilation into American society smoother.

Monica Marconi was immediately taken by the dashing Santiago, who displayed ostentatiously his new-found wealth. Up until this point, Santiago's world revolved around his Colombian neighborhood, and he rarely ventured into other areas. The population of the city was comprised of pockets of many different ethnic groups who settled in neighborhoods with people of similar European or South American backgrounds. Italian, Colombian, Hungarian, Yugoslavian, Romanian, Irish, Russian – they all were represented in closed communities that perpetuated the cultures of their respective homelands. The Catholic Church in many of these areas was required to assign priests who spoke the language of the inhabitants in order for the older folks who struggled with the new language to go to confession.

Diego and Monica danced that night under the watchful eye of her chaperone mother, and subsequently, Santiago began courting her in a formal way by calling on her at her home and spending time with her parents. When they announced they wanted to marry, there was significant push-back from her parents. They always envisioned she would marry a man of Italian extraction, and she would be the first to break this unwritten code if she married an outsider. But eventually Monica convinced them that he would be a good provider, and she would give them the grandchildren they wanted.

The couple were married in a formal Catholic service, and a typical Italian reception was held in celebration. Santiago's parents and friends sat on one side of the room, and all the guests of the bride on the other, showing the union was not fully blessed by either side.

Monica moved to the Colombian neighborhood where Santiago had bought a house, and she gave birth to two children within the first five years of the marriage. She immediately asserted herself as an extremely strong matriarch of the family. Although Diego was the power figure in all his business activities, Monica was the backbone of the family and the force that sustained it in the difficult times experienced by Santiago's operations. She was strong-willed and unbending in support of her husband, emulating the strength of her mother and grandmother, who had a powerful influence in molding her character. Monica's marriage to Diego was an enduring one based on strong family values. She died when Santiago was 65 years old, but the impact on the family was sustainable and ongoing.

Of their children, Barbara Santiago was the older, and Roberto Santiago followed. Barbara developed into an outspoken advocate of women's rights, a trait obviously inherited from her mother. Although Santiago was a traditional old-world father not born into a society that willingly accepted equality in women, he nonetheless gave her free reign to express herself. She was the light of his life. Barbara identified more with her mother's ethnic background rather than her father's, so it was only natural that when she found a husband, he would be an American of Italian descent.

Her marriage to Damian DeRiso, whose family lived in the Italian neighborhood, was the social event of the season. Santiago threw a lavish party with over 500 people in attendance, including many politicians and ranking giants of industry, the arts, and the sports world. Nothing was too good for his little girl. DeRiso was a talented man with a degree in marketing from the University of Pittsburgh. He accepted a job with Alcoa Aluminum, whose headquarters was in Pittsburgh, and the two spent the first five years of marriage in that city. Barbara had already completed two years of schooling at St. Vincent College in Latrobe, Pennsylvania, so she was able to transfer her credits to Duquesne University in Pittsburgh, where she earned a degree in accounting. Both are catholic institutions. Santiago was impressed with Damian's abilities. He offered him a position in Central Penn Warehousing, believing his skills could promote and expand the business. Barbara was happy to move back home, and since she had become a Certified Public Accountant while living in Pittsburgh, she had an easy time finding a job with a national CPA firm in Harrisburg.

The marriage was a happy one in Pittsburgh and for a few years in Harrisburg, but as so often happens when both are professionals with their own careers, the excitement of married life tended to wane.

It was, however, many years before Damian DeRiso roamed away from the loyalties demanded of married life. He was overly attracted to the head of the law department, even though she was twenty years younger than he. He soon found out the attraction was mutual. DeRiso and Jennifer Ambrose had a torrid, secret affair that lasted for about a year, but the fear of having DeRiso's father-in-law learn of it was greater than her lust, so she ceremoniously called an end to the affair. DeRiso had a very difficult time accepting it, even though he knew that doing anything to cross his father-in-law was asking for more trouble than he could ever imagine.

Basso was in his office when the phone call came. It was Susan Aspect. "Mr. Basso, I have something I must explain to you. Would it be possible for us to meet away from my office?"

Basso accepted the invitation, and the two met in an out-of-the-way coffee shop outside of the city.

"I was not totally honest with you when we first talked. I told you Jennifer had not confided in me and that I had no knowledge of her dating anyone. I do know the name of a man she was seeing, but you must understand that at the time, I was extremely afraid to tell you for fear of losing my job or worse. Well, the more I thought about it, the more I realized I could not keep silent, not with what has happened to her. The man she told me she was seeing was Damian DeRiso, the son-in-law of our employer. You can see how this is something I would not want to discuss, particularly not in a company office. It also wasn't truthful when I said she was not involved in my cases. I think professional pride overtook common sense, and I wanted to shield her as much as possible, but I realize now that was wrong."

"Yes, I do understand, and I am very thankful to you for coming forward with this information. How many others know of this affair?"

"To my knowledge, I am the only one. Jennifer was deathly afraid Santiago would find out, and everyone knows he has a very bad temper."

"Was the affair still going on at the time of her death?"

"No, she broke it off a while ago. She said they were in lust, not in love, and the pressure on her was too much to handle, so she told him it was over."

"How did he take it?"

"Not very well. His marriage with Santiago's daughter was not going well; they led different professional lives. Barbara's job frequently caused her to travel to other cities. Sometimes the trips lasted a week or longer, so they were often apart."

"I really appreciate your volunteering this information. It took a bit of courage. I am thankful for your actions now.

As they parted, Basso's mind was turning, trying to fit this latest piece into the expanding puzzle.

CHAPTER 14: THE FUNERAL

The funeral service for Jennifer Ambrose was sparsely attended. Her ex-husband Gregory, some members of the district attorney's office, and most of the office employees of the Santiago Harrisburg staff were there, but there was a conspicuous absence of others not associated with her business life. As Gregory Ambrose had told them, she did not have a large circle of friends outside her professional life. She was baptized a catholic, but she had not been a practicing one for many years; still, a standard catholic two-day viewing, mass at St. Anthony's Church, and a funeral procession to the gravesite ensued, albeit somewhat mechanically. Father McGinty made some general but not very personal comments about her, making his sermon sound uninspired. He had never met her, so that was to be expected. Basso and Curto were also in attendance, but they stayed out of sight of the other guests, preferring to monitor the event from afar to see who else was there. They hoped to get a glimpse of someone other than people from the business side, but that did not happen.

The day before, Basso had talked to the undertaker who owned the Stultz Funeral Parlor where the viewing was to occur. He asked him who had taken care of the administrative matters, and who was paying for the funeral. At first, Stultz was hesitant to respond, but Basso reminded him that the lady was murdered, and any questions he asked were aimed at finding an answer to her death. Stultz acquiesced and told him the administrative assistant to Diego Santiago, Grace Fuller, had planned everything. She had picked out the casket, dictated the viewing hours, and arranged for all other related matters including the financial piece. Fuller also planned a luncheon at a local restaurant after the burial. She was responsible for the multitude of funeral flower baskets that decorated the space around the casket during the viewing period, suggesting a wider circle of loved ones than existed. Santiago provided Cadillacs and Lincolns for the procession to the burial site; he rode in the first car.

While she was still married to Gregory Ambrose, they had selected and paid for the cemetery plot, so it seemed ironic that although they did not have a solid union in life, their bodies were destined to remain side by side for eternity.

Ambrose was very systematic in her planning, so the cemetery plot was not out of character. Most of her married life had been organized in a similar fashion. She had already passed the bar exam when she met her ex-husband, and he had already established his dental practice, so the union was somewhat akin to a business arrangement. When Basso had interviewed Gregory Ambrose earlier, he had asked him if, during the time of their marriage, he was in love with his wife. He answered somewhat matter-of-factly that he was terribly fond of her. This told Basso all he needed to know about their relationship. He felt if Jennifer Ambrose were alive to be asked the same question, her answer would be similar.

Basso mumbled under his breath *"Was this woman capable of loving another human being?"* With all her physical assets and financial stability, she should have been an attraction to most men who felt they could play in her league. From what Biantano told them plus what they learned from the surveillance tape, there was someone recently who had penetrated her tough exterior. *"Was that person DeRiso or someone else."* He felt learning that person's identity was the path to solving her murder.

Although all members of her law department were on hand, Basso was a bit surprised that none of the people she and her staff represented legally were there. Maybe this was on orders of Santiago, who knew the place would be watched by the police, so there was no need to expose them to any possible question and answer game – not at a funeral at least.

Basso made a short appearance at the after-burial luncheon, again hoping to catch a glimpse of someone other than those who had a corresponding LinkedIn account, but that was not the case. Curto remained in the car out of sight. Later, Basso asked Curto for his impression of the services. He remarked, "The woman was strictly professional in life, so why should we expect her funeral to be something other." Most funerals both men attended had always had some overriding sense of sorrow and sadness, but those emotions seemed to be seriously lacking at this one. Not that she wasn't an extremely well-respected person in life, she just did not give off the impression of being loved. Basso evaluated all this information and concluded silently *"All indicators point to her life revolving around her work, which suggests strongly that the killer was part of that crowd today."*

As they were pulling away at the restaurant, they were confronted by Joan McCabe, a ten-year veteran as a reporter for the Harrisburg Tribune, the smallest newspaper based on circulation in the city. The murder of a prominent attorney was big news in town. There was coverage on all the network TV news shows and the few remaining newspapers, but the Harrisburg Tribune, leaning typically toward sensationalism, made it headline news. They wanted to follow up with a feature about the specifics and the suspects. McCabe typically covered less than sensational news, but she pleaded with her editor to let her dig deeper into the Ambrose murder, and he agreed to let her try. She hailed the car, and Curto rolled down his passenger-side window. She had previously met Curto, so she directed her questions at him.

"Mr. Curto, I am interested in the human aspects of this case, specifically the life of the victim. What can you tell me about her job, her relationships, her friends?"

"Ms. McCabe, you probably have heard as much as I have about her. She was a lawyer, she was divorced, she was young, she was pretty, and now she is dead. We have some clues, but we are a long way from making an arrest."

"But I have already been doing some talking to people she worked with at Central Penn Warehousing, and if I read between the lines, there is more to it than you are saying. Was this a crime of passion? Was a jealous lover involved? Was she sexually assaulted?"

"Ms. McCabe, I am sure you were at our press conference, so we have told the press everything we know at this point. I am sorry, but we have nothing more to add now."

McCabe backed down, but she was determined to find out what they were hiding. She knew there was some dirt buried somewhere beneath the surface.

CHAPTER 15: THE TRIP

The weekend after the funeral, Curto was committed to taking his wife and two sons on a short holiday to the Choo Choo Barn, a miniature railroad layout in Strasburg, Pennsylvania less than an hour away. The display included a 1,700-square foot layout with 22 operating trains built to the O gauge standard of a quarter inch to the foot. Curto knew the boys would love seeing this wonderful display; as a young boy, he had been enamored with model trains and built his own layout in the family basement. The hobby started as a Christmas display under the tree but grew to much larger proportions as he became enthralled with constructing houses, stores, factories, and the like to complement the three model trains he operated.

Nine-year-old Robert, and seven-year-old Ronald Curto were very excited about the trip and highly anticipated a weekend with their father away from his demanding job. Both boys showed all the signs of growing up to be very handsome, which would be expected given the genes they inherited from both parents. To them, he always seemed to be working, always seemed to get phone calls during dinner, always seemed to have more time for the job than for them. This feeling of being neglected was not solely the children's view. Eszter had experienced the same sense of neglect. And with their third child due to arrive in a few months, the sense of abandonment heightened. It was hard for her to understand how a job could command so much of his time when supposedly he was off duty.

Initially she thought she was imagining it, but over a period of time, she started to entertain the idea that possibly it wasn't always the work that took him away from the family. *"Could he possibly be having an affair,"* she wondered. *"Has he lost interest in me."* She noticed how when shopping together, women would glance at him and smile. Other times when attending or hosting a neighborhood cocktail party, she noticed a few of the women getting overly friendly, but she attributed it to the ladies being a little tipsy. These thoughts of unfaithfulness played on her mind, and she hoped and prayed she was wrong in her assessment of the situation.

Since arriving in the USA with her husband after his tour of duty in her home country of Iraq, she had seen the magic of their relationship gradually decline, although this change happened very slowly. When they married in Iraq, life was blissful. The thought of moving to the USA was overwhelmingly exciting to her, and she knew she would be free of the rigid controls of Sharia Law, a set of guiding moral principles derived from the teachings of the Prophet Mohammed. She also knew she most likely would have to make some sacrifices career-wise. Eszter Abadi was a rarity among women in Iraq, a male dominated society. Only about 3 percent of Iraqi women out of a population of about 20 million acquire an education above the high school equivalent level, but she was in that group. Her parents were free thinkers who believed that women should have equal rights, but this kind of outlook was not shared by the masses. They learned very early that she was gifted intellectually, so they did their best to open opportunities for her in the restricted environment in which they lived. Through their open-mindedness, she was not subjected to genital mutilation so often fostered on women to curb sexual promiscuity. They were able to enroll her in The College of Sciences for Women at Baghdad University where she eventually received a Bachelor of Science degree in Biology.

She met Julius Curto in Baghdad at the marketplace while he was on a three-day pass. Although she wore the long abaya gown and hijab head scarf, Curto could see she was a beautiful woman. They talked at length in the open market, then she invited him back to her home where she felt more comfortable speaking with him away from glaring eyes. Curto saw immediately during their initial conversation that she was extraordinary in relation to other Iraqi women he had met. Her broad scope of conversational subjects singled her out as highly educated. Her parents accepted him immediately; Curto could charm most people he met. He continued to visit the home during off-duty hours with the approval of her parents, and as the relationship continued, it blossomed into love.

Curto proposed marriage and she immediately accepted, even though she envisioned her current career as a biochemist doing biomedical research would be over. As required when a person in the US military marries a foreign national, he completed numerous government forms, underwent counseling, a medical examination, and obtained the permission of his commander. Eszter was required to undergo a security background check, which highlighted nothing that would preclude her getting married. She also had to have a medical examination. Curto was required to attend classes and convert to the Muslim faith, since Islamic law prohibited a non-Muslim man to marry a Muslim woman in Iraq. Since he had no intention of practicing the faith, a second ceremony in the Christian faith was performed by the base chaplain but not made public. After completing all these procedures, Iraq's Social Status Court then recognized the marriage and issued a marriage contract that was signed by the two of them. Her parents were required to be present at the court when this happened. The United States Embassy in Iraq also officially recognized the marriage. From start to finish, the process took three months. She continued to live with her parents rather than move onto the base, but she did gain all the military benefits including medical coverage and commissary privileges.

In the car on the way to Strasburg, Eszter attempted to put these feelings of insecurity behind her, but it was difficult. She tried to be light-hearted while starting a singing session with the boys to lighten the tension she could feel brewing. But the fallout from her suspicious mood resulted in her snapping at Julius when he mentioned something disagreeable to her. He had been overly distant for much of the trip, and her tone set him off. What ensued was so typical of married people who sense a lack of trust. A verbal battle began and threatened to ruin the trip for the boys. She never directly brought up the subject of his suspected infidelity, but the inferences were great and further annoyed Julius. Ronald became afraid and started to cry.

Fortunately, or maybe unfortunately, Curto's cell phone rang. He answered it using the Bluetooth link connected to the car radio and speakers. It was Basso on the other end, and what he said was disastrous to everyone in the car except Curto. "Julius, I know it is your day off, but I need you in the office as quickly as you can get here."

"Gene, I am about a half hour drive outside of town. I was taking Eszter and the boys on a weekend excursion."

"I am sorry to do this to you, but you know I would not ask it if it were not extremely important. You'll have to give my apologies to them, but this is necessary."

The trip back to Camp Hill was extremely subdued, and no one spoke. They arrived back home, Eszter unloaded the car of the overnight bags she had packed for them, and she and the boys went into the house as Curto drove off to the precinct.

He was almost glad that Basso had put an end to the weekend trip. It had started off badly, and he suspected it would go downhill from there. He was disappointed for the boys, though; they really were looking forward to seeing the trains. He had talked to them a lot about his own layout, so their anticipation was very high. *"Whatever happened to all those trains I had,"* he wondered. *"After I left for the marines, Mom probably discarded them,"* he surmised.

CHAPTER 16: THE BAR

The Friday night before Curto left on his family outing, the law staff at Santiago's company were all working late. Each of the lawyers was heavily into structuring their respective defenses. At around 10 p.m., John Halbrook announced that he was pooped, and he extended an invitation to all. "Why don't we all call it quits and get a drink at the Pleasure Bar? Tomorrow is Saturday, and we could all use a change of scenery."

Although the offer was unexpected, both Susan Aspect and Ruth Biantano, plus the paralegal June Curtis, accepted. They had met socially as a group on several occasions previously, and these outings gave them a chance to let off steam. Although they at times sought feedback on their respective cases during these sessions, those topics were generally not on the agenda. These outings were designed to be work-free.

At the Pleasure Bar, they secured a table in the corner of the room and ordered drinks. "Great idea to get out of that office," said Aspect. "I was starting to see double reading all that text."

Halbrook joked, "If we stay here too long, the same thing could happen."

The group laughed at his witty remark. They all got along well both in and out of the office, which made for a favorable environment for all. This time, however, the mood became a bit maudlin. They recalled the times they had been at this very table and Jennifer Ambrose was with them.

"I still can't believe she's gone," Biantano uttered.

"Who could have done such a thing," chimed in Curtis. "I did not get to know her well in the month I have been here, but she certainly seemed like a decent person."

They agreed to stop discussing the matter in public, so the evening went on more amicably as the talk turned to fashion, then sports, and then politics.

Around midnight, the group decided to call it quits. Each had driven to the bar separately, so they took one last sip of their drinks and headed for the parking lot.

Aspect had the longest drive to make. Her commute each day was about 45 minutes each way. The others all lived closer to the job. She had not consumed a lot of alcohol, so her head was reasonably clear as she began the trip home.

Around 1 a.m., she arrived at her home, which she had owned for many years. She bought it after graduating from law school at Villanova University in Philadelphia and passing the bar exam. Aspect had several employment offers from larger law firms, some in downtown Philadelphia, but she was not raised as a city girl, so the offer to locate in central Pennsylvania with its rural surroundings appealed to her. At 48, she no longer could be called a young woman, but she was attractive, maintained herself well, and was in good health. Aspect had never married; she had a disastrous romantic affair with a married man when she was younger, and the breakup left deep scars on her. The man refused to leave his wife for her, resulting in her forming a life-long opinion that all men were bastards. Now at this point in her life, she was comfortable financially and reasonably happy not having a man in her life. Her job and her gardening hobby allowed her to feel content and secure in her person.

Aspect put her car in the attached garage, unlocked the door leading from the garage to the kitchen, and flicked on the lights. The neighborhood consisted mostly of upper middle-class professionals, with property values steadily rising. The area was considered a safe place to live and raise a family. She placed her handbag on the kitchen counter and poured herself a glass of water. As she was about to take off her suitcoat, she thought she heard a noise. Aspect walked into the living room, put on the lights, but saw nothing. *Am I imagining things*, she thought. The house was a one-floor design, and she always felt safe in it, since the neighborhood had no history of burglaries or other crimes. The only time she ever heard of a disturbance, a domestic squabble was at the root.

Just to be sure, she walked into her bedroom and bathroom, thinking to herself, *"I know I heard something."* Being satisfied she was wrong, she went back to the bedroom to change out of her office clothes. Although there was no official office dress code, most professionals adhered to the smart business casual style, while others dressed in more formal attire that was the norm in America a few decades ago. Before she could start undressing, she heard another noise in the kitchen. Still holding the water glass, she went back to the kitchen and instantly screamed. The glass slipped from her hand, crashing and breaking on the tile kitchen floor.

"What are you doing here, and how did you get in?"

"I have been waiting for well over an hour for you," he responded. "What took you so long?"

Then in a sudden forceful lunge, he grabbed at her, rotated her body around and up against his, and immediately wrapped a rough-edge cord around her neck. Aspect was caught so off-guard at the unexpected attack that she could in no way respond to it. As he pulled harder and harder on the cord, she grasped at it, trying to pry it away from her neck, but his gloved grip was much too strong for her. Coughing and crying out in a muffled voice that increasingly became quieter and then inaudible, she slowly felt her lungs being denied precious breath. Her hands began to release their grip on the cord, her head drooped, and she slumped to the floor. He checked her pulse and assured himself she was dead.

He made sure there were no traces of anyone other than Aspect being in the house, put back in place anything that might have been disturbed during the long period he was waiting for her to return home from work, and then cleaned up the broken glass on the kitchen floor, using a sponge to sop up the water. He placed the broken glass in a small paper bag and slipped it into his coat pocket, not wanting to leave it in the trash bin.

When he was certain that everything in the house was in place with nothing out of order, he took the car keys from her handbag, turned off the lights, and carried her body through the kitchen door into the garage. He placed her body in the truck of her car and pushed the button to raise the garage door.

The world appeared peaceful and silent at 1:30 a.m. There were no cars moving on the street; it was rare in this neighborhood that anyone would be on the streets at this time of night. A subdivision security service patrolled the neighborhood, but since it was a very low crime area, their trips were infrequent. All the stars seemed to be out, the sky was clear, and a half-moon cast its dimmed light over the surroundings. Confirming it was safe to pull out of the garage unnoticed, he headed for Wilson Park. Using a back road to avoid being noticed on the highway, he made the trip in less than an hour. Pulling up to the trail across from the bridge, he made sure there were no spying eyes of the security guard or any other. The body was unloaded from the trunk and quickly dragged down the grade to the general area where Jennifer Ambrose was found but out of sight from anyone standing on the bridge.

Climbing back up the hill, he was about to get into the car when his eye caught sight of a flashlight beam as someone walked across the bridge. Without starting the car, he put the gear lever into neutral and pushed it fully out of view from anyone standing on the bridge. His heart was pounding as slowly the light beam scanned the landscape, covering a wide spectrum of the hillside. The adrenaline rush was exhilarating; danger seemed to agree with him. Crouching flat on the ground, he was able to see that officer Josh Brady was making his rounds around the park. Apparently, this was a nightly ritual.

When Brady had moved on to another area of the park, he went back to the car and drove to Aspect's home, where he put the car back in her garage, placed the keys back in her handbag, and ensured he left no telltale signs of having been there. His car was parked several blocks away on a deserted street, and he made the short walk feeling very pleased with himself, musing *"That went very well, didn't it?"*

CHAPTER 17: THE SHORTCUT

Early Saturday morning, two boys were cutting across the park that served as a shortcut from their home to a gym operated by the Boys Club of America organization. The gym hosted a Saturday morning pick-up game of basketball that drew other teenagers in the deprived area. Surrounding the park on two sides was the neighborhood of Greenfield, which was once considered middle-class, but now it was a run-down assortment of deteriorating homes, abandoned businesses, boarded-up store fronts, and burnt-out automobiles. Low income workers inhabited it, most of them Black or Hispanic who had been bypassed in achieving the American dream they so desperately sought. Everyone in the city considered it a tough and unsafe neighborhood, so an outsider was rarely seen within its boundaries. It was said the neighborhood harbored escaped convicts, illegal immigrants, and army deserters, but the police were at a loss to apprehend any of these suspected criminals. For this reason, Wilson Park, which at one time had been the jewel of the city available to everyone as a haven from urban life, was now very rarely used, and all the amenities the park offered went mostly untapped.

Demetrius Johnson, street name Yoyo, and Antonio Jackson, street name Speed, were a product of this crumbling environment. As they made their way through the park to the gym, one of them spotted something under the bridge. They moved closer and discovered the body of Susan Aspect. Looking around to ensure they were alone, they removed the bracelet and wrist watch from her arms and a ring from her finger. Although they were pleased at the stroke of good luck they had just experienced, they were quite put off by not finding any money or credit cards on the body. In a fit of anger, one of the boys kicked the body viciously in the side. After venting this anger, they proceeded quickly on their way to the gym.

Despite the condition of the surrounding neighborhood, the city continued to maintain the park grounds, benefiting from a government grant through the National Park Service intended to support historical recreational facilities not directly under their administrative responsibility. Marcus Washington was steering his wide-blade riding lawnmower across the hillside under the bridge when he spotted the body of Susan Aspect later Saturday morning. When he realized what he had found, he immediately called 911, and within the hour, the area was swarming with policemen and an emergency ambulance crew.

Gianni Basso was also mowing his lawn when he received the call. He went into the house, took a quick shower, and made the call to Curto, insisting he cut short his weekend trip and meet him as soon as possible at the station.

He arrived at the station just as Curto was pulling into the parking lot. "Don't bother to get out. We have another murder on our hands." He jumped into the passenger side of the vehicle, and the two sped away to Wilson Park with the siren blaring to clear the way. Cars scattered to let them through the unusually heavy traffic for a weekend.

"Did you give my apologies to Eszter and the boys?"

Curto confirmed he did. As they approached Wilson Park, Curto spouted "This is getting to be a habit with this place."

Jeff McIntyre was already there, crouching over the body in an all-too-familiar pose.

"What do we have this time, Jeff."

McIntyre said in a depressing tone, "Another female strangulation, very similar to the Ambrose killing."

Basso was shocked when he looked down and immediately recognized the body of Susan Aspect. Although he routinely saw dead bodies and felt he was used to it, this one took him back a step, given he knew the victim and had recently talked with her. It was rare for him to know the identity of most of the dead bodies he encountered, let alone to know them personally.

"Are the strangle marks on the neck the same as on Ambrose?"

McIntyre replied "Yes, they show the very same pattern of a rope that has a nasty edge to it. It could be a wire rope from the looks of these neck marks or a thin cord with wire in its interior. Her blood has already coagulated, so it looks to me like she was killed about 11 or 12 hours ago. As to where, same conclusion as with Ambrose. The killing occurred elsewhere. There is one difference to this killing, though; she has evidence of being kicked very hard in the side, but she was already dead when that occurred. Bruise-like symptoms can appear post-mortem. If you want to talk to the worker who found the body, you will find him over there with those two policemen."

Marcus Washington was visibly shaken. Although in his neighborhood he saw drive-by shootings and people lying in the street, they always had a sheet covering them. Finding the body in such a raw state was a big shock for him. Curto was first to approach Washington.

"What time was it when you saw the body?"

"It was just after 11 a.m. I remember thinking that lunch time was coming soon, so I decided to make one last swoop of the hill with my mower before going back to my car to get my lunch. I was the only one of the crew working today. Needed to get in some overtime."

Curto returned to the body, telling Basso that the city worker was not much help. "Seems he just stumbled onto the body while mowing this hillside."

"Julius, notice that the woman is not wearing any rings, watch, or bracelet. When we interviewed her, she had on all three of those pieces. It seems odd that she is still dressed in a smart business suit and heels, yet she does not have on any jewelry. Let's try to find out right away what time she left her job. You check with Ms. Biantano by phone, and I will contact Mr. Halbrook."

"Will do, Gene."

Basso asked about the patrolman on duty last night. Another officer said it was Josh Brady, but he went off duty at 8 a.m. "Get him on the phone right now," Basso demanded. Brady answered his phone in a somewhat dazed manner, having been asleep for just a couple of hours. Working the night shift was not easy duty.

"Brady, this is Detective Basso. When was the last time your patrol route took you over the bridge at Wilson Park?"

Brady looked at his log and answered "Looks like I walked over the bridge around 1:50 a.m. I recall scanning my flashlight all over the area, but there was nothing unusual going on. Why do you ask?"

"We had another killing and the body was dumped under the bridge. Just wondering if you saw anything while making your rounds."

"Sorry, but as I said, it was very quiet; the weather was very nice for that time of the night, and I simply continued my rounds over the bridge and proceeded to the other sections of the park. It's a big place, as you know."

"Thanks, Brady. I'll let you know if we need anything else."

This new crime baffled Basso. He thought, *"It is no coincidence that both women worked for the same company, so there has got to be a connection to Santiago. And isn't it odd,"* he continued, *"that Susan Aspect was the one person so far who could have been a link to more information on the Ambrose murder. On the other hand,"* he wondered, *"could we possibly be dealing with a serial killer."* The thought certainly had entered his mind.

The medics were loading the body into the ambulance when Basso got off the phone with Brady. "Julius, go with them and McIntyre to the lab to see if we can get an early clue from the examination. I'll drive your car back to the station."

Before leaving, Curto questioned and searched Marcus Washington. He was reasonably sure Washington had not taken the jewelry. The man was still highly unsettled from finding the body.

Basso looked at his phone contact list and made a call to John Halbrook. "Sorry to bother you on a Saturday, Mr. Halbrook, but I wonder if I could come over to your house to have a word with you. Would that be convenient?"

Halbrook agreed to meet him, but Basso gave him no indication of what he wanted to discuss. Halbrook thought he was through with all this.

CHAPTER 18: THE LAWYER

John Halbrook's home was in Hershey, a short distance east of Harrisburg. His community, nicknamed 'Chocolatetown', is famous as the location of The Hershey Company, world-renowned maker of chocolate candy. The town also boasts the Hershey Park theme park, host to more than three million visitors annually.

Halbrook opened the door to admit Detective Basso upon his arrival, sporting an obvious quizzical look on his face. He ushered him into the living room, and the two sat down. Halbrook's wife came in, and he introduced her. "Detective Basso, this is my wife, Annette."

"Pleased to meet you, Mrs. Halbrook. I am afraid I have some unpleasant news for you. We just found the dead body of your co-worker Susan Aspect in Wilson Park." Halbrook was aghast. He was in total shock, and so was his wife, who had met her on several social occasions.

Not wanting to do any questioning of Halbrook in front of his wife, he asked, "Would it be possible to speak to your husband alone, Mrs. Halbrook?"

"Certainly," she said trying unsuccessfully to hold back sobs of sincere sorrow and utter disbelief. A sense of fear overtook her, realizing that two people in his department had been murdered. She did not want to continue the line of thinking overtaking her thoughts; it was too frightening to even imagine.

"Mr. Halbrook, Ms. Aspect was found strangled, and it appears it happened last night. What can you tell me about your work day yesterday? To your knowledge, when did she leave the office?"

Halbrook went into lengthy detail to explain they were all working late, and at about 10 p.m., the entire department decided to have a drink at the Pleasure Bar. "We, that is Ms. Biantano, Ms. Curtis, and Ms. Aspect, and I stayed there until around midnight, and then we all left in separate cars. Susan lives about 45 minutes away, but she was not inebriated and was perfectly able to drive."

"What was she wearing."

"As I recall, she had on a stylish business suit, but with slacks rather than a skirt."

"Did she have on any jewelry?"

"I am not an overly observant man, but I do believe she had on a bracelet, and, yes, also a watch, because at one point I asked for the time, and she responded."

"When you left the parking lot, did you notice any other cars in the lot? Could someone have followed her?"

"It was just about closing time for that bar. They don't stay open until the legal limit of 2 a.m., so the parking lot was pretty much deserted. I believe our four cars were the only ones in the customer section of the lot."

"What time did you arrive home?"

"I arrived home around 12:30. Not much traffic that time of night, and my wife was still up watching a movie when I came in."

"I know we went over this in our meeting at your office, but in your mind, did you think any of the people you were defending was a threat? Were you fearful of anyone?"

"No, as I said before, everything we were doing was routine."

"Well, thank you Mr. Halbrook. I am sure we will learn more after we examine the body. I am sorry to have been the one to break this news to you."

"May I ask something before you leave, Mr. Basso? Does Ruth Biantano and June Curtis know about this tragic event?

As you know, our department is very close-knit, and since we were all together last night, I don't want to be the one to break the news unless you don't intend to notify them. I certainly don't want to panic them into thinking there is a plot against our group. You know lawyers are not the most loved people in the world. You don't think there is a vendetta targeting our department, do you?"

"No, Mr. Halbrook, I have no reason to believe that these crimes are specifically directed at lawyers or at your company's lawyers. You are at liberty to communicate with them, but I believe someone on my staff is in the process of alerting them. In situations like this, we prefer those with close association to the victim not learn about it on the evening news."

Halbrook's wife returned to say goodbye, but she was highly unnerved. Her voice cracked as she tried desperately to hold back the feelings of dread that overcame her. Halbrook was himself in a daze. He said to his wife, "You see someone one day, and the next day they are dead. This whole situation is almost too emotional to tolerate."

Basso left the house, satisfied about confirming his presumption that Aspect had been wearing jewelry that evening. He also was genuinely moved by the sincerity Halbrook showed in his reaction to what he told him. "Unless he is an academy award-level actor, his emotions are fully believable."

His mind started down the path it typically takes when he has a difficult problem to solve. Basso was a very logical thinker and had substantial training in the art of problem resolution. He had taken courses on the subject that were offered primarily to business people to solve business-related problems using the case study instructional method pioneered years ago by the Harvard Business School. The courses stressed the key to resolving a problem was to isolate the changes or differences in the information presented. In fact, *Change Analysis* was the title of one of these courses, and its concepts applied to all problems in life, not necessarily business ones. Students were presented a scenario containing ambiguous information, but there was no specific question asked. Students had to uncover the problem as well as the solution from analyzing the scenario.

So, he thought of the similarities of the two murders and the differences. Obviously, the method of killing was the same, the location of the bodies was the same, and the occupation and employer were the same. He realized very quickly, though, the first body did not have any signs of trauma other than on the neck, while the second one was bruised on the side. The first body showed no sign of a robbery, but the second one did. He also realized that the first body was found almost immediately after being dumped under the bridge, while many hours passed before the second one was discovered. *"What if there are two crimes here – a murder and a robbery? The timeframe for discovering the second body certainly would allow that."* He took out his notebook and wrote a message to himself to have a patrolman from the precinct canvass the local pawn shops to learn if any jewelry had been pawned very recently.

He also planned his next move in information gathering. They had not yet talked to most of the others in Santiago's company other than the professionals and the foreman Rojas. It was time they broadened the scope, since the second murder put the direction of the investigation squarely on that company.

Central Penn Warehousing Inc. employed about 60 people in total, including the professional staffs of traffic managers, marketing and sales specialists, and accountants, in addition to the lawyers he had already interviewed. The non-professional group consisted of warehousemen, truck drivers, forklift operators, and general laborers plus the group of hired parolees. He selected the parolees as the people he wanted to review first, and Raphael Pino was at the top of the list, given his connection to Aspect and what he had learned about his pending case from Curto. Officially, his job with the company was forklift driver, but his rap sheet confirmed he had extracurricular activities.

CHAPTER 19: THE TOUR OF DUTY

Curto rode back to the city in the ambulance with the paramedics and the body of Susan Aspect. His thoughts wandered during the ride, mainly to the argument he had with Eszter and the disappointment the boys experienced from having the trip stopped before it began. *"When had things started to go wrong? Why have we grown distant? Was she to blame, or was I?"* These questions rattled around in his brain as he disassociated himself from the body lying in the back of the ambulance. Over the years, he had become somewhat calloused to death; uncomfortableness was the extent of the emotion it stirred. His tour of duty in Iraq had exposed him to all the death a human should have to encounter. Curto wondered how he would react to the death of his boys or Eszter should that occur.

Curto spent his whole career after college in law enforcement, including his six years in the Marines where he was assigned to the Provost Marshall's staff. He was born in California, but his parents relocated to Pennsylvania when he was six due to a job promotion his father attained with a chemical company where he was Vice President of Marketing and Sales. He was brought up in an upscale neighborhood in Bucks County, did reasonably well in school, and enrolled at Temple University in Philadelphia where he majored in psychology. This provided him with ample tools to better understand human behavior. He was always an astute judge of character and prided himself on being able to predict the behavioral direction a person would take in any given situation. Curto was also part of the Navy Reserve Officers Training Corps (ROTC) program at Temple and selected the Marine option, which required his entry into the military right after graduation to fulfill his obligation for the scholarship they provided.

His marine tour of duty took him to Iraq right at the end of Gulf War 2, also known as Operation Iraqi Freedom. He arrived in May 2003 just after the invading forces of the USA, UK, Australia, and Poland had captured Baghdad. The coalition had an express goal of ridding Iraq of weapons of mass destruction, but speculation was rampant that the USA's motivation was strongly influenced by the 9/11 attack on the World Trade Center. The armed conflict was short, lasting from March 20, 2003 to May 1, 2003. After the fall of Baghdad, the country was in chaos, making the need for deterring violence and establishing control vital, not only with the civilian population but among the troops as well. As a captain in the law enforcement arm of the Marines, he was in a strong position of authority, and he embraced this status wholeheartedly. He loved being in charge and relished the concept of playing a vital role in ensuring the security of the people.

Danger was a given in doing his job. On one occasion, Curto was assigned to head up an investigation of two marines who were reported as having deserted their post. The morning report of personnel changes from the previous day listed Marine Corporal Joseph Bennett and Lance Corporal John Hanratty as AWOL, citing their absence from roll call. Curto assembled a team of four military police under his command to retrace the steps of the missing men from the night before. He began by interviewing the men who bunked above and next to them. He learned that Bennett and Hanratty had a pass allowing them to exit the post for six hours, but they had not returned to the base before the midnight curfew. He then talked with the base bus driver who transported them and learned they were dropped off the previous night at a hotel bar in the city. The bus driver said they were not at his last pick-up stop at 11:45. Curto's team went to the drop-off location to talk with anyone who had seen the two marines. They learned the two men had entered the hotel bar around 8 p.m., reputedly wanting to relieve the tension of military duty. After the regime of Saddam Hussein fell in 2003, whiskey, beer, and wine once again were available in Baghdad for a short period of time.

Curto then questioned the staff on duty the night before. At first no one would tell him anything, so using strong language and displaying prominently their weapons, they were able to pry out of the bartender what had happened. But not before Curto used intimidation and brute force to show he would not tolerate silence. He learned the marines were sitting at a table enjoying a beer, a cigarette, and the bar's music when six members of the militant Al-Qaeda burst in, shooting their rifles into the air to gain attention. Everyone in the club froze in silence, realizing these extremists were dangerous and fanatical. They smashed bottles, upset tables, and harassed the locals for consuming alcohol, but when they saw the US marines, their anger rose tenfold. Four Al-Qaeda members approached the marines and forcibly dragged them away from the table while the others held the crowd at gunpoint. The crowd could not stop Bennett and Hanratty from being kidnapped, nor would they if they had the opportunity. The Al-Qaeda exited with the two marines after putting cloth sacks over their heads and tying their hands behind their backs.

Curto demanded to know where they were taken, and one waiter who saw how the bartender was treated yielded to the pressure and offered a possible location known to harbor these dissidents. The M.P. team and Curto went to the address on the perimeter of the city, and with weapons drawn, burst into a filthy basement room to find Bennett and Hanratty strapped to chairs, still with the cloth sacks over their heads. They caught the Al-Qaeda gang, who had been torturing the marines off and on all night, by surprise, allowing the invading force to open fire and kill all the Al-Qaeda present. Bennett was sobbing in pain; his index finger and middle finger that held his cigarettes had been amputated as a symbol of the Al-Qaeda's disdain for the use of tobacco. They cauterized the open wounds with a red-hot branding iron. Hanratty had cigarette and iron burns over his face, back and chest. Curto's team extricated the prisoners from the basement before any others in the immediate area could react, and they were able to get both to the base hospital for emergency treatment. What intrigued Curto most about the operation was the satisfaction saving these men gave him. He realized he could never perform a desk job when he returned to civilian life.

It was during this period of turmoil that he met Eszter. Maybe it was the desire to be away for a while from the violence he encountered daily, maybe it was his loneliness for intelligent conversation, maybe it was the need for female companionship. Whatever the reason, he was drawn to her immediately after their encounter in the marketplace. He was learning very quickly the customs of the Iraqi people, and he knew military personnel were not the most loved souls by the Iraqi people. When she invited him into her home to meet her parents, he was immediately thrilled by the situation. His visits to their home became a haven from the turbulence he was forced to endure in this war-torn country.

But all that seemed to change when he was discharged from the marines and returned to the USA. Excitement no longer surrounded him daily. Exposure to a constant diet of that lifestyle can become infectious, and he craved the satisfaction being in control gave him. It was only natural that he gravitated toward a job on the police force.

Curto was mustered out of the military through the Indiantown Gap Military Reservation (The Gap) in Annville, Pennsylvania. This military base northeast of Harrisburg played a strategic role in many of the armed conflicts the USA faced. During World War II, it was a major training facility used to amass thousands of soldiers who were then sent to Europe for the war against Germany. It became important again during the Korean War as a training ground for thousands of replacement troops. The National Guard used the base extensively in the 1960s for training summer camp reservists. The Gap became a refugee camp for thousands of Vietnamese and Cambodians after the Vietnam War, and again in 1980 as a refugee camp for the mass emigration by boat of Cuban aliens seeking asylum. It was a mobilization center in 1990 for units deployed in the first Persian Gulf war. While Curto was on active duty, The Gap was again a mobilization center for troops destined for Bosnia and Kosovo, as well as for operations in Iraq. The base also became a training headquarters for the Pennsylvania State Police Academy.

Curto decided to settle in this area. He and Eszter chose central Pennsylvania, thinking it would provide a better environment for their soon to arrive first child as opposed to the densely populated eastern part of the state. In 2010, Forbes Magazine rated Harrisburg as the second-best place in the USA to raise a family. His military assignments had given him solid credentials for this work, and he was hired onto the Harrisburg police force immediately after he applied.

After the mandatory schooling at the Police Academy, he had an opportunity to choose the area of specialization he preferred. He sorted through his options, but he was intrigued with the work the undercover police did. They were not subject to the disciplines of other police sectors, and the free-wheeling methods of the assignment appealed to him. He could once again personally oversee the direction his work took.

Like most cities in the USA, drug use had proliferated nearly unabated in the poorer neighborhoods. There were the corner thugs who pushed the product onto youths who became increasingly dependent on the illegal substances. But arresting these pushers who preyed on downtrodden citizens was not the answer to the problem. His assignment was to infiltrate the organization to learn the source from which this river of destruction flowed. Doing this was a time-consuming job that took patience, self-confidence, and perseverance if success was going to be realized.

The Greenfield suburb surrounding Wilson Park was the logical place for him to insert himself into this culture. His daily wardrobe matched the dress of the people living there, being drab, unkempt, and lacking any semblance of well-being. He took on the name of Stefano Grassi and was provided with adequate identification and a falsified background of previous criminal charges that would support his claim of being who he was not. He grew a full beard, had his black hair dyed light brown, had contacts inserted to change his eye color, had removable tattoos professionally drawn on his arms, and made other adjustments to make it difficult to recognize him as Julius Curto. He rented a sparsely furnished third-floor walk-up apartment in Greenfield, which was to be home for him while this assignment lasted. Given his ability for winning over the confidences of others, he gradually wormed his way into the organization by living fully the life of a sleaze. He could only revert to the more affluent lifestyle he provided his family on limited occasions. The job required Curto to be away from them for extended periods of time. It was rare that an undercover agent could enjoy a family life, but he was able to juggle both roles effectively, even though he only saw Eszter and the boys when he could temporarily cast off the undercover role.

Stefano Grassi né Julius Curto's leadership ability was soon noticed by several underlings of Tomás Rojas, who Curto learned was in direct control of the men who provided the pushers in the neighborhood with their illicit product.

Rojas' men had talked to him about this guy they called Grassi and suggested he could be helpful to the organization. They judged him street-smart and willing to take controlled risks, qualities that would make him a useful tool in their profit-motivated schemes.

He was, however, given several severe tests to confirm he was a fit in their organization. So, for the first time in his military and civilian life, he was required to break the law instead of enforce it. They also checked his background, which revealed the history the police had fabricated. Curto had to show a violent side when asked to take care of a user who had gotten in debt due to his unaffordable drug habit. In view of Rojas and the others, he showed no mercy to the man, beating him severely. He passed this test, but felt obligated to tell Rojas that acts like that don't put any money in their pocket. "It is not about money," he countered. "When word gets out what happened to this man, it will cause many others to reconsider stiffing us."

After several other tests of his willingness to do despicable things to detestable people, his reputation as a tough guy with brains grew. He learned the ins and outs of the drug trade, all the while growing more confident in his ability to pull off this charade. Only on rare occasions was he asked to give a status report of his progress to the head of the undercover division. They would meet in a nondescript car in a remote area away from Greenfield and Wilson Park, and

Curto would brief him on his escapades. He gave leads to the police on occasion as to when a new supply of drugs would be hitting the street, but he was cautious not to do this frequently. The last thing he wanted was for someone to suspect there was a rat in the organization. When the police did make a bust, he made sure the information he had given could have logically come from an alternate source. It was an approach he learned when reading about Britain's tactic, code-named Ultra, used during World War II with intercepted wartime data sourced from having broken the code of highly-encrypted enemy communications on Hitler's planned strategies.

Eventually, word of Curto's talent reached the head of the organization. Rojas told Santiago about his guy they were using who had proven himself an asset in maintaining control of the Wilson Park suburb. He was not surprised when Rojas finally invited him to take a ride, guessing correctly they would be going to meet the head man. He was ushered into the warehouse and told to wait in one of the back aisles while Rojas went up the stairs to the second-level offices. In about fifteen minutes, Rojas came back and said, "Follow me."

He went into Diego Santiago's office with Rojas behind him, and introductions were made. "I have been hearing a lot about you, Grassi. Tomás has been telling me how you have helped us. I can use a man of your talents in my organization. You could be making a lot more money than you are now.

And it would certainly improve the way you dress." Grassi noticed immediately how stylishly Santiago was dressed, almost too fashionable for the warehouse environment they were in.

After having been undercover in the streets for some time, Curto realized he was finally getting a chance to do the job he was assigned to do. He gladly accepted the offer and thanked Santiago for the opportunity.

From that point on, the man called Stefano Grassi became increasingly useful to Santiago. His innate ability to win over one's confidence worked to perfection with Santiago, who took a liking to the man who reminded him of himself when he was just starting out.

Curto was awakened from his reveries when the ambulance pulled into the morgue's parking lot and the body of Susan Aspect was ceremoniously placed on a long table in McIntyre's near-frigid all-white laboratory. "Let's see what else this unfortunate girl can tell us," McIntyre muttered.

CHAPTER 20: THE DROP

Upon Basso's orders, Raphael Pino was picked up by the police and taken to the station for questioning. Basso was in the interrogation room when Pino was brought in by two officers. "Am I under arrest," Pino asked in a belligerent tone.

"No, I just want to ask you a few questions. I would suggest you call your lawyer, Pino, but as you are well aware, she is dead."

"What are you talking about – dead. I spoke with her Friday at her office, and she was just fine."

"Well, she is not fine now. Someone strangled her Friday night and dumped her body in Wilson Park. We want to know what you know about this. Keep in mind you are a two-time felon, so the next conviction will put you away for a long, long time."

"Are you suggesting I had something to do with this? You are way off base. What reason would I have for killing her? She was my attorney, and I relied on her to keep me out of trouble."

Using the theory prompted by Curto, Basso said, "We heard your current scrape with the law was not going so well. Did you think she was not putting forth the full effort on your behalf? We have seen more than once where an attorney sacrifices the client on orders from higher-up."

"Wait a minute. You got this thing all wrong. I am a forklift driver for Central Penn Warehousing and nothing more. I know nothing of any murder, and I certainly would not want to kill the person who was defending me against your bogus charges. I want to talk with Mr. Santiago. I want him to send a lawyer down here right now. You have no right to accuse me of anything."

"Unfortunately, Mr. Pino, your past actions give us every right in the world to accuse you. You could hardly be considered a model citizen. But I am through with being nice to you. If you don't stop this play acting, I am going to forget about all the rights you supposedly think you have." Basso went around the table and pulled Pino backwards until his chair was tilted on two legs. As he was about to drop the chair, a loud rap on the observation window caused Basso to stop. He gained his composure and pushed the chair forward, causing Pino's chest to be jammed by the edge of the desk.

"I am not saying another word without a lawyer. And I am going to sue the police department for this brutality. If I am not under arrest, I demand you let me out of here."

"You are free to leave anytime you want; I just thought you would want to cooperate with us in this terrible matter, but apparently you prefer to play hard ball. But I can get even harder and become your worst nightmare."

"Cooperating with you is like dealing with the devil." With that, Pino left the station immediately.

As Pino was exiting the precinct, Joan McCabe of the Harrisburg Tribune confronted him. She had been hanging around the station hoping to get an exclusive on the murder case. "Mr. Pino, did the police question you about the murder of Susan Aspect?"

"Lady, get out of my way before I make you do it. I have no comment."

Back inside Basso's office, he and Curto continued to discuss the case. "Gene, we should talk to the DA to see if we have grounds to hold him." Curto had witnessed the interrogation from behind the one-way glass separating the interrogation room from the viewing area. "Look at the facts: he was being defended by her; she wasn't doing her best; Ambrose pulled all the strings on cases; Ambrose answers to Santiago."

"Julius, all you have there is conjecture. If we had one shred of evidence to link him to either or both murders, I would do it in a heartbeat. But as of now, we have no other alternative than to let him go. Besides, we always know where to find him."

"Gene, you are forgetting about one piece of significant circumstantial evidence. Pino's blood type is AB positive, which as you know is an extremely rare type found only in a small percentage of humans. All the same, I think I will talk with Nancy Kowalski to get her opinion. She has been able to make a case stick more than once on circumstantial evidence." Kowalski was the senior Assistant District Attorney on the staff of District Attorney George Ziegler, who was in his second term of office for Dauphin County.

Basso wanted to wrap this thing up as much as Curto did, but he did not want to be embarrassed by charging a person and then finding he could not get a grand jury indictment, particularly when the man worked for someone as powerful as Santiago.

"Julius, I'll talk to some of his co-workers to see if I can learn more."

The media had not yet released the news of Aspect's death. Basso felt he would soon be under a lot of pressure from Mayor Bixby. Two killings involving employees of the same company would make headline news, not to mention

Santiago would be leading the call for prompt action. Joan McCabe would be going to press very soon.

Raphael Pino was more than anxious to get out of the hands of the police. He, Tomás Rojas, and Matias Martinez were making their quarterly run to the Philadelphia docks that evening. As routinely happened, they were to meet an arriving ship from Colombia whose cargo had not yet been cleared by customs officials.

The cargo ship Santa Marta arrived at the Philadelphia docks around 3 p.m. that afternoon. The vessel was a medium sized carrier loaded with 8,000 20-foot metal containers. This ship typically operated with a crew of 30, including the ship's master, three deck officers, three engineering officers, and 23 ratings, the name given to the non-officer crew working in either the engine room, cargo area, or kitchen. The ship primarily transported Colombian coffee, a product much in demand by aficionados of the beverage. Included in the rating crew were six men recruited by Alejandro Moreno to carry out his illicit drug operation.

Santiago owned under an assumed name a large spacious powerboat that he kept at a private berthing site near the commercial docks. Two of the Colombian crew slipped off the ship unnoticed around 11 p.m. and made their way to the dock where they boarded Santiago's boat. The craft was outfitted with a large open deck area with protective railings and could accommodate as many as 40 crates. The boat maneuvered through choppy waters to the side of the Santa Marta not facing the dock.

Meanwhile, the other four ratings in Moreno's employ volunteered for night watch duty, which was easy to attain since it was undesirable duty normally requiring an officer to order men to it. After the long ocean voyage, the entire crew was anxious for some rest and relaxation, and although not permitted to disembark the ship, they passed the time playing cards or dice. Some at times gambled away their entire earnings from the trip. Heavy work awaited them in the morning when the containers were to be unloaded, but on arrival day, it was free time for most.

Being careful to avoid the watchful eyes of the deck officer on duty, the four Moreno ratings located the deck-level container that had been specially marked and positioned for ease in opening. The front portion of the container held crates filled with high-grade uncut cocaine Moreno was shipping to Santiago. Similar markings were on the designated cocaine crates within the large container. The drugs were packaged in plastic bags buried within the center of vacuum-sealed institution sized No. 10 coffee cans. Each of the 20 crates contained four cases or 24 cans, and each can normally held three pounds of coffee. Roughly half of each can was cocaine, so this shipment represented about 720 pounds of cocaine. Since the USA street value of cocaine is $150 per gram, this shipment was valued at $50 million uncut and nearly double when cut.

The men flipped the latches and pulled outward on the two heavy levers to open the locking rods securing the right side of the container. Then they duplicated this effort to open the left-side door. Previously that day, they ensured the container's center lock box was open. Clandestinely, the four men moved the marked crates to a portable crane they had maneuvered to the ship's side, below which sat the powerboat bobbing in the water.

The entire mission was perilous. Coast Guard vessels routinely patrolled these waters, and avoiding their large, probing searchlights was a challenge. They had, however, perfected the routine over time and knew precisely the schedule for the Coast Guard's trips. Periodically, one of the men supposedly on guard duty reported in to the deck officer on the bridge to announce all was well.

Using the heavy-duty crane, they slowly dropped the crates, which were bundled in a large cargo net for lowering down to the powerboat. The water line of the boat dropped with each additional crate put onboard. This procedure had to be conducted before morning when customs officials would board the ship and inspect the contents of many 20-foot containers selected at random. Rather than chance any of the tainted coffee crates being selected for inspection,

Santiago opted for the unloading procedure before the checking began.

The entire operation took a little over one hour. When all the crates were off-loaded to the boat, it sped away from the ship to a secluded cove about four miles away. Rojas and his men were waiting with an unmarked truck to take the goods back to the Santiago warehouse.

This operation had been carried out countless times without any difficulty, so there was no reason to believe this night would be any different. When the powerboat approached the cove's landing dock, it flashed its lights to signal its arrival. Rojas and his team were waiting to acknowledge the signal. The boat docked, and the crew started to pass the many crates to Rojas's men. The crates were stacked on the dock by hand, which was tedious, time-consuming work. The powerboat driver and his helper handed each crate to Rojas and his men, and the routine went smoothly under the cover of darkness.

But to the team's dismay, when there remained only a couple of crates to transfer to the dock, a glaring, highly luminous spotlight concentrated on them. From the ground area behind them facing the dock, a voice announced using a powered megaphone, "This is the Harbor Patrol; you are to cease and desist what you are doing and put your hands up." Rojas and his two men were blinded at first by the light and stunned at the unsuspected intrusion. The powerboat driver, however, ignored the order, and his helper released the line tethering the boat to the dock. They sped away under a hail of bullets from the Harbor Patrol with the remaining few crates still onboard. Rojas and Martinez realized they were outnumbered and at an extreme disadvantage, so they immediately ran for cover in the surrounding bushes and trees away from where the megaphone voice emanated. They were able through crouching and crawling to make their way laboriously to the truck without being detected. The truck was out of sight of the Harbor Patrol, hidden by densely clustered trees on a deserted dirt road.

On a normal operation, once the crates were on the dock, the truck would be brought out of its hiding place to the dock for yet another labor-intensive handling. Rojas was pleased with himself for having devised this multi-step maneuver, which paid dividends this time. Raphael Pino, being too proud or too dumb, stayed behind. He made an immediate move to pull his gun tucked in the small of his back, but before he could fire, he was greeted with a multitude of gunshots from the entire perimeter secured by the Harbor Patrol. He died instantly.

Rojas and Martinez witnessed Pino's execution, which in their minds was closer to a suicide. After a few minutes the shooting stopped, and the Coast Guard squad made its way to the dock to take possession of the crates. Rojas and

Martinez waited patiently for over an hour while the Harbor Patrol confiscated the crates. When the area cleared, and they felt it was safe to leave, they sped away back to Harrisburg, fearful of having to tell Santiago what happened. They had no idea what went wrong, but they knew Santiago was intolerant of failure regardless of who or what was deemed responsible. Although losing an entire shipment was unacceptable to their unsympathetic boss, their fear extended much deeper. They feared for their very lives.

CHAPTER 21: THE BACKLASH

When Rojas and Martinez returned to the Santiago warehouse, they drove the van into the facility and parked it in the rear out of site. Normally, this was the interior parking spot where the crates would be unloaded and the drugs extracted for processing, packaging, and eventual distribution. With no crates in the van and Pino dead, they were quite fearful of what was to come Monday morning when they would have to face Santiago. They did not have to wait that long. Although Pino had no identification on him, nor did the others, the Philadelphia police, who took possession of his body from the Harbor Patrol, were easily able to make his identification based on several mug shots they had on computerized files. As a two-time convicted felon, his face was well known to the Philadelphia police and available to every police station in the country through this online database of criminals.

Philadelphia police notified Harrisburg police, since that was his last known address, and the news of his death became public knowledge very quickly. Santiago was having lunch on Sunday at the local country club with several politicians when he received the notification. He excused himself from the table and left promptly for his office, notifying Rojas to have everyone there immediately.

Rojas rounded up his team, and they were all there at the warehouse when Santiago came in. To say he was angry is putting it mildly. "I will try to remain calm. We lost product having a street value of nearly 100 million dollars. Do any of your feeble brains comprehend the magnitude of this loss? The supply for the entire eastern seaboard will be significantly affected by your stupidity. We run the risk of losing long-time customers. The door could be opened to any number of competitors anxious to jump at the chance to take our business. Someone tell me what happened."

Rojas went on to explain the entire scenario. He told of the ship being unloaded clandestinely, the crates transported by boat to the assigned docking location, and the crew's efforts in unloading most of them onto the dock. "That is when all hell broke out. The place lit up like Veterans Stadium. The harbor police were there waiting for us. There is no way they could have known we would be there."

"Is the entire cargo lost?"

"Yes, all except a couple crates that had not been unloaded, but the powerboat got away, and I don't know what happened after that. Pino pulled out his gun, and that signaled the police to open fire. Martinez and I were able to escape – no way we were going to get into a shootout with them, but that crazy Pino did. And he paid for it."

"I'll tell you what happened to the rest of it," Santiago said smugly. "The boat was apprehended minutes after it pulled away from the dock, which is a very expensive loss to me in addition to the product loss. Did you think the police would not have the entire area surrounded, included the cove's waterway?"

"We could not do anything about it," pleaded Martinez, upon which Santiago picked up a small plank from the floor and viciously slammed it into Martinez' shoulder. He crumbled to the floor as Santiago shouted, "I don't want excuses from any of you. I pay you for results."

All of Rojas's men crouched in fear, and not a word was heard from any of them. Santiago realized that the quarterly routine of picking up a new shipment had become a sloppy operation predictable by not varying the process. He had no reason to suspect that anyone in his organization was responsible, but he wondered if it were possible. "Get that man out of my sight. I never want to see him around here again." Rojas lived in deathly fear of Santiago and his fits of rage, so he did not have to be told twice what to do. Martinez disappeared, and his name was never mentioned again. It was as though he never existed, but the lesson was not lost on the others. "Don't screw up or else," was their byword.

Basso received word about the Pino killing on Sunday as well. He was out of town with Gerri Allen at an outdoor weekend jazz festival on the campus of Franklin & Marshall College, 40 miles southeast of Harrisburg, where the two felt safe from being recognized by anyone they knew. These festivals were typically a three-day affair, with four or more performances happening each day. American jazz enthusiasts became enthralled with the outdoor festival concept when the very popular Newport, Rhode Island Jazz Festival began its long run of successive annual events in 1954 on the lawn of the Newport Casino, a national historical landmark built in 1880. Since then, indoor and outdoor festivals have proliferated all over the world and especially in Europe, where the masses more readily accept the art form than in its USA birthplace.

Allen had packed a picnic basket, and they were sitting on a blanket listening to the advanced, instantly composed music of the William Parker-led quartet In Order to Survive when his phone vibrated. "Sorry, Gerri, but we have to leave. This job is a 24-hour affair, and we have to get back to it." He called Curto with the news and the order to be at the station in two hours. Allen was dropped off at her home so she could drive to the station on her own.

Back at the precinct, Basso asked, "Julius, what does this all mean. First Ambrose, then Aspect, and now Pino – all connected to Santiago but nothing tying the threads together."

"This Pino thing in Philadelphia seems to be unrelated to the murders. I contacted Philadelphia police, and they referred me to the Harbor Patrol, who advised me they had received an anonymous tip about a drug deal going down at that specific cove where Pino was killed. I checked with my former boss, and he told me he did not have anyone in his undercover crew who had infiltrated the Santiago gang, so he was at a loss to know who made the anonymous call. He guessed it had to be someone within the organization who had a beef with Santiago."

"No, Julius, I do not believe the Pino death is unrelated to the other two. I appreciate that coincidences do happen, but it is a giant stretch to believe that Pino, whose lawyer was Aspect, and whose boss was Ambrose, died in unrelated incidents within such a short period of time. That would test the imagination too far. There has to be a connection."

"But Gene, how could it be known that Pino would be killed? He could have surrendered and been taken into custody."

"You forget he is a two-time loser, so any arrest would mean he could spend the rest of his life in prison. People like that would not accept that alternative over attempting to shoot it out and escape."

"I guess you are right, Gene, but I still have a hard time piecing it all together. What about considering the possibility that Pino killed both Ambrose and Aspect, so his death by the police closes the case. That certainly could be what happened."

"It is one theory, Julius, but what evidence do we have to support that conjecture?" Basso asked Allen, "Is there any way to tie the drug deal to Santiago?"

Allen, who had been in touch with Philadelphia police, answered, "No, I am afraid not. There is no link directly to Santiago, and any good lawyer could have an easy time selling the proposition that Pino and his buddies were acting independently. It would not be the first time a small-time criminal set out on his own. Pino did not have a shred of identification on him. The police said he was not alone, but the others escaped in the darkness. They found truck tire marks in a muddy area away from the dock, but nobody saw the truck."

"I understand they apprehended the boat that was trying to get away. What did that yield, Gerri?"

"They found two crates of coffee, but buried inside each vacuum-sealed can was a bag of powder that proved to be pure uncut cocaine. The cans contained no company name, label, or trademark. Again, no possible way to connect that with Santiago. We have the DEA trying to trace the shipment back to the shipper, but this may not be easy. Very unique packaging. The police have in custody the two people they apprehended in the boat. They are Colombian nationals who were part of the large crew for the vessel carrying the cocaine. The men were easily traced to one of the few ships arriving that day. The police talked with the captain of the vessel, but the officers could not draw any connection between the ship's owners and the cocaine. They surmise the operation was perpetrated by a few crew members and not by the shipping company owners."

"What about the owner of the boat? Do we have any information about that?"

This time Curto answered. "No, Gene. The boat was registered under a false name, and the address of the owner turns out to be the middle of the Delaware River, according to what is showing in the Harbor Patrol's records."

"Thanks, both of you. Amazing how that man can run a major illicit operation right under our noses, and we can't do a thing about it."

The Harrisburg Tribune came out with a critical article on police handling of the raid at the Philadelphia harbor. Although successful in stopping one shipment, it was not successful in making any advances in getting to the source of the drug problem in the city. The story by Joan McCabe highlighted the death of Raphael Pino and made the obvious direct connection to his employer and the employer of Jennifer Ambrose and Susan Aspect. The media were crying for action from the mayor and the chief of police to show progress in this series of deaths they claimed were tied together in some way. This headline article caused the other newspapers to jump on the story, and the entire city administration was under attack by the press.

Basso was called into the office of the Precinct Captain Ralph O'Brian to give a status report of his progress on the two murders and their link to the drug bust and Santiago. "Gene, I am tired of seeing my face on the evening news making excuses for our lack of advancement in these cases."

"Ralph, we are not making much progress on any of this, so I won't make excuses either. We have interviewed a lot of people, learned a lot about the operation of Central Penn Warehousing, but we have not been able to make the connection of the two deaths to Diego Santiago or to associate them in any way to the drug dealings by Santiago. We know a lot about the dead women, but we don't know if they were crimes of passion, crimes of revenge, or crimes to silence them for some unknown reason. My team has several people yet to interview, including most of the men who work at the warehouse under the parole arrangement they have with the State. We don't know who tipped off the police on the Philadelphia drug run that led to Raphael Pino's death and the confiscation of the entire shipment of drugs."

"Gene, not only is my boss and the mayor on my back, now we are getting interference from the Feds who think maybe they should take charge of this thing. They claim they have jurisdiction because of the link between the women and Santiago. I don't want that to happen; they were murdered in our city, and it is up to us to prosecute the guilty party, not the FBI. The drugs might involve interstate commerce but not the murders."

"I am planning to set up another meeting with Santiago to put some pressure on him. You know I must do these things alone since we can't risk anyone at the warehouse making the connection between my partner and Stefano Grassi. So, the going is slow."

"Have you spoken with anyone on George Ziegler's DA staff to see what it would take to make a charge stick on any of those hoodlums they call rehabilitated criminals?"

"Curto and I went over that thoroughly, and I contended there is not enough to tie any of them into this, but we still have much to do in that area. Curto is going to pursue the matter with Nancy Kowalski, but I don't expect it to amount to anything. We thought we had something that would link Pino, and Julius still believes in that, but it just isn't there right now. I will keep you personally posted if anything even comes close to resembling a breakthrough."

CHAPTER 22: THE SOURCE

B asso prepared for his revisit with Santiago by reviewing all existing police files on him, plus he wanted to get a list of every employee working for him in the Harrisburg area. A meeting was scheduled for Monday morning, and Basso arrived at the Central Penn Warehousing facility around 9 a.m. Mrs. Fuller offered him coffee in her sitting area. While waiting, Basso noticed many framed photographs on the walls showing Santiago posing with either professional athletes, federal, state, or local politicians, CEO's of major corporations, or prominent members of the clergy. It was a who's who gallery of important people. He recognized all those pictured, but the shot of Santiago with Mayor Bixby particularly caught his attention. Within minutes, Santiago emerged and invited Basso into his office.

"Mr. Santiago, you are aware of the events that happened at the Philadelphia docks Saturday night. Raphael Pino worked for you, and he was killed while involved in criminal activities. What role did you play in this crime?"

"I am shocked to hear you ask me that, Mr. Basso. We both know that Pino had a criminal record, and I told you previously I was attempting to rehabilitate him. But he obviously went off the deep end again, and he acted absolutely on his own. I am a respected businessman in this community, and I have earned the esteem of the people who pay your salary, so I deeply resent the implications you are making."

"Well, I am sorry you feel that way, but in a very short timeframe, we have three dead people, all of whom worked for you, so I do not think it would be out of the question for me to probe into what your involvement might be."

"Well, you have probed, and I have answered, so let us put the accusations to rest. I had nothing to do with what Pino was doing when he was shot. And I fail to see any connection between his rogue activities and the death of two of my star lawyers. Why aren't you out trying to find their killer instead of making wild accusations against my character?"

"Whether you accept it or not, it is no coincidence that these three deaths involved employees of this company. Hell, it would not take a rocket scientist to make a connection back to you."

"I repeat, you are totally off base, and I resent it. Is there anything else?"

"Unless you would prefer to conduct this interview down at police headquarters, I suggest you lose the attitude and start being straightforward with me. I am not one of your lackeys you can order around, so start giving me straight answers. What was Pino's role in that drug drop, and what other employees of yours were with him."

"Mr. Basso, I also am not one who can be coerced, and your position does not frighten me. I told you once, and I'll tell you again. Pino was a grown man who had ambitions higher than his capabilities. He obviously was out of his league in getting involved in drug trafficking. And to my knowledge, he was not accompanied by any other person in my employ."

"Mr. Santiago. You must take me for a fool. Regardless of all the fancy clothes you wear and all the important people you know, you are no better than a two-bit hoodlum in my book. Your money can go only so far in protecting you."

"Mr. Basso. I will be speaking directly with the mayor and your boss about your bullish behavior and insolent remarks. Now, unless you have any valid questions or requests, I suggest you leave this office."

"I'll go, but first, I want a list of every employee you have in this company."

"Fine, Mrs. Fuller will have that sent over to your office as soon as possible. Good day, Mr. Basso."

To the misfortune of Santiago, word of the murders and of the drug deal gone wrong reached Alejandro Moreno in Bogota. He was informed of the deaths of the lawyers, of the confiscation of the last shipment of cocaine, of the killing by the police of one of Santiago's men, and about the heavy pressure the police were putting on Santiago in trying to implicate him in these deaths. Moreno was seriously disturbed at this news. Santiago and Moreno had a flourishing business going ever since Santiago visited him years ago. Since then, drug shipments increased substantially, but more importantly, profits skyrocketed. The flow of cash through the bank laundering scheme Santiago established worked to perfection, and Moreno had little exposure from the whole operation, as he preferred.

Moreno concluded early in his career that it was best to involve as few people as possible to carry out these transactions. Finding the right men who would be employed as crewmen on the ships going to the USA was preferred over getting the ship's officers or the ship's owners involved. He became simply an indirect customer of the shipping companies, but the key was the planting of five or six crew members who would be responsible for seeing that his crates reached their intended destination without interference from the law. The ships he used were all Colombian registry and

Colombian crew, making it easy to place his people with the Maritime Employment Office.

Knowing how much was at stake because of this botched operation and the murders, Moreno decided to handle the matter on his own. He had been required to do such things personally before, such as the time years ago when a distributor for his product decided to go into business for himself. He learned about the betrayal from an associate. The amount of business lost was not overly significant, but the fact that a trusted ally would intentionally cheat him was more than he could tolerate. Above all, he valued trustworthiness as a man's most important character trait. Moreno bided his time; he gathered facts on how the treachery had been accomplished to preclude future such occurrences.

When he thought the traitor was comfortable in his success, he stopped his supply source. Moreno had an iron-clad grip on the entire country's output of cocaine and heroin. The man came pleading to him to restore his supply chain, but Moreno simply laughed at him. Moreno had two of his men strap the man to a table where both arms and both legs were immobilized. The man groveled for pity. Then, one by one, wielding a giant scissors used for shearing sheep, Moreno methodically and slowly cut off every finger and every toe. Screaming in agony, the man very slowly died of loss of blood. Moreno had a reputation for brutality before this, but this execution firmly cemented his name as the most feared in the nation.

Given this current upsetting situation with Santiago, Moreno flew to the USA shortly after hearing the news. He showed up at Santiago's office unexpectedly and unannounced. He traveled under a falsified passport, since his name was in the immigration database with instructions to detain. Mrs. Fuller buzzed Santiago and told him he had a visitor in the lobby. When Santiago came out and saw Moreno, he was petrified. For more years than he cared to remember, he was the king of the mountain. Everybody bowed to him. But when he saw Moreno, he realized that his position of authority was fully undermined by this one man.

Trying to act as nonchalant as possible, he said "Alejandro, what a pleasant surprise. What brings you to the States?"

Moreno was not one for small talk and went right to the point. "You know full well why I am here. What has gotten into you? You botched up a shipment which will cost me substantially, but more importantly, you are getting high-profile notice by all the wrong people. And if you are in the spotlight with the police, that jeopardizes me and my organization. I cannot allow that to happen."

Santiago knew better than to make excuses. "I have it under control, Alejandro. We have taken care of one of the men who allowed this to happen, and the police took care of the other, so I assure you things will be back to normal."

"They have confiscated our shipment, so they know how the drugs are getting here. Fortunately for you, the containers cannot be traced back to me. There are two other layers insolating my organization from the shipment. All the same, I will not tolerate inefficiency. If there is one more incident involving you that hits the newspapers, you will be sorry we ever met."

"Be reasonable, Alejandro."

"I am being as reasonable as possible given your current performance. Do you understand the damage this has done to my ability to use that shipping line again? Even though I am not the known party of record, the people I used to interface with the shipper have now been fully compromised. And the Colombian government is making a protest to your government about detaining two of its citizens."

"Alejandro, I have run a tight ship for all the years we have been associated, and you know that. As I said, I have things under control, and you have nothing to worry about."

"You are the one who has something to worry about. You know my distaste for violence, but when it is needed, I do not hesitate to use it to get my point across. You are inches close to being out of business or worse. And you know what

I mean by worse. Given our long association, I thought it best to tell you personally rather than send a messenger, but the next message will be swift and direct."

With that, Moreno ceremoniously left Santiago's office, leaving the once-unbreakable giant in a state of utter confusion and disbelief. At 70 years old, he had always been the threatener, not the threatened. He screamed at Mrs. Fuller "Get Rojas in here immediately."

Rojas came in slightly out of breath, knowing he should not dally in getting there.

"Tomás, what are the names of the men in your department?"

"Well, let's see, there are the Garcia brothers, Jose and Juan, Felipe Rodriguez, Jose Caderas, Joaquin Gonzalez, Lucas Lopez, and Rodrigo Sanchez. They have all been with us a number of years."

"Well, tighten the screws on all of them. At first, I thought this happened because we had gotten sloppy, but now I am convinced somebody tipped off the police, and a good starting point is with your guys."

Rojas left his office, and Santiago sat at his desk with his head in his hands thinking of what approach he should take. He realized Moreno was not to be taken lightly. At risk was everything he had worked for his entire life, so resolving what had gone wrong within his organization was the most important thing he had to do. As his mind replayed the possibilities for the leaked information, he decided to wait until Rojas reported back on his interrogation of his staff, since that was the most likely source of the betrayal. "Mrs. Fuller, I am leaving the office early today. Cancel and reschedule any appointments I have. If you need me, you can reach me at my home."

Santiago lived outside the city limits in the most affluent neighborhood of the area. His home of 10,000 square feet was a stone English Tudor mansion on five acres of land with an extended driveway leading to the circle at the main entrance. The property was gated and fully enclosed by an eight-foot high black iron fence with embedded alarm sensors. There was a guard at the gate 24 hours per day, making it a true fortress. Security cameras mounted intermittently scanned the entire exterior of the property. All cameras were monitored from a basement command post by guards on duty in three shifts around the clock. Two other guards per shift walked the perimeter of the property accompanied by Doberman Pinschers.

Despite all his money, Diego Santiago was a lonely man. His wife died five years ago, leaving him to ramble around the cheerless house in solitude except for all the servants and guards whom he routinely disregarded. Barbara had not provided him with any grandchildren, and Roberto was nowhere near ready to settle down. He had just about given up on Roberto ever becoming a stable family man. Santiago realized he had probably given Roberto too much too soon. He spoiled his children in contrast to the poverty-ridden life his parents endured in Colombia and their early years in the USA. He took the blame for the man Roberto turned out to be.

The servants were surprised to see him home so early; Santiago's work ethic seldom allowed for leisure time. His cook asked him if he wanted anything special for dinner, but he walked past brusquely without acknowledging her and went to his study. The room was lined with built-in floor-to-ceiling bookcases containing many first editions. When he was younger, he and Monica would ride the sliding library ladder with drinks in hand, laughing and loving the time they spent together. Now, the study was a gloomy prison with no gaiety there or anywhere else in the house. Even when he hosted elaborate dinner parties for the rich and famous at the 20-seat glass table in the ornate dining room, he could not bring himself to join in the laughter and merriment his boisterous friends fostered.

He had come to realize that all the money in the world cannot buy happiness if there is no one near and dear to share the lifestyle. But it did provide him with something he relished, something that kept him motivated daily. It was the power money gave him – power to influence the direction he wanted a business deal to take, power to command respect, power to dominate any situation, power over other people, even power over those who considered themselves powerful. This is what sustained him in the years following the death of Monica.

He poured himself a glass of 25-year-old McCallan scotch from a Waterford crystal decanter and sat in his high-backed Italian leather chair behind his ten-foot wide mahogany desk. His mind kept forcing him to remember that his power did not extend to Alejandro Moreno. Santiago was not the dominant person in that relationship, and it galled him when he had to bow and scrape to any other person. How to deal with the threats made by Moreno weighed heavily on him.

As he contemplated the situation, a shrill alarm jolted him out of his reverie. One of the guards knocked at the door and entered, saying an intruder had tried to penetrate the property security and was captured immediately. He was being held in the lower level by the security guards.

Santiago put down his drink glass and followed the guard to the holding area where the intruder was being fiercely interrogated and physically abused. "Stop that," Santiago shouted. "I want to talk to him while he is still capable of speaking."

Santiago demanded, "Who are you? Who sent you?" His first thoughts were that Moreno had gone back on his word and was taking immediate retaliatory action. The man sat silently and refused to answer, upon which one of the guards slapped him forcefully in the face. Realizing he was in no position to resist and fearing he was close to being killed, he decided to talk.

"My name is Carlos Martinez. I am the brother of Matias Martinez, who works for you. We live together on the other side of the river. Matias has not been home for several days, and he always kept me informed if he was going to be late or away. When I went to the warehouse where he works, I was told he no longer worked there. They would give me no information and in fact were quite rude, so I decided to see if I could learn something from you. But I was denied access at the gate, so I tried to climb the fence and was immediately attacked by a dog who bit deeply into my thigh. Then your guards dragged me down here. I am just trying to find out what happened to my brother."

"Who else lives with you?"

"Nobody else, just the two of us. My brother and I came to the States from Honduras several years ago, and we have no other relatives in this country. I run a small shoe repair shop, and Matias sometimes helps me out, but now I am alone there. I can't go to the police, since I don't have a green card to allow my business to operate."

"I will call our Human Resources department to see if I can help you." Santiago left the room and pretended to be making a call. When he returned, he informed the man that Matias Martinez had quit without notice and left no forwarding address. "They still have a check for back wages but have nowhere to send it. Trying to break into my home was not a smart move. You are lucky to survive such a dumb stunt."

Santiago told the guards to escort the man off the property and warned him not to come back. He then called Rojas and told him what had just transpired. That evening before closing hours, a fire broke out at Carlos Martinez' shop, burning it to the ground. The firemen found the dead body of the owner burned almost beyond recognition. He had not been able to escape the fire and fumes, and the officials were unable to determine the cause of the blaze. The man apparently was an illegal immigrant, so no information on next of kin was available. He was buried in an unmarked grave at a cemetery used for unknown or indigent people.

CHAPTER 23: THE INTERROGATION

When officer Jack Bearden and his partner Otto Schmidt made the rounds of the pawn shops in the Wilson Park Greenfield area, they were equipped with a rendering of the jewelry Susan Aspect was wearing the night she was murdered. Ruth Biantano and June Curtis had collaborated and given the descriptions to a sketch artist, who drew the watch, bracelet, and ring. There were five shops within the area, and all did a thriving business. Given the poverty level of the people living there, pawning one's valuables to make ends meet was a common practice.

They knew the owners of these shops since they had been patrolling the area by squad car for two years. The area was too dangerous to patrol on foot. They showed the picture to three shop owners within proximity of each other, but these visits yielded nothing. The owners were cooperative but did not recognize the jewelry. On the fourth stop at Saul's Pawn Shop, they found success. The owner Saul Bernstein recognized the pieces immediately. He had not yet put them in his safe, so he was able to show them immediately to the officers.

"Who are they, Saul? I know you have their names in your log book."

"I don't want any trouble officers. I have to work in this neighborhood, and you know how mean these kids can be."

"I can get a lot meaner, Saul. We are investigating a homicide, not a theft, so unless you want to be charged as an accessory, I suggest you look in your little book and give us the names."

Reluctantly, Saul told them their street names were Yoyo and Speed, but he did not know their real names. He had lowballed the price, but they did not hassle him over it and accepted it immediately. "They usually hang out at that diner over on 10th street."

"I am afraid we are going to have to confiscate these, Saul. After all these years, you would think you'd know better than to buy stolen goods. Did you think one of their mothers died, and they inherited this stuff?"

It did not take long for Bearden and Schmidt to learn that Demarcus Johnson and Antonio Jackson were Yoyo and Speed. They could not find them on the street, but they did have their home addresses on file. Both lived in the same government housing project. Calling for police backup, they approached the dilapidated building and proceeded up one flight to the apartment address of Johnson. With weapons in hand, they banged on the apartment door with the butts of their guns, announcing, "Open up. This is the police." When no response was heard, the door was smashed open by the backup police. Spotting an open window leading to a fire escape, they saw Speed and Yoyo taking two steps at a time down the flimsy metal ladder, but waiting for them at the bottom were three armed officers. "Not so fast, you guys. You are under arrest."

Kicking and screaming, the boys were transported to police headquarters and handcuffed to chairs in the interrogation room, but not before Yoyo had to be subdued from behind with a police baton pressed against his neck. Curto and Basso watched the two young boys from behind the one-way glass as the youths squirmed in their seats. "They're only high school kids," Basso noted.

The interrogation was fast and conclusive. Both boys had juvenile police records. But it became apparent very rapidly that these boys did not kill Susan Aspect. Their story and timing about finding the body on the way to the Boy's Club gym were believable."

"Why did one of you kick the dead body?"

"We was mad at not findin' no cash or credit cards. The bitch should have had some dough on her."

"Well your temper along with your greed is going to cost you this time, and it won't be as a juvenile offender either. Attacking a corpse along with larceny are serious charges."

"Well, you called it correctly, Gene. Two separate crimes."

"Yes, but now we are back to square one, Julius. Our first suspicions were directed at Santiago, but he had a solid alibi. Then our next leads were the lawyers' cases, and that did not pan out. Then our third assumption pointed to Raphael Pino, and that fell through. Now this situation with those kids turns out to be unrelated. So, we do not know anything more than we did at the start."

"We can't let Santiago off the hook, regardless of his alibi. We know he pulls the strings and could simply have ordered it. He never gets his own hands dirty. And don't forget what you told me about his son-in-law. That is definitely a subject requiring clarification."

"I agree. I am scheduled to interview Damian DeRiso tomorrow. Are we still on for the squash game tonight, Julius? Has your hand healed?"

"Yes, looking forward to beating you again, old man."

The two had a standing weekly match at the Harrisburg Athletic Club where they both had memberships. Although older than Curto by 15 years, Basso continued to keep himself in shape. Playing a rigorous sport like squash inspired him to stay in the peak of good condition. A few weeks earlier, they were absorbed in one of their usual highly intense matches. They started the set at the standard time of 8 p.m. at the court on which they have a standing reservation. The pace was faster than normal, and both men enjoyed the exhilaration this one-on-one sport provided. Shortly after the start of the match, Basso made an amazing save of a shot Curto had not expected him to retrieve. Curto was not fast enough to get out of the way of Basso's return swing. His racket clipped Curto's hand, cutting him on the finger. After a first-aid treatment, they decided not to continue, since Curto appeared to be in significant pain. There was swelling and bruising as well as bleeding.

"I had you on the run, Gene. No way you were going to recover from my shot."

"If you were not so confident, you would have had the sense to get out of the way. We can pick up where we left off next time, assuming you are able to play. I had the feeling I was in the driver's seat tonight, and you go and mess it up by getting hurt."

CHAPTER 24: THE ALTER EGO

Curto, as Stefano Grassi, was with the undercover bureau of the force for about four years, during which time he had been successful in alerting the police to several drug deals involving smaller members of the Santiago organization. Arrests and convictions were made, and a small amount of the product was taken off the street. However, the department was looking for the big payoff, the one that would allow them to arrest Santiago and put his huge operation out of business. But they also could not do anything to put Grassi's life in danger. He was deeply planted in Santiago's organization and was extremely helpful, but the operation was not able to be taken down completely.

In his fourth year as Stefano Grassi, Curto was looking for a change. He told the department he was getting very nervous about his double life. Although he managed to get close to Santiago, he was not ever able to alert the police of the major operation that would allow them to close in and arrest him. Right after he made this plea, he learned information on a major shipment that could possibly be the break for which the police were looking. The pattern of delivery was being altered from ship cargo to plane cargo. Their plan was to fly a plane from Colombia to one of the remote islands in the northern Bahamas, and from there use a small aircraft to fly the cargo to the USA. He learned it was possible to fly under the radar of the FAA, since typical radar systems are line of sight operations. Signals are sent out and bounce off an object to return the signal to its origin. Small aircraft could fly at a low enough altitude to elude detection if the landing site was not in a large metropolitan area.

The Commonwealth of the Bahamas is made up of over 700 islands, cays, and islets, many of them unpopulated. The island chain is thought to have been inhabited as early as 300 or 400 A.D. by people known as Lucayans, but the first European to land was Christopher Columbus on October 12, 1492 on the Bahamian island of San Salvador. Because of its shallow sea, he described it as baja mar, hence the name Bahamas evolved. The Bahamas have not only some of the shallowest parts of the Atlantic Ocean but also some of the deepest. It was a colony of the British Empire starting in 1649, but in 1973, it became an independent Commonwealth realm while still recognizing Queen Elizabeth II as the head of state.

Santiago was successful in purchasing land rights to one of these isolated islands through a sham company, ostensibly for purposes of building an exclusive retreat catering to the ultra-rich. The first step in his private island project was to build an airstrip, which was to be used to receive its first plane from Colombia under this newly hatched scheme.

Santiago cleared the new plan with Alejandro Moreno in Bogota, and the first shipment was sent. The pilot landed successfully at the island in the Bahamas, transferred the cargo to a smaller seaplane, and took off to a destination on the coast of northern Florida. From there, the plan was to transport the drugs by truck back to a warehouse destination in Pennsylvania. Although the pilot was extremely nervous about flying at such a low altitude even though the distance was not great, he managed the operation without a problem. Santiago's men were waiting on the deserted coast when the seaplane landed in the water, signaled with a flashing light, and made its way to shore. The cargo was unloaded and reloaded onto an unmarked truck having Florida license plates. The plan was for the driver to change to Georgia plates when crossing the Florida line, to South Carolina plates when in that state, and so on until it was away from the southern states. A vehicle having a license plate from a northern state was more likely to be hassled when making its way up the southern coast.

Curto as Grassi informed his boss of the plan, which the brass thought would be the one leading to the elimination of the Santiago organization. But they also thought it was an excellent opportunity for them to extricate Curto from the Santiago organization and bring him back in. To do this, they hatched an elaborate plan. When the truck with the seaplane cargo reached its designated point in Pennsylvania, Grassi would be part of the crew on the receiving end. The police would move in, a gun battle would likely ensue, and in the firefight, Grassi would be killed. His body would be commandeered by the police, his death announced publicly, and Julius Curto would emerge as a new man on the police force.

The truck made its way through Georgia, South Carolina, North Carolina, Tennessee, Virginia, Maryland, and finally Pennsylvania. But before reaching Pennsylvania, the truck detoured to a scheduled rendezvous point in Maryland, and the product was redistributed to four other smaller trucks that took varying routes back to another facility owned by Santiago in Scranton, Pennsylvania. Santiago had learned to be cautious when delving into something new, and his gut feeling was to switch the plan without telling any of the people in Rojas's group, which included Stefano Grassi. As his closest confidant, Rojas was told.

The original truck sans drugs proceeded on its prescribed course, arriving at 2 a.m. at an abandoned warehouse about three miles from Central Penn Warehousing. The driver opened the truck's rear doors, Rojas's men came out to begin unloading, and the police in their concealed position announced their presence. The first reaction by Rojas's men was to pull their weapons and begin firing at the police. Grassi made sure he was in open sight of the police, who on signal, fired at him. Of course, he was wearing a bulletproof vest, and the police were careful only to fire one shot at his chest. He fell instantly from the stunning force of the bullet and dragged himself forward, appearing to attempt to shoot back at the police. Under the cover of heavy fire, the police pulled his body out of the line of fire and continued the assault on the opponents.

Realizing they were outnumbered, Rojas and all but two of his men escaped through the rear of the abandoned warehouse. The two unlucky men, who Rojas had enlisted specifically for this operation, were killed in the gun battle. They were not employees of Central Penn Warehousing. The truck driver was still in the cargo area of the truck when the police took control. What they found were boxes marked Owens Corning Glassware, and when they opened the boxes, they found only stemmed glassware. Santiago's alternate plan had been a success, and the police once again had been outsmarted.

Joan McCabe of the Harrisburg Tribune was the first to learn of the news. She had been tipped of the story by a friend on the police force, so she was on hand when the gun battle ensued. Instead of writing a story about a significant drug bust and the arrest of the perpetrators, she wrote a scathing story of a police operation totally bungled and of innocent lives lost. She reported the death of Stefano Grassi in addition to the other two. The driver of the truck was released, threatening to sue the police for an unwarranted attack on decent people.

Curto was taken by ambulance to an area hospital where Stefano Grassi was pronounced dead. He exited the rear of the hospital and began the process of reverting back to his original self. The police, however, wanted to debrief him very quickly, so he was smuggled into the station to tell what happened. Curto was at a loss to explain. According to everything he was told, the truck was supposed to have drugs in its hold. He stressed the point that obviously, Rojas and his men believed they were on a drug run as well. They would not have started the gunfight had they been aware of a change in plan. The Police Commissioner came under considerable fire for the plan gone awry, but Curto was commended for his brave actions and for the time he spent as Stefano Grassi. He was considered a hero for risking his life.

He shaved his beard, dyed his hair back to its original color, took out the contacts, removed the tattoos, and Julius Curto began life all over again. Eszter was overjoyed at his reverting to the status of a normal citizen. Although she continued to be fearful for his safety, she felt he was a lot safer as a detective than an undercover policeman. His promotion to the homicide division was in recognition of his covert service in his undercover role.

CHAPTER 25: THE SON-IN-LAW

"Mr. DeRiso, this is Detective Gianni Basso at police headquarters. I wonder if it would be convenient for you to visit with me in my office? I would prefer to talk to you in person away from your work."

"Certainly, Mr. Basso. I can be there around 3 p.m. if that time is convenient."

DeRiso drove to the station at the scheduled time and climbed the stairs to Basso's office, wondering how a building like this had not been torn down years ago.

"I am pleased you could see me on short notice, Mr. DeRiso. I have some concerns about the unfortunate deaths of two of your work colleagues. Could you please tell me how well you knew Jennifer Ambrose?"

"Obviously, I knew her and knew of her fine reputation as a lawyer, but being in the marketing side of the business, I seldom interacted with her."

"Mr. DeRiso, if we are going to have any success from this discussion, it will hinge on you being totally honest with me. I know for a fact that what you just said is not true."

DeRiso was caught off guard. To his knowledge, his affair with Ambrose was a secret, so he was quite surprised at Basso's comment.

"Well, why don't you tell me what you know, so we can start on a level playing field."

"I know your relationship was not strictly professional, so why don't you take it from there."

"I underestimated you, Mr. Basso. Okay, I saw Ms. Ambrose on occasion privately. Given my marital status being married to the boss's daughter, I certainly would not make such an action public if not necessary."

"Given she was murdered and was pregnant at the time of her death, that relationship is of prime interest to me. How long were the two of you seeing each other?"

"I was totally unaware of her pregnancy until I read it in the paper. I occasionally had coffee with her in the company lunchroom. We talked about patent rights on a company warehousing product, about our trademark, and various other matters of a legal nature. This was in full view of others and often in the company of others. But I saw something in her eyes that encouraged me to pursue a more personal relationship. I called her at her home one night, and we talked for about two hours. We seemed to click on an intellectual level. These calls went on for a week or so, but at one point, she suggested we could converse a lot easier at her home. Barbara was out of town on one of her typical audits, so I drove over. Well, within a few minutes, we were not talking about patent rights. She was an aggressive woman who appeared to crave sex. At first, I was taken back by her libidinous behavior, but I soon got over that. We both had physical needs, so a very heated affair ensued that satisfied both of us."

"Was it still going on at the time of her death?"

"No, a few months ago, completely unexpectedly, she told me she did not want to see me again. I was confused and hurt, since I did not see anything like that coming."

"How did that make you feel? Were you angry? Did you want revenge? Did you want to hurt her?"

"Absolutely not. I accepted it as just one of those things. We had fun for a time, and the fun ended. Neither one of us was looking for a permanent relationship. We simply filled each other's needs for a while, and when it was over, I accepted it as over."

"Are you telling me you are not the jealous type? That you were not very upset about being rejected?"

"I am telling you the affair ended, and I accepted that."

"Do you think you are the father of her unborn child?"

"I have no way of knowing. She never told me about it, but I guess it is possible from a timing standpoint, although she generally demanded I use protection. But I repeat, I knew nothing about the pregnancy, and I definitely had no reason to kill her. I have too much to lose from my marriage to Santiago's daughter."

"To your knowledge, was she seeing someone else during the time of your relationship or after it?"

"I always suspected I was not the only man she used as a sex toy."

"What gave you that impression?"

"It was just a feeling. She would cancel a rendezvous with me at a moment's notice, she unwittingly left tell-tale signs around her house suggesting someone else had been there, and other actions that made me think there was another or others."

"I assume you have an alibi for the night she was killed?"

"Absolutely. I was with my wife at a dinner party hosted by some friends. At least ten people can vouch for me."

"Thank you for coming in, Mr. DeRiso. If we decide it is necessary, would you be willing to take a blood test to establish if you are the father? That is, if we decide it is relevant to the murder case."

"Yes, I would do that. Just let me know."

After DeRiso left the office, he wondered to himself why a man in his position would risk his career and home for a fling. But the thought suddenly struck him that, although his relationship with Gerri Allen was not illicit, he was taking a similar risk career-wise. *"I am in no position to judge him,"* he thought.

As these thoughts were going through his mind, his phone rang. His ex-wife Janice Turner was on the line asking if she could see him.

In the three years since his divorce to Janice Turner, she lived in the Cleveland, Ohio area. She reverted to her maiden name and used her Education degree from Penn State to good advantage, getting a job in a local high school in a suburb about a dozen or so miles west of the downtown area and close to the shores of Lake Erie. She enjoyed her work with the children, and living in a middle-class, mostly Caucasian neighborhood created a feeling of well-being for her. Although English as expected was once the predominant language of the area, over the years, many Middle-Eastern people emigrated to the district for the job opportunities the well-located, industrialized area offered, making Arabic the first language of about 15 percent of the population. Many of Turner's students went on to college, giving her great satisfaction. The town boasted a 50 percent rate of adults with a bachelor's degree or higher.

From a social standpoint, however, life was not as satisfying. She had several relationships with either men from her school or those she met at the local country club, community theater where she volunteered her time, or the upscale shopping areas with their many fine restaurants. But she did not find that love interest to sweep her off her feet. Most relationships lasted a short time, cut short mainly by her loss of interest and her inability to fill a void in her life.

Now in her early 50s, while still maintaining her looks and shape, she was starting to worry about where her life was going. So, on a whim, she decided during the summer school break to revisit her hometown of Harrisburg. And while reminiscing about her life there and remembering the happier times of her marriage, she decided to give her ex-husband a call. The beautiful thing about the mind is that it allows one to forget about the bad in the past and remember only the good. She did not know what to expect from the call. They had not been in touch since she relocated to Ohio. The parting, although painful for her husband, was not acrimonious.

Basso, being fully caught up in two murder cases, answered the phone rather gruffly, and then when realizing who was calling, softened a bit. "Well, what a surprise to hear from you. Not a word since the day you left town."

"At the time, I thought it was better to have a clean wound rather than a jagged one. But enough about that; how have you been, and what have you been up to lately?"

They continued with polite small talk for a while, until Turner asked if they could get together for lunch. She was staying at a local hotel and suggested the restaurant in its lobby.

They met the following day for lunch. Basso was surprised at how good she looked. The divorce for him had not been easy, but as time passed, he grew to be free of old feelings and was fully over her. Seeing her now, to his amazement, did not rekindle any old passions, and this surprised him. He was proud of himself, not knowing how he would react when he first agreed to meet with her.

To his further amazement, Turner asked about the possibility of their getting back together again. Basso was shocked. "Don't you have a good job in Cleveland? Are you saying you want to move back here?"

"I did a lot of soul searching, and I thought since we invested a couple decades of our life in each other, maybe it was not wise to throw that away."

"Well, you are blowing me away with this proposal coming so unexpectedly. When you phoned and suggested lunch, I thought the conversation would lead to reminiscing rather than this. I never in my wildest dreams thought you wanted to start over. You have caught me off-guard."

Then, getting a firm grip on reality, he decided that directness was the best approach for him in this case. "Look, Janice, when you left, I was devastated. But I got over it, although it wasn't easy. Now, I have someone else in my life, someone who is not against the job I do. Someone who is supportive of my work. If you force yourself to recall, my job was your biggest problem, and nothing has changed over the years."

Basso saw the sadness darkening her complexion and for a moment, thought she might cry, but she bit her lower lip lightly and said "I understand. It was crazy for me to come here, thinking I could turn back the clock." She had bared her soul, and she was rebuked.

They finished lunch with a dark cloud hanging over them. It was quite uncomfortable for both. Basso was relieved when the check came. They gracefully departed, and Turner drove back to Ohio that day.

Back in his office, he mulled over whether he should tell Allen about this strange turn of events. He was not ready to experience any form of domestic upheaval. Eventually, he decided there was no reason to do so. He had no intention of ever getting back with his ex-wife, so there was no need to bring up the subject. *"At least I can close this case,"* he thought.

CHAPTER 26: THE SON

The list of Central Penn Warehousing employees arrived on Basso's desk. It included all the employees at the Harrisburg facility, including the names of several students who worked during the summer on a part-time basis. As Basso scanned the list, sorted by departmental responsibility, his eye caught sight of the name Roberto Santiago, the son of Diego Santiago.

Younger than his sister Barbara by two years, Roberto was pampered all his life. He was doted over, spoiled, and indulged. Given the traditional prima-donna status of a first-born male in the Colombian culture, he was demanding, unsympathetic, and intolerant when anything did not go his way. His father gave him the best of everything – a pony on his 12th birthday, a sports car for his 16th birthday, trips to Europe with two other friends during school summer break, and other overly generous materialistic gifts. This excess attention had its impact on his motivation. Since everything was always given to him, he did not feel the need to strike out on his own or to make an effort to achieve success. He firmly believed it would automatically come to him. He truly thought he was of the entitled class.

In high school, his grades were mediocre only because he put forth no effort. His intelligence quotient was very high, but it did not show in his grades. Nonetheless, his father was able to get him admitted into Rutgers University in New Jersey. Because of his above average intelligence level, he coasted through his classes without any real dedication. Occasionally, the mean streak he had developed came out. In one instance, he started a fight with another student at a local bar and broke the arm of his opponent. The boy's father wanted Roberto arrested, but Diego Santiago interceded and made financial amends to make the matter go away. Four years of fun and fraternity life later, he emerged with a general business degree. Knowing his father would always have a place for him in the company, he did not experience the anxiety typically realized by college graduates when searching for the right opportunity to put them on their career path.

Following a year of traveling around Europe after graduation, he joined his father's firm on the sales force soliciting new warehousing opportunities from area businesses. His father attempted to shield him from the more nefarious elements of the business, although Roberto was in no way a naïve person. He learned very early in life that the wealth his family enjoyed was not likely the result of any business enterprise that stored boxes on shelves. Everybody knew he was the boss's son, so the privileged state that had been his right since birth continued. He did little on the job, usually coming in late with a hangover from the previous night's partying.

Roberto was also a womanizer. He often dated three or more women at a time, and as could be expected from his character traits, he was not always gentle. More than once, he became overly rough with his partner, but there never were any repercussions. He never expected any – he always squirmed out of these predicaments, usually because of his father's belief that spreading money around could solve any problem.

He did not always separate these extra-curricular activities from the business. He dated several of the women in the firm and not just the professional staff. He frequently had one-night stands with the hourly-paid women in the less skilled departments. But he was always careful to keep his affairs secret from his father, because he knew he would not approve.

It was, therefore, no accident that Jennifer Ambrose caught his eye. Being a divorced woman who was beautiful, blond, and intelligent made her fair game for this Romeo who had all the machismo that goes with his Colombian heritage. Ambrose was intrigued by this handsome young man who did not fall under her spell as did so many men with whom she had been involved. That, of course, was the overriding trait of Roberto; he used women, occasionally abused women, but never succumbed to women. They, to him, were tools to be used and then discarded when no longer of interest.

His affair with Ambrose was, however, an ongoing thing, notwithstanding it was intermittent. He would see her when he had a need, and she would contact him when she had a need, but it never was an unbroken or committed relationship. Ambrose was wise enough not to discuss this matter with anyone, not even Susan Aspect, with whom she shared details of her other encounters. She told Aspect about the affair with Damian DeRiso, but she never mentioned the one with Roberto Santiago. Whether it was fear or maybe common sense, she kept all her irregular encounters with the boss's son to herself.

There was, however, one time they were together for an extended time, during which period Roberto appeared to be transformed temporarily into a kinder, gentler person. They managed to sneak off without anyone's knowledge for a ten-day trip to Italy. They took a direct flight to Venice, where Roberto hired a speedboat water taxi at the airport to transport them to the waterway doorstep of the luxurious Boscolo Dei Dogi hotel, a work of art in a country full of art. It was originally built in the 16th century on one of Venice's many canals for the noble Rizzo family. Over the centuries after the Rizzo clan died out, it was a monastery and then embassies for two counties before becoming a five-star hotel. It boasts fine Venetian stuccoes, classic glassware from master craftsmen on the nearby island of Murano, multicolored marble, and other Venetian architectural elements.

In Venice, they visited the Murano glass works, toured the famed Piazza San Marco, took a gondola ride through the maze of canals seeing the historic home of Casanova from their water view, sipped wine at outdoor cafés, visited numerous museums including the Doge Palace, and walked the intricate narrow streets whose complexity can even get residents lost.

From Venice, they took a train to the art capital of Italy – Florence. They visited the Academia, which houses Michelangelo's marvelous statue of David, shopped on the famed Ponte Vecchio where shops selling gold and silver jewelry adorn both sides of the bridge, visited the famed Pitti and Uffici museums, toured the incredible Duomo standing out as a city treasure with its multi-colored architecture, walked the Piazza della Signoria with its outdoor statutes standing guard over the square, and shopped in some of the most exclusive brand-name stores for which Italy is famous.

Next, they trained to Rome for another three days while staying on the famous Via Veneto at another luxury hotel. The Roman Coliseum, Trevi Fountain, the Piazza del Popolo, the ancient Forum, the unmatchable Vatican Museum, its adjoining centerpiece, the Sistine Chapel, were all on their touring list. They marveled at the Pantheon, had a drink at a café in the Piazza Navona, viewed Michelangelo's Pietà in St. Peters Basilica, and spent a small fortune shopping on the Via Condotti where every famous Italian brand was on display.

Ambrose relished the beauty of the trip, but she was too wise a woman to be misled by Roberto Santiago's change in demeanor. She realized a leopard cannot change its spots, but she was happy to have experienced a human side of him for a change.

She was correct. Once they returned home, Roberto Santiago reverted to type. He was flippant and uncaring with her when they could sneak in an evening away from watchful eyes. Ambrose accepted it for what it was and nothing more. The affair was engulfed in passion but devoid of romance.

Gianni Basso called Roberto Santiago's office and spoke with his secretary, only to learn Roberto was playing golf that afternoon with a potential customer. She took a note to have him call Basso in the morning.

When he called as requested, Basso asked "Is there somewhere we can meet privately to talk?"

They agreed to an out-of-the-way bar across town. Basso arrived first but fully expected Roberto Santiago to be late, which he was. When he did arrive, Basso made a short introduction and explanation for the meeting request.

"Mr. Santiago, as you know, we are investigating the murder of Jennifer Ambrose. What can you tell me about your relationship with her?"

Not knowing what Basso knew or did not know, Roberto decided to be straightforward. "I knew her quite well. Jennifer was a woman who had needs, and I guess you could say I fulfilled those needs."

"Were you the only one she was seeing socially?"

"Heavens no. Jennifer and I had an unspoken agreement of no strings attached to our relationship. She saw whomever she wanted, and I certainly did the same."

"When did you last see her outside the office?"

"I believe it was about four or five weeks before her death. She contacted me, and I agreed to meet her for dinner out of town."

Basso was aware of Roberto's penchant for rage, so he asked directly, "Was the relationship always amicable? Did you ever have any disagreements that led to more than just talking?"

"If you are asking did I ever hit her, the answer is yes. Jennifer was into rough sex, but I never struck her out of anger or rage. Any physicality was always related to sex."

"Can you account for your time on the evening she was killed?"

"As I recall, I had a particularly bad day from the lingering effects of a hangover, so I spent the night at home recuperating."

"Alone?"

"Yes, I was alone. And I am afraid there is nobody who can confirm that."

"Before you read it in the newspaper, did you know she was pregnant?"

"No, she never told me. I guess if she had and suggested I was the father, I would have forced her immediately to have an abortion."

"Do you know your blood type, Mr. Santiago?"

"Yes, it is A positive."

With that answer, Basso switched his line of questioning. "How well did you know Susan Aspect?"

"That woman, I can assure you, has never been in my life or my bed. From everything I saw and heard, she was a man-hater. Nothing about her did I find attractive, and the grapevine told me she preferred women over men. I have no solid evidence to support that statement, but rumor does have it."

"Well, I think that is all I have for now. I may want to talk to you later. Are you planning on any trips?"

"No, I will be at my office if you need me."

Basso left the bar confused about this relationship, but even more confused by what he continues to learn about Ambrose and the men in her life. But this interview had opened a new channel in this on-going saga. He wondered, *"If Aspect was involved with a woman, who was it?"*

CHAPTER 27: THE CONFESSION

Not knowing if there were any connections between what Roberto Santiago said about Susan Aspect's sexual preferences and her death, he decided to explore the matter further. He made a call to Ruth Biantano and scheduled a meeting at her home that evening.

Biantano lived a short distance west of Harrisburg in the medium-sized town of Carlisle, home to the U.S. Army War College. This senior-level military educational institution, with origins dating back to 1751, offers graduates of its two-year program a master's degree in Strategic Studies. The town's tree-lined streets house numerous historical landmarks and museums to attract visitors. Notably, George Washington mustered troops in Carlisle in 1794 when he led the militia that suppressed the Whiskey Rebellion in Western Pennsylvania.

"What can I do for you, Mr. Basso? I thought we answered all your questions satisfactorily."

"You did, Ms. Biantano, but something has come up that requires clarification. Unfortunately, the deaths of two women in your department are obviously related; it would be too much of a coincidence to think otherwise. And given that, I have the unpleasant task of getting into matters that would normally be considered personal. We have learned a considerable amount about the lifestyle Jennifer Ambrose led after her divorce, and much of it complicates this case. We learned of her personal involvement with others working for your company. You told us of your suspicions on this matter, and our investigation has substantiated your assumptions were correct. Are you certain you do not know any specifics?"

"No, it was just office gossip I heard, but I felt obligated to mention it to you."

"Fine. Jennifer Ambrose was your boss, so it would be natural for her not to confide in you as her employee. But what about Susan Aspect? She was a co-worker. What can you tell me of her romantic involvement with anyone at your company?"

"I know nothing about that."

"Ms. Biantano, I do not believe you are being totally honest with me. Working side by side, surely you discussed personal matters, maybe even matters that to you would seem very delicate."

"What are you getting at, Mr. Basso?"

"You force me to be direct. We have learned that Susan Aspect might have had an alternative lifestyle when it came to sexual preference. Was Ms. Aspect having an affair with any woman in your company?"

At this point, Ruth Biantano began to cry. Sobbing while struggling to get out the words, she muttered faintly, "Mr. Basso, you have to understand I am a very conservative woman with Christian values. I do not endorse what others do, but at the same time, I don't condemn them. God gave us a free will to act as we see fit. But yes, it became obvious to me after working with Susan that she was still very angry about a relationship she had years ago with a married man, which caused her to distrust all men. As a result, she found comfort in the tenderness and compassion shown by women to her. This is something I never would willingly discuss with another, so you must understand why I held back."

"Who was the woman who showed the tenderness, Ms. Biantano?"

"One night we were working late, and I needed to retrieve a file from the central filing room. Although I was not seen, I was horrified to see Susan and Jennifer embracing in the most passionate manner. I never mentioned it to a soul until now. It was something of a shock to me."

"So, you never brought it up with Ms. Aspect?"

"Goodness no, I was much too embarrassed to do that."

"What was your relationship with Ms. Aspect after you witnessed this event? Did you remain friends? Did you shun her?"

"I did my best to be pleasant with her at all times. Never did I let on that I had seen her with our boss, and never did Susan ever mention anything to me. I treated it as though it never happened, but I must tell you, the episode shook me. It is not something one observes routinely."

"You may have already answered this, but I'll ask again. Did either Ms. Ambrose or Ms. Aspect have any enemies – anyone jealous of their success – anyone who felt they had not been treated fairly? I am looking for any hint as to why they are both dead."

"I assure you, Mr. Basso. I can't imagine a soul who would want to do either of them harm."

Learning that Ruth Biantano could not provide anything more than a confirmation of what Roberto Santiago told him, he thanked her and left her home.

The affair between Ambrose and Aspect was one sided. Aspect was a very vulnerable woman looking for love, while Ambrose was a confident woman with physical needs that appeared to know no boundaries. The flirtation amused Ambrose. She was adventurous enough to experiment with a different side of the sexual equation, while Aspect was naive and thought the compassion and tenderness Ambrose showed to her were sincere. The so-called romance did not last. Ambrose, as always, became bored with the arrangement. Although she was able to satisfy her sexual appetite, she saw that Aspect was getting far too involved to the point of wanting to establish an open relationship. Ambrose could not, of course, allow that to happen, nor would she be satisfied with such a relationship. Even though she realized she had a bi-sexual leaning, it was not the preferred route she wanted to take other than as an occasional divergence. It ended as quickly as it began, and once again, Susan Aspect was left alone and dejected.

In the car, Basso realized he had added another piece to this enigma. Jennifer Ambrose had sexual relations with two men and one woman with her company. Any of the three could possibly have a reason for killing her, but it left a huge gap in any theory as to why Susan Aspect was killed. Aspect would have been a suspect given this new information, although she might not have had the strength to choke her victim. But she could have had help. All that theorizing went out the window with her death, though, and left Basso as confused and frustrated as ever. Talking aloud to himself, he speculated "If Aspect learned anything from Ambrose about Ambrose's relationship with either Damian DeRiso or

Roberto Santiago, would that be motive enough for either of those men to kill her?"

Back in his office, he brought Julius Curto up to speed on all he had learned about Aspect and Ambrose. Curto was not stunned by his comments. "Gene, from what you have learned about Ambrose's libido, I am not at all surprised or shocked at what you say. What I don't understand is what makes a woman like that tick. As we have pointed out many times, she was given more physical and mental assets than most women, yet she did not seem to be able to use those assets to bring her happiness. She appeared to be a searching soul looking for some unknown elixir that would make her happy. Looks like she never found that."

"All that is well and good, Julius, but the most perplexing thing about her case is the association with Aspect's murder. Even though the women are tied together by employment and by their physical relationship, there is nothing to tie their two deaths together."

CHAPTER 28: THE DAUGHTER

Curto was sitting in Basso's office talking about the case when Allen approached. She had been mulling over the cast of characters in this melodrama, and the thought occurred to her that Santiago's daughter Barbara might have some insight. "Although she does not work for Central Penn, it must be a major part of her life. Her father founded it soon after she was born, and her husband also works there. Who knows what she has learned or overheard from either of them."

Barbara Santiago DeRiso grew up around her father's business, since it played such a significant role in his life. She knew he was an important businessman in the community, and this importance extended outside of Pennsylvania as well. On more than one occasion, she met congressmen from Washington who were present at some of the elaborate dinner parties her mother and father hosted. The guest list typically extended to notables from all parts of the country.

"How do you suggest we approach her, Gerri? Do we conduct a typical interview, or is there a better way to get her to open up with what she knows or has observed?"

"Seems to me Julius would be a good candidate to speak with her, as long as he never met her while he was Stefano Grassi. He enjoys charming women into telling him what he wants to know," Allen said as she glanced in Curto's direction and smiled.

"You give me too much credit, Gerri. But you might be correct in thinking I am the one for this job. In the entire time I was undercover, I never had the occasion to meet her. She never came to the office, and of course, in my lowlife position with the firm, I was never invited to the big house. So, I think it is safe to assume she would not know the other me."

"Take a shot at it, Julius. We have nothing to lose, and we desperately need a lead to advance this case. Thanks, Gerri, for the suggestion. I would never have thought to put her in play."

"You don't think as a woman does, Gene. If she had the slightest hint that her husband at one time had an affair with Ambrose, I am sure it would spark some fire into her. She might not have been capable physically of strangling anyone, but with her money, she certainly had the resources to pay someone to kill Ambrose if she felt it was the only way to get back at her husband. You know the saying about hell not having the fury of a woman scorned." Her paraphrased proverb dates to a line in a play written in 1697 by William Congreve called *The Morning Bride,* and its message has been consistently proven true over the centuries.

Curto added another point. "If her father was aware of the affair her husband had with Ambrose, who knows how he would react. Would he be angry enough to call a hit on her to protect his daughter? Up until now, we have not deduced any motive on Santiago's part, but this could possibly do just that."

Curto made a call to the downtown Harrisburg CPA firm where Barbara DeRiso worked. She joined the firm when she and her husband moved back home after he left his job with Alcoa in Pittsburgh to become part of the family business. She told him she could meet with him for a short period, but scheduling was tight since she was juggling audits of three major corporations. Curto said he would not mind meeting after business hours if it made it more convenient for her. They agreed to meet at a downtown restaurant the following night. Curto went as far as to tell his wife about the appointment to preclude any problems later.

"It was good of you to see me, Mrs. DeRiso. I appreciate your finding the time to talk."

"You are welcome. It is a very busy time for me right now. I am more than happy to talk with you, but I really don't know what I could possibly add to your information base on these murders. And please call me Barbara."

"Sometimes the slightest thing can lead to a breakthrough. What can you tell me about Jennifer Ambrose? Since she was your father's general counsel, I am sure you have met her."

"I only know what I learned from my father. She was an excellent attorney who did wonders in protecting my father from the many people who want to bring him down. He has many enemies who are jealous of his success. I met her on several occasions at my father's house at dinner parties, and she always conducted herself in a professional manner."

"Did you ever hear any rumors about her social life outside the office? Did your husband ever speak of her?"

"Julius, why don't we stop this charade. I think I know what you are getting at, so why not be straightforward and just ask me if I knew my husband had an affair with her."

Curto was thrown off course by her bold statement. He expected he would have to use his boyish charms to gain her confidence, but she turned out to be a very intuitive woman. "You impress me, Barbara, with your insight. Yes, I was hoping to find a delicate way to broach the subject, but your forthright manner made any pretext unnecessary."

"I learned about it on my own. You see, I have my own methods. But it might amuse you to know that Damian told me about it himself. I guess he was feeling guilty, so confessing to me was a form of soul cleansing."

"How did your learning of the affair affect you? Were you angry?"

"Of course I was angry, but not angry enough to do anything about it, and certainly not angry enough to kill her. He told me it was short-lived, and I believed him. I knew her before and after her divorce, and I saw the change in her that being free and reasonably well off made. I might have done the same thing if I were in her shoes."

"Did he tell you why he broke it off?"

"Yes, he said she was the one who terminated the relationship. Damian firmly believed she had found someone who really meant more to her than just a casual fling."

"Did he ever tell you who that person might be? This would be very important to our case."

"No, he knew by intuition he was right, but he never could learn who the other party was. I guess I should be grateful to that person, whoever he might be. Taking Damian's ego down a peg or two worked wonders for our relationship. Ever since we returned from Pittsburgh, our careers clashed, and that had a negative impact on our marriage. But his affair made both of us realize we were not putting forth the right effort in our marriage, so you might call it a wake-up call for both of us."

"Barbara, since you suggested we be direct, I won't couch my words. I have learned during this investigation that your father has a temper when provoked. Did he ever learn of Damian's affair?"

"You shock me with that leading question. Do I think my father is capable of extracting revenge against anyone who harmed me? The answer is yes. He loves me dearly. Do I think he did anything to cause the death of Jennifer Ambrose, the answer is a definite no. I had the common sense not to tell him, and neither Damian nor I ever suspected he learned about it from any other source. Certainly she would not be the one to tell him, and according to Damian, nobody else was privy to that sordid detail."

"I am afraid you are not correct there, Barbara. We learned that Ambrose confided in Susan Aspect about her affair with your husband, so if she knew, then it is possible your father learned. Aspect told us directly. That is how we knew, and of course, during our interview with your husband, he confirmed it."

"What are you suggesting?"

"One could reasonably tie both murders together, if Aspect was the only other person to have knowledge of this. How far would your father go to protect you?"

"I will not allow you to throw suspicion on my father about this fling Damian had. And to be frank with you, I firmly believe that if my father had ever learned, he would have taken his pound of flesh out of Damian, not Jennifer. I don't mean to be rude, but if there is nothing else, I must be leaving."

"But we have not yet ordered dinner."

"Thank you for the drink. I must be going."

Trying to salvage the interview, Curto blurted, "One last question. Was your husband despondent over being rejected?"

To which Barbara DeRiso simply looked at him and said, "Good night, Mr. Curto."

It was not often that Curto was put in his place so forcefully. The next morning, he returned to the station to brief Basso and Allen. "Looks like we have hit another dead end. She was aware of and not outraged by her husband's affair with Ambrose, and she came right out and admitted that if Santiago learned about it, he would have killed DeRiso, not Ambrose."

Allen and Basso were a bit disappointed at his failure to learn anything new, but they were amused when they heard how brusquely Curto had been dismissed by a female. It must have been a first.

CHAPTER 29: THE TWINS

Continuing his review of the employee list received from Grace Fuller, Basso decided to get comfortable with the group of men reporting to Tomás Rojas. He had Gerri Allen bring him the police files for eight men who were hired through Santiago's arrangement with the parole board. Basso thought there were two ways any of these men could have been involved with the murders – as a lover of Ambrose, or through acting on orders from higher-up. If it was simply on command, it made getting an answer quite difficult. His first approach to the files, therefore, was to concentrate on the lover angle. He immediately eliminated six of the eight names based either on their old age, or on their obvious lack of anything resembling good looks. Ambrose was a classy woman, and even though she led a promiscuous life, she did confine her activity to people who were handsome or good-looking. That left the two Garcia brothers, Juan and Jose.

The brothers were twins born in Chile who were brought to the USA illegally by their parents when only eight years old, but because of the permissiveness of the US government and its immigration policies, they were allowed to stay, even after attaining a criminal record. Being sponsored by Santiago and given a job had significant weight in their not being deported back to Chile.

As he was reviewing the list, Allen entered his office with a surprised look on her face. "Gene, you are not going to believe this. I have just been notified by Reading police that a body washed up from the Schuylkill River in their town. The police identified the man as Matias Martinez, another product of Santiago's social rehabilitation program.

The Schuylkill river has been an important commercial waterway since coal was discovered in the Anthracite Coal Region in northeastern Pennsylvania, allowing millions of tons of the product to be transported by water to many of the country's largest iron and steel plants along its route. Running from west to east, it stretches 135 miles and eventually flows into the Delaware River at Philadelphia as a significant tributary. In 1682, William Penn chose the left bank of the confluence with the Delaware River to establish the city of Philadelphia.

"I am really blown away by that, Gerri. Another death, another person in the employ of Santiago. Is this turning into a war? What do we know about the way he died?"

"There are significant bruises on his body, but the coroner states the cause of death was a blunt object struck to his temple. He died immediately after that blow. Being that he was in the water a good while and floated down from the scene of the crime, no murder weapon could be found. It probably is at the bottom of the river somewhere along the way."

"I was just going over the files on those social misfits, so it appears we can strike another off the list. This will eventually come back hard on Santiago; he can only dodge so many bullets before his luck runs out."

Basso arranged for the Garcia brothers to be brought in for questioning. They came with a struggle, feeling the police had no right to drag them down to the precinct without probable cause. Both were sitting in the interrogation room while Curto and Basso observed their behavior from behind the one-way glass.

"I would prefer to talk to them separately, Julius, but we can't risk one of them recognizing you. I'll start by talking with them together, and if necessary, I'll split them up."

Neither of the bothers was a tall man, but they did have a distinguished air with their slicked-back jet-black hair and razor-thin mustaches. They were identical twins, making it extremely difficult to distinguish one from the other.

"What do you two gentlemen know about the death of your co-worker Matias Martinez? We found his body today, and someone gave him a pretty good beating."

Both men feigned any knowledge of the death. "We haven't seen him in a long while," volunteered Juan. "We thought he just quit the company and found another job. Had no idea he was dead."

"Martinez is not the reason we brought you in today. I want to know what your relationship was with Jennifer Ambrose?" Basso had already reviewed the case files on the two brothers and found that several years ago, Ambrose was successful in getting charges dismissed on them on an assault accusation before it went to a grand jury. George Ziegler did not have enough evidence to hold them when the victim refused to testify.

Jose was the first to answer. "She is a lawyer for the company we work for. She helped us one time when we were wrongly accused. Seemed like a nice lady."

Basso thought for a moment and decided to make up a story to see if they would give themselves away. "Look, guys, I am not playing games here. I have evidence showing you or your brother or both of you had more than an attorney-client relationship with her. If you do not come clean and tell the truth, I am going to have both of you held at the Dauphin County Prison and charged with murder." Basso continued the fake scenario. "I know your reputation as lady's men, so if you want to save yourself a lot of trouble, you better start telling me the truth."

The twins both started to laugh. "No way you can threaten us with Dauphin," said Juan smugly. "Without grounds, we walk."

"You guys aren't too smart. This is a murder case, and I can hold you for 24 hours, and with one phone call, it will be 96 hours. You pretty boys will be fresh meat to those animals up there. You won't be smiling so much in a few days. Or maybe you will be."

The brothers could not discern whether Basso was bluffing or not, and they resented his insinuation. They talked privately to each other, and Juan took the lead. "We'll tell you about her, but first, we want you to know we have five or six witnesses who can testify we were in a poker game that lasted nearly all night on the night she was killed."

"Okay, so tell me,"

"When she had our case thrown out of court a couple of years ago, she proposed we should celebrate. We went to a club, had a few drinks, and about an hour later, she suggested going back to her place where the booze was cheaper. Everybody knows money was not a problem with her, so we caught on right away. The three of us went to her house. She was one hot lady. Never been with a woman like that before. We no sooner had our drinks poured when she attacked Jose, ripping his clothes off while passionately kissing him. She did the same to me. We drank and made love every way you could imagine until the sun was almost up. It was the best threesome either of us has ever experienced. Around 6 a.m., she jumped out of bed, took a shower, and told us bluntly we should leave right then. Jose and I dressed, left her house, and we never could get close to her again. It was as though it never happened. At the warehouse, she totally ignored us, and given her position versus ours, we left it at that. We never tried to have an encore. We never even had an occasion to speak to her after that, and that's the God's truth."

"Would each of you be willing to take a paternity test to eliminate you as the father of Ambrose's unborn child? If it came out negative, it could support your contention you never had the reprise you dreamed about."

"Our lawyer has constantly advised us never to volunteer anything to the police unless they have a subpoena, and you can't get that without probable cause. Besides, she insisted on protection, so you would be wasting your time."

"I think your statements today would qualify as probable cause, but at this moment, I don't intend to do that."

Basso left the room to speak with Curto in the adjoining room. "What do you make of it, Julius?"

"Well, seems like they are being straightforward with you on the threesome, but I find it hard to believe they would not go back for seconds."

"You could be right, but for now, all we have is confirmation of the others' stories on Ambrose and her sexual appetite. I don't think we can hold them, but I am amazed they went for my bluff so quickly. I guess the thought of going back to that prison put the fear of God into them."

"By the way, Gene, I finally was able to get some time in with Nancy Kowalski. I told her all the circumstantial evidence we had on Pino before he was shot, including his blood type. You were right. She said we would not have been able to make a case on what we had, even though the circumstantial evidence was plentiful."

"Julius, tell me. Do you recall when you were undercover at Central Penn whether the men clocked in and out on their job? I'm trying to ascertain if there really was a late-night card game the whole crew uses as an alibi for the night of Ambrose's killing."

"Yes, there are time clocks for the hourly-paid class at the warehouse, but that won't help in this case, because they would have been required by policy to punch out after the normal work day, even though they stayed in the facility. Why don't you talk to the cleaning staff working that night? I recall they work from 6 p.m. to 2:30 a.m. They would know if the group was there. I can't do it. One of them might recognize me."

"Good idea, Julius. I'll do that."

CHAPTER 30: THE ATTEMPT

The investigation as it related to Santiago was slowed by the death of his 95-year-old father Sebastian. Santiago lost his wife Monica, the true strength of his family, five years earlier, and his mother ten years before that. Now losing his father, he was without the last remaining link to his life as a boy in Colombia. His father kept his position as janitor until he retired despite the overwhelming protests of Santiago, who tried to reason with him. "Pop. I have all the money you will ever need to live a wonderful life, so why do you insist on doing this menial job?"

"It has served this family well for all these years in America," Sebastian snapped.

While they were alive, Santiago's mother and his wife were overly supportive of him against all his detractors, but his father did not condone the lifestyle his son led, or the way he earned the money to perpetuate that lifestyle. But there was never a loss of respect by Diego Santiago for his dad; he knew that he and his mother were responsible for his success by making the bold and dangerous decision to emigrate to America when he was only twelve years old. His father, when he became particularly agitated about reading negative comments about his son in the newspaper, was extremely critical of him. "We left Colombia with nothing more than the clothes on our back to get you away from the violence and crime of that country, and here you are doing the same thing in this country. I sometimes wish you were not my son."

"Pop, I am just trying to make life better for you. Mom died fifteen years ago, yet you continue to live in this crummy place when it is absolutely not necessary. You should have retired years ago."

Nothing he could say would make his father accept him. His death was a blow to Santiago despite his father's age. He realized in all the years of his life, he had never uttered the words 'I love you' to him, nor had he heard them from his father. Now it was too late. He planned a huge funeral that included a who's who list of city dignitaries, state politicians, high-ranking members of the church, and even famous showbusiness celebrities. Santiago had used money all his life to solve his problems, and he attempted to do the same thing with this funeral to appease the ill will his father had for him. Although most of the attendees never met his father, they came to pay respect to his son. The funeral was a sign of the power and influence he had in this country.

The body was laid out for viewing at a funeral home in an affluent part of the city. After the two-day viewing, the casket with the remains of Sebastian Santiago was moved to St. Anthony's Church, where the Jennifer Ambrose mass celebration took place just a few weeks earlier.

Basso attended the funeral of Santiago's father and sat in the rear, marveling at the class of people there. He mused, *"They probably think I'm the bad guy for hassling him. Wonder how many of these people have accepted bribes from Diego Santiago. I would love to see his little black book of favors due him for his generosity to these people."*

Of course, Curto could not be there for fear of being recognized. He looked totally different today from his alter ego Stefano Grassi, yet the police force did not want to take any chances. Less than welcome guests included FBI and DEA agents, but they behaved in a respectable manner. They sighted other kingpins of crime from New York and Philadelphia, but note-taking was as far as it went.

Sitting in the rear close to Basso was a Black woman of about 50 years of age who showed signs in her wrinkled face of a hard life. Her dress was a bit shabby and stood out in comparison to the fineries displayed by the prominent people at the funeral mass. Basso was curious what her connection was to Santiago or his father, but he let the thought slip from his mind as he concentrated on the priest's words.

Father McGinty went into a fairly long dissertation on the life of Sebastian Santiago, emphasizing his fleeing from Colombia and its political oppression for the opportunities America offered in giving his son Diego a better chance at success. He was prepared better than he was for the Ambrose eulogy. As he was speaking in front of the closed casket, which shortly was scheduled to be transported in a lengthy procession to the gravesite, the Black woman sitting near Basso rose and walked slowly towards the alter and the expensive casket of Sebastian Santiago. People in the pews were puzzled as she walked down the aisle. Although in retrospect, they thought it was an unusual move, nobody even gave more than a cursory glance at her.

When she reached the first pew where Diego Santiago was sitting with his children Barbara and Roberto, plus Barbara's husband Damian, the woman's demeanor changed from solemn to fierce. She interrupted the priest by shouting out in a vicious tone while looking straight at Diego Santiago, "Murderer, you killed my son." Of course, nobody knew at the time, but this woman, Minnie Robinson, had lost her son very recently to an overdose of crack cocaine.

She shouted an obscenity at him and spat in his face, and before anyone could react, she pulled a pistol from her handbag and pointed it directly at him, screaming while tears flowed profusely down her cheeks. "You'll pay for all the evil you have done." Her slight hesitation was her downfall.

Standing at either side of the alter were two armed police officers there to ensure the safety of this large crowd of notable people. One of the officers lunged at her with his gun in hand, wrestling her arm to the ground and her gun away from its pointed direction. People started screaming, the priest was in shock, and Santiago's first reaction was to cover his daughter from any harm. As the police officer struggled with her, his gun unintentionally went off, and Minnie Robinson fell to the floor bleeding heavily from the chest wound the gun shot inflicted.

The church became a place of mass hysteria. People in the pews poured out and ran toward the church exit, some stumbling in the panic and falling, while others tripped over the fallen. Someone grabbed the microphone from the priest and shouted, "Please, everybody, remain calm. There is no longer any danger."

But that did not stop the unruly exiting of the churchgoers. Basso, although still in the rear, immediately made a 911 call for an ambulance. It arrived in minutes, but Minnie Robinson was already dead.

It took quite a while for order and sanity to be restored. The church emptied of all the affluent people, and the parking lot emptied of all the expensive cars. Any planned showing of respect at the gravesite was abandoned by the crowd. Santiago kept his composure while still holding tightly onto his daughter. He made some comment about the woman's mental health while mumbling over and over, "I have no idea who she is."

The only people left in the church were the immediate family, the priest, and the authorities. Even the altar boys abandoned their post. Father McGinty knelt over the body trying to ascertain if life still remained in this unfortunate woman while saying a prayer she could no longer hear. In minutes, the paramedics arrived to replace him. They checked her pulse and determined there was none. The urgency to get her medical help was abandoned. Basso made a call to Jeff McIntyre to alert him to the new customer he would soon be receiving.

The only person undisturbed about the whole event was the honoree of the day, Sebastian Santiago. A woman was shot down in front of him, but in death he stayed oblivious to it.

There remained the duty to bury the body, so Santiago enlisted the help of the police to transfer the casket to the waiting hearse. What was planned as a 50-car procession turned out to be a parade of two vehicles. Father McGinty accompanied the family to the gravesite and said something solemn to the four attendees. The ancient ritual of throwing dirt on the casket ensued. A huge luncheon at the country club for all the influential people attending the funeral mass was cancelled.

The family remained in a state of confusion and shock as they realized how fortunate they were to have escaped the rage of a woman who came so close to ending their father's life. The unknown collateral damage was to Santiago's reputation. How many of the influential people in attendance would now distance themselves from him was indeterminable, but it was inevitable.

CHAPTER 31: THE RIOT

What followed that night and over the next several days was an even greater tragedy. The headline in the Harrisburg Tribune read, *Black Woman Shot Dead by Police in Church*. Joan McCabe's written article was somewhat factually accurate, but by not knowing and printing the reason for the killing, it caused an immediate adverse reaction in Minnie Robinson's community of Greenfield, which surrounds Wilson Park. Most people never read further than the headline, and the calm of the neighborhood turned to chaos. At first, it was only a couple of male teenagers expressing their anger of the police. They kept shouting about a Black woman not being safe even in church. A few in the group had a reputation as instigators and took the opportunity to rally the crowd. Soon the crowd became larger, their voices became louder, their anger became deeper, and their insistence on justice became a rallying cry.

And as so often happens when crowds lose control of the ability to reason and cease distinguishing right from wrong, destruction of property began - their own property, but it began. First a rock was thrown through a storefront window, then a car was rocked until it toppled, then the spilled gasoline from the car was ignited causing the car to burst into flames as the crowd cheered. From there, the rage of the unruly crowd overflowed to all the adjoining streets. As more businesses were trashed, the looting began. People who were struggling just to exist in this improvised area were now seeing what little they had go up in flames or out the door on the backs of looters.

Panic continued into the night as mob rule took over Greenfield. Some people frantically called 911, but the reaction of the police to restore calm was apparently not a pressing issue. At least, that is the impression the residents of Greenfield felt from the lack of action. The community was the regular beat for officers Otto Schmidt and Jack Bearden. They were circling the blocks when the outbreak began. Their immediate reaction was to call for backup, but they were told to stand back. There was enough history on this type of outbreak to conclude that two lone policemen in the eye of a hurricane would only lead to someone being critically injured or killed.

The burning continued, the looting continued, and the aging residents cowered in their meager apartments in fear for their lives.

On the second day of the riot, Mayor Bixby called a special meeting with the chief of police. The discussion centered on whether the Pennsylvania National Guard should be brought in to quell the rioting. They decided to hold off for one day to see if it would die a natural death. When it did not, Bixby contacted the Governor, and martial law prevailed over a neighborhood previously ruled by gangs. Equipped with weapons with rubber bullets, troops poured into Greenfield while tanks closed off the access roads. All semblance of normal life ceased to exist starting on the first night of the riot, but the addition of the military made living conditions intolerable.

The mayor pleaded with the ringleaders to stop this senseless violence. Eventually, a negotiating team was able to talk with the riot leaders, who first demanded justice for the killing of Minnie Robinson. They did not want to be confused by the fact that she tried to kill another person; the situation had gone far beyond that. As the turmoil snowballed, the original reason for the riot was lost on the crowd. Mayor Bixby promised a full inquiry would be held, and if there was any wrongdoing on the part of the police, action would be taken.

On the fourth day, calm returned to Greenfield. The damage was accessed in the millions. Area hospitals were overloaded with injured people, but amazingly, no one was killed. The real tragedy was the enormity of loss to the poverty-stricken residents who could not afford the burdens they were already being forced to carry.

Saul Bernstein was one of the big losers. When the violence started, Bernstein returned to his pawn shop in the center of Greenfield where most of the looting and arson were occurring. He had a 12-guage shotgun behind the counter which he took with him to the locked area behind the floor-to-ceiling cage separating his inventory from the customer counter. He decided he would stay the evening in the shop, hoping his presence and the shotgun would be a deterrent to any troublemakers. The first hours passed uneventfully, although he heard plenty of shouting and the sound of an occasional gunshot, but it did not seem to be near his store. Just about 2 a.m., he was jolted awake from his drowsy position in his chair by hollering in the street, followed by forceful slams against the shop door. The door burst open from the force of the blows, and about a dozen males, all seemingly teenagers, invaded the store.

Bernstein's reacted by pointing the shotgun through the cage opening and demanding they leave at once. Of course, they laughed at him, insisting he come out of the caged area immediately. One asked sarcastically, "What you gonna do with that gun, old man? You not gonna shoot nobody."

Bernstein refused, which angered the youths, who then started upsetting displays, overturning shelves, and destroying anything they could get their hands on. To stop the trashing of his store, Bernstein exited the caged area, still holding the gun. One of the mob grabbed the gun and slammed its butt into Bernstein's chest, causing him to reel from the pain. He collapsed to the floor as the gang invaded his inventory area. More people poured into the shop as the pillage of Bernstein's pawned goods continued unabated. Competitors fought over the more expensive items, at times destroying them in the process.

Bernstein rose from the floor in another attempt to protect his possessions, but he was greeted again by a forceful blow to his face and jaw. Angry mobsters outside hurled bricks into both storefront windows. The pawn shop was in total shambles, every tangible item on shelves behind the cage door was taken as the intruders ransacked the entire area. They carried away everything in sight, including Bernstein's shotgun. Bleeding from the mouth and not yet realizing his jaw was broken, he moaned in excruciating pain from the three broken ribs he suffered. Bernstein crawled behind the counter and waited for the storm to abate. Eventually, calm returned in his area when there was nothing left worth taking.

Bernstein knew a few of the boys, but many he had never seen in the neighborhood. Two he did recognize were Antonio Jackson and DeMeritus Johnson, although he only knew them by the names Speed and Yoyo. Both were out on bail posted by Jackson's mother. She pledged her wedding ring and car title to secure the bailout. *"Why did they do this,"* he pondered. *"Was it because I cheated them on that jewelry they stole? Did they learn it was worth more? Did they come to get even with me?"* All sorts of thoughts raged through Bernstein's mind as he suffered in silence on the floor behind the counter.

Bernstein dozed off and on throughout the night. In the morning, he managed to call his son to extricate him from his horrible position. His son cautiously navigated the dangerous streets and was successful in reaching the shop to rescue his father. The hatred in his son's heart was enormous, but Bernstein tried to calm him. On the way to the hospital, Bernstein said in slurred words almost too painful to utter, "Who do you kill when something like this happens? They are all to blame, and none of them are to blame. We must pick up the pieces and go on with life. Revenge will not solve anything."

A race-related riot is not an isolated event in the USA, nor are the reasons for the calamity always accurate. By comparison, though, the Greenfield riot was small in relation to two that occurred in the Los Angeles area.

From August 11 to August 16, 1965, a devastating riot occurred in the Watts neighborhood of Los Angeles. A Black motorist was stopped for reckless driving by a White traffic policeman, an argument ensued, followed by a fight. Somehow, this altercation with the police was falsely rumored to have involved a Black pregnant woman reputedly hurt in the scuffle. This was the trigger point for a riot that involved six days of arson and looting. The Los Angeles police were not able to quell the disturbance, forcing the Governor to send in 4,000 California National Guardsmen. When peace was finally established, 34 people were dead and property damage was more than $40 million.

The Watts riots, however, were surpassed in devastation, cost, and loss of life by the Rodney King riots, also in Los Angeles, whose cause in this case appears to be fact-based. King was brutally beaten by police after a high-speed chase when he tried to elude the police after their failed attempt to make a traffic stop. He was tasered and savagely beaten, including 56 strikes with a police baton. Unfortunately for the police, the entire incident was filmed on a video camera by a bystander. The video was given to a local TV station, and from there it found country and worldwide coverage. The four officers were indicted and put on trial for the excessive force used against King, but a jury acquitted all of them. This triggered a five-day riot that cost the lives of 63 people. Local police were unable to contain the demonstrations. It took the use of the Californian Army National Guard, the Army's 7th Infantry Division, and the 1st Marine Division to quell the violence. Over 8,000 troops were on patrol. In addition to the dead, almost 2,400 were injured. The police made 12,000 arrests during this time. The cost in terms of property damage exceeded $1 billion.

Mayor Bill Bixby spoke on a special TV broadcast to reassure the entire city the situation in Greenfield was under control. His call to have the matter investigated did nothing to reassure the people of Greenfield. Minnie Robinson was buried by her family, and the Santiago family made a public statement regretting the incident while reaffirming the accusations against Diego were baseless. This statement also fell on deaf ears.

CHAPTER 32: THE TRIAL

Basso was feeling the pressure even more with this current turn of events. District Attorney George Ziegler came to his office for a progress report on the two murders.

"George, we are not making much headway. It is obvious the killings have something to do with Santiago, but we can't seem to make that breakthrough to connect the dots. We talked with a lot of people working for his company, and although we learned a lot about the personal lives of the victims, we can't seem to make the right associations. They are related yet seemingly unrelated."

"Well, Gene, you know Mayor Bixby is breathing down my back wanting to see an arrest to get the press off his back. The Tribune has been brutal in their criticism of our handling of this whole mess. There must be a connection to Santiago. This ugly business in Greenfield and at his father's funeral is just adding more fuel to the fire. Santiago must be the common thread piecing together these things."

"What is happening with the trial of Jose Caderas that's to be defended by attorney John Halbrook. I might be grasping at straws, but I am hopeful something emerges during that trial that will give us the break we need."

"It actually begins tomorrow morning. Don't know how well Nancy is going to do. The victim, Joe Benjamin, is her crucial witness, but he lacks credibility because he has a record. And, he is getting cold feet about testifying. I believe he was threatened again and is afraid to speak openly. If he refuses to testify, Nancy will not be able to do much."

"Well, if she can link the assault and attempted murder charge against Caderas to Santiago, it would be wonderful. Everybody knows Caderas is not a rocket scientist, so he in no way planned and acted on his own. He was simply taking orders, but how do you prove that without the victim testifying as to the motive. The motive for the assault is the key, and if provable, would link to Santiago, I am certain."

The trial of Jose Caderas began the next morning. Nancy Kowalski was the attorney for the state. John Halbrook as defense counsel sat with his client, who had posted a $50,000 cash bond when originally arraigned. Everyone knew he could not possibly afford to post a bond in that amount, nor could he likely pay the fee of a bail bondsman to do it. After the preliminary trial formalities, Kowalski delivered an impressive opening statement summarizing the evidence she would present. "Ladies and Gentlemen of the jury, I intend to prove to you that the defendant, Jose Caderas, did viciously attack the victim, Joe Benjamin, leaving him nearly dead in an alley." She went on to explain the specifics of the attack and how the defendant committed them. Halbrook countered with his rebuttal statement, stating no evidence will be shown that links his client to the crime.

The trial began. Kowalski first called the emergency room doctor who attended Joe Benjamin when he was brought in by the paramedics. He gave a graphic picture of the condition of the victim, volunteering the likely object used in the attack while stating they were fortunate to save his life. Halbrook partially discredited the testimony by showing the doctor was not qualified to rule on the specific object causing the injuries unless it were produced into evidence. He suggested, "The man might have been hit by a car, for all we know."

Kowalski also proffered as a witness the man who found the victim bleeding in the alley. His description of the man's condition was even more graphic. Of course, Halbrook countered by asking the man what medical training he had, and when he responded he had none, Halbrook discredited his testimony as simply a glorification of the situation. "Did you see the attack?"

The witness answered, "No."

"Then you did not see my client commit any crime, is that true?"

"Yes, that is true."

"No further questions," Halbrook exclaimed triumphantly, and the witness was excused.

Kowalski was at this point prepared to call Joe Benjamin to the stand, but he had not yet appeared in court. Kowalski asked if there could be a recess, since her next witness, the victim, was yet to arrive. Benjamin assured her he would make an appearance, but he was an hour overdue from the appointed time. The judge denied the request, citing he was not going to delay the trial because the prosecutor could not control her witnesses. Halbrook immediately requested all charges be dropped since the prosecutor had not been able to establish a *prima facie* case that a crime was committed, let alone his client's involvement.

Before the judge could rule, Kowalski asked, "May I approach, Your Honor."

"What is it, Ms. Kowalski?"

"Your Honor, we have a serious crime here where a man was badly beaten and left for dead. It is a miracle he is still alive. We are convinced the defendant is responsible, and I believe he is somehow involved in further intimidation to preclude my witness from testifying against him. If I could have an hour for the police to find him and bring him to court, I am sure we could convict on his testimony."

"I am sorry Ms. Kowalski. The wheels of justice may grind slowly, but once they are in motion, it would be improper for me to halt them. They grind for the prosecution and for the defense. If your witness does not appear in the next ten minutes, I have no other option but to sustain defense counsel's motion.

To everyone's surprise and Kowalski's relief, before the ten minutes elapsed, Joe Benjamin appeared in court. Kowalski scolded him privately for being late and directed him immediately to take the stand for questioning. She asked first about his drug habit to clear the air before the defense brought it into play. Benjamin admitted he was an addict but was getting help to kick it. He was in a state-sponsored drug rehabilitation program.

She then asked him to recount the events on the night of April 25th. Benjamin told the court he was walking to his car after work when he was accosted by a man who demanded money from him.

"Why did he want you to give him money?"

"I owed him $5,000 for drugs I purchased and did not have the money to pay for them."

"What did this man do then?"

"He pulled a baseball bat from behind his back and struck me in the knee, then in the shoulder, and then in the mid-section. I fell to the ground pleading for him to stop, but he continued to beat me. I spent two months in the hospital recuperating."

The courtroom crowd moaned, and the judge reprimanded them to be silent.

Nancy was ecstatic. She was going for the kill with the next question. "Do you see the man who beat you in this courtroom?"

Benjamin scanned the courtroom carefully from left to right and answered, "No."

Again, the crowd reacted in vocal amazement, and the judge demanded order in the court.

Kowalski was stunned. "Mr. Benjamin, did you not pick out the defendant from a lineup as the man who inflicted those grievous injuries on you?"

"I did pick out a man from the lineup, but that man is not in this courtroom." Again, the crowd buzzed.

"Mr. Benjamin, do you know that lying under oath is a serious crime that could result in your imprisonment? Have you just now perjured yourself?"

Before he could respond, Halbrook jumped up and demanded an immediate dismissal of all charges. The judge had no other alternative but to grant the motion. The case was dismissed with prejudice, but not before the judge admonished Kowalski for wasting the court's time and money on a baseless case.

Nancy Kowalski could not believe what just happened. She was on the threshold of convicting a man for assault and attempted murder, but more importantly, she intended to link Caderas directly to Santiago as the supplier of the drugs at the center of the case. She was devastated.

Jose Caderas walked out of the courtroom a free man, leaving the District Attorney's office embarrassed and frustrated.

Ziegler informed Basso of the trial results, which he had anticipated losing all along, but certainly not in the calamitous way it abruptly unraveled. "Once again, Gene, we come close to putting a noose around Santiago's neck, and once again, he slips out of it with ease. His luck has to run out at some point."

"I think we should have the police pick up this guy Benjamin to see why he perjured himself. I can threaten him with jail time if he does not tell the truth, even though we can't use it against Caderas. We could use it against Santiago."

Basso ordered the police to find Joe Benjamin and bring him to the precinct, feeling certain he could intimidate him into telling the truth. The police first went to Benjamin's place of employment and were told he was not working that day. They then approached the operators of the rehabilitation center where Benjamin claimed he was receiving treatment. They had not seen him for several days. Even though it was midday, they concluded he must be at home.

Benjamin lived in Greenfield on the top floor of a five-story apartment building without an elevator. It was a dilapidated structure that should have been razed years ago. The landlord steadfastly refused to do any repairs, and the tenants were in no position to force him. They all suffered from the same condition – pauperism. Although it would not pass any of the inspections required of the fire department's code, no citation was ever issued against the owner.

Two police officers cautiously climbed the wood frame steps with service revolvers in hand, since they had no idea what to expect in this neighborhood. They rapped on the door of his apartment with the butts of their guns, ordering Benjamin to open the door for the police. When no response was heard, they smashed it open. To their surprise, the filthy apartment was vacant except for two large rats gnawing at some leftover pizza sitting uncovered in the stained, rust-colored sink.

The police radioed to headquarters that Benjamin was nowhere to be found. As they were returning to the station, the police car radio crackled. "Get over to Wilson Park right away. They found Benjamin."

Officer Brady had traded with a coworker his normal midnight shift for personal reasons. As he walked his familiar beat, which seemed somehow different to him in daylight, what he saw startled him. Joe Benjamin was swinging listlessly from a rope tied around his neck attached to a pillar of the stone bridge. He was hanging directly above the location where Brady previously found the body of Jennifer Ambrose. Joe Benjamin was dead of an apparent suicide.

CHAPTER 33: THE REASSESMENT

When Basso remarked at the crime scene where Jennifer Ambrose's body was found that Santiago was made of Teflon, he couldn't have known just how accurately his assessment would ring true. He would wait for McIntyre's report, but he in no way believed Benjamin committed suicide. He told Allen, "My guess is they could not risk Benjamin changing his tune if faced with a charge of lying under oath, so they eliminated the possibility. And with the body of Matias Martinez found floating in the Schuylkill River, the case Ruth Biantano was defending involving a rival drug dealer was obviously deleted from the court's calendar."

No evidence was found in Benjamin's apartment or on his person to suggest anything other than a suicide, with one exception. There was no note typically left by suicidal people. Otherwise, the bridge site gave off no clues of foul play, and his room was clean of other fingerprints or indication that he tried to fight off any intruders, if in fact he had been abducted from his apartment. With no evidence to the contrary, it was concluded that Benjamin walked to the nearby bridge and was solely responsible for his own death. Most people who read this account in the newspaper did not believe the story was factual.

Benjamin's life, just like his death, was a disaster from start to finish. He became hooked on cocaine in his early teens, and he became progressively more dependent as the years went by. Without holding down a steady job for longer than a few weeks, he grew deeper and deeper in debt to his drug supplier. He settled the financial score the hard way by paying with his life.

The next day, Allen and Basso attended a memorial service for Susan Aspect, whose body was cremated a few days earlier. She had no family in the area other than her mother, who was listed in the employment records at Central Penn Warehousing as the beneficiary for the company-paid life insurance policy. Santiago agreed to pay all expenses, as he had done for Jennifer Ambrose. The service was sparsely attended, with only a handful of people from the company being there in addition to Basso and Allen. Her aging mother, being bedridden, was too ill to attend.

When they returned to the precinct, Basso asked Allen to recheck the blood types of all the men in Rojas's organization. It was an easy task, since all were listed in their criminal database. She confirmed what she had previously said; the only one of the group who had a blood type of AB positive was the deceased Raphael Pino. He reviewed their alibis again, which he originally suspected were rehearsed by each of them covering for one another. They claimed to be playing cards as a group in the warehouse lunchroom late into the night. But the card game and the participants were confirmed by the cleaning staff working the night of the Ambrose murder. The custodial crew complained about the mess the gamblers had left in the lunchroom. He went over his interview notes of Damian DeRiso, Roberto Santiago, the Garcia brothers, and ex-husband Gregory Ambrose. Nothing jumped out at him to push the investigation forward. He even checked with immigration authorities to confirm that Ambrose's earlier boyfriend, Daniel Steele, had not reentered the country in the last several months.

He asked Curto to come to his office. "Julius, you reviewed the list of all her phone calls, didn't you?"

Curto retrieved the list to answer Basso with details. Flipping through the pages, he said, "Yes, Gene, I went over the calls to and from her office phone, which turned out to be all business related. The phone calls from her home were minimal. She called local businesses such as her hair dresser, her doctor, her housekeeper, but nothing was of a personal nature. There were no incoming calls for the last month on the home phone. From her cell phone, all the calls were to and from her office. They all involved Central Penn employees. So, nothing shows up to suggest she called anyone for personal reasons unless any of the calls to other employees was not business related. That would confirm what we have suspected all along. Her involvement was with a co-worker."

"Then there were no calls to restaurants to set up a reservation?"

"No, nothing showed up like that in the two months of records I reviewed. If we did not know already to the contrary, one would think she led a monastic life."

"It is quite possible, being a lawyer, she was overly cautious. She could have used a cheap, throw-away phone where you buy a prepaid card to make personal calls. Those are not traceable. By the way, have you checked with the company in Pittsburgh that Santiago claimed he was visiting on the day of the murder?"

"Yes, I talked to the individual personally, and he named the specific restaurant at which Santiago said they ate. It matched the name on the credit card receipt."

"So, not only do we not have a definitive motive, we appear to have solid alibis for everyone on our potential list. And we do not have a connection to the Aspect murder either. This is quite frustrating."

Ralph O'Brian entered his office while all three were talking. "Gene, we have that scheduled press conference in five minutes in the conference room. Do you know what you are going to say?"

"Yes, the same thing I said last time."

Basso addressed the group of reporters, couching the truth in opacity by stating they had several leads yet to pursue, but at this point he could give them nothing new to report.

Joan McCabe raised her hand. "Mr. Basso, is there any connection between Joe Benjamin's suicide and the two murders that are yet unsolved?"

"To our knowledge, Mr. Benjamin's apparent suicide is unrelated to those two cases.

"Do you not agree, then, it is a strange coincidence that his lawyer was on the staff that included the two deceased?"

"Coincidences do happen, but we have nothing to support they are connected."

"Come on, Mr. Basso. You're suggesting the bridge site where three bodies have been found is happenstance? You don't really believe that, do you?"

McCabe's question was considered rhetorical and not answered.

Another reporter asked, "What about the attempt on Mr. Santiago's life and the death of Minnie Robinson – how do they relate to the Ambrose and Aspect killings?"

"Again, I can tell you from the evidence we have seen, those events are unrelated. If we are able to make a connection, we will announce it in this room."

"And the killing of Matias Martinez who worked for the same company as all those others mentioned today – is that a coincidence also?"

"I am afraid it is. That will be all, ladies and gentlemen."

With that, O'Brian and Basso left the podium, happy to escape from the hounding reporters looking for any scrap of newsworthy print.

After the disastrous press briefing, Basso was desperate to find a breakthrough. He thought he would contact Grace Fuller. It was after work hours, so he called her home and asked if she was available to speak to him. She agreed, and Basso drove immediately to her home on the outskirts of the city.

Fuller was the stereotypical example of the stern looking protector of the boss's affairs - the proverbial office wife. Her desk in front of his office was a road block to anyone wanting access to Santiago. And her no-nonsense personality contributed to the intimidation she exerted over others. She was in her early sixties and had been a widow for 15 years. Fuller wore her hair in a bun on the top of her head and dressed with extreme conservatism. In the office she typically wore tweed suits, with the skirt at out-of-style long length, lace blouses buttoned to the neck, and black lace-up oxford shoes with thick two-inch heels. When she began working as a young girl, her position was called secretary, but now in this world of political correctness she was known as an administrative assistant – a title the prim Mrs. Fuller disfavored but tolerated.

"Thank you for seeing me on short notice, Mrs. Fuller. I just have a few questions. First, tell me about your background with Central Penn Warehousing. How long have you been employed there?"

"I am very proud to say I have been assisting Mr. Santiago for nearly 30 years. I have seen the business grow and prosper over the years due to his fine leadership."

"You were there when Jennifer Ambrose was hired?"

"Certainly. I have the most continuous service of any employee in the company, including Mr. Santiago's operations outside the city."

"You seem to me to be a very observant woman. What can you tell me about Ms. Ambrose's private life? Was she seeing anyone socially during the period just before she died?"

"Of course, you know there are always rumors floating about in any company, and she was not immune to that idle gossip, but Ms. Ambrose was always very professional in the office and never was less than discreet."

"But surely you were privy to some details. In your position, I am sure you become more aware than most of what is going on."

"Well, I can tell you I observed a change in her in the last month or so. A woman can see those things. She seemed to be less tense, laughed a bit more, was more inclined to talk about non-business events, and was less prone to bark at anyone. She seemed a lot more at ease with herself and with everyone else."

"Sounds to me like you are describing a woman in love. Could what you observed match my perception?"

"Well, I did not want to come right out and say it, but yes, you are very astute. I made the same assumption. But she still never let down her guard to give me any clue as to whom her affections were directed. She still remained the consummate professional in the office."

"I am very pleased you told me this, Mrs. Fuller. What about Ms. Aspect. What can you tell me about her?"

"Susan Aspect was a lonely woman. She was unhappy, and it showed. To my knowledge, she was not involved with a man the entire time I knew her. There was a period maybe a year ago when I thought I saw a spark of gaiety in her eyes, but I must have been misreading her, because that look disappeared quickly, and she reverted to her sullen self. She performed her job admirably and was respected by her co-workers, but she seemed to be a person who was not enjoying life. I felt sorry for her."

Basso thought to himself, *"I bet that happy period was during the time of her affair with Ambrose."* Aloud he said, "Can you think of anyone who would want to kill either of these two women?"

"Absolutely no one. Both women to my knowledge had no enemies. They were extremely well liked within the company. I hope I was of some help. This is a very difficult time at the company, but we will cope with it."

Basso refrained from probing into anything involving Santiago. He knew Fuller would be overly protective of him to the point her comments would not be useful. The next morning, he discussed his interview of Fuller with Curto and Allen. "Guys, my talk with Mrs. Fuller was very interesting. We have been assuming all along that Ambrose was an emotionally detached woman who used men to her own advantage and pleasure. But Fuller saw something recently that might refute that. From the way she described her change in behavior, someone finally broke through the thick exterior of the woman. She was in love."

Allen spoke first. "That is significant, Gene. Find out who she was in love with, and maybe, you find the killer. Of course, it could play out the opposite way. If it truly was love, someone else could have been jealous enough to do it." Curto and Basso agreed.

CHAPTER 34: THE CAMPAIGNS

Gianni Basso's older brother Francesco sat in the office of Mayor Bill Bixby discussing the upcoming campaign for Bixby's third term as mayor. Francesco was the campaign manager for Bixby in both of his successful elections, and with the fine record Bixby amassed over the years, he saw no reason a third term could not be realized. The city has no term limits for the office of mayor. He was concerned, however, about the financing side of the campaign. There was no shortage of political contributions; to the contrary, his concerns came from the source of the plentiful funds available to them.

That morning, Francesco Basso had gone to the office of Central Penn Warehousing's Chief Financial Officer John Caravacca to discuss campaign financing. Caravacca acted on a *pro bono* basis as campaign treasurer for Bixby's reelection, and he served in the same role four years ago for Bixby's second term as mayor.

"John, we seem to be having no problem with contributions to Bill's reelection effort. Would it be possible for me to review your records? I want to be knowledgeable about our contributors so I can recognize their support when writing Bill's speeches. He always likes to give credit to the ones who support him."

"Sure, Francesco. Feel free to look at the most recent data I compiled today. You are right. We are having a good year fundraising, and the way Bill spends money, we certainly need it. I chide him sometimes about being too lavish. It could have an adverse effect on the less affluent class."

Francesco sat in John's outer office with John's ledgers giving full details of contributions and contributors. Most of the names were individuals giving nominal amounts that in total were significant. He had a lot of backers. There were also large contributions from Political Action Committees. But from a dollar standpoint, one entry stood out. The largest amount contributed directly to the campaign was from Central Penn Warehousing, which Francesco realized immediately was a violation of the law. Corporations, labor unions, and other organizations were prohibited from making direct contributions to a politician's campaign.

"John, you are aware, aren't you, that corporations are not allowed to contribute directly to any elected official's campaign. Yet the largest contributor is Santiago's company. Why did you allow that, particularly since you work for this company?"

"I suggest you talk with Bill about that. All I do is account for the cash in and the cash out."

"To the contrary, John. You have a fiduciary responsibility to see that the laws are followed. You simply can't shirk this off as Bill's responsibility."

"As I said, Francesco, speak with Bill."

Francesco left Caravacca's office and headed straight for City Hall and burst into Bixby's office. "Bill, I was curious as to why I have so much money at my disposal for the new campaign, so this morning I approached our campaign treasurer John Caravacca about it. He allowed me to look at the financial records. What I saw concerns me. There is a very large donation coming from Central Penn Warehousing. You know they are registered with the Securities and Exchange Commission as a publicly traded company, and the law forbids a corporation from giving money directly to a candidate running for public office. You are not allowed to accept that donation. To make matters worse, John is the Chief Financial Officer of Central Penn, so this large donation really is suspect."

"Francesco, you are being much too conservative. Santiago is a very patriotic person who wants the best for this city, so he is only trying to help all of us help the people. He volunteered John's time to us for our second campaign, and you recall things went a whole lot smoother than the first. Now once again we have access to his fine financial skills for our new campaign."

"All the good intentions in the world will not help if this donation is ever questioned when the mandatory campaign reports are filed with the state. If your political enemies or nosy reporters go snooping, we're sunk. Potential political ramifications aside, you could even be prosecuted for violating the election code. Besides, in the last two years, you have been down to his resort in the Bahamas at least twice each winter, and there has never been a record of the expenses for those trips being reported as required by law. Is Santiago picking up the tab for all of that? You take your entire family at times, which means those trips cost tens of thousands of dollars, particularly at a place like his, which I understand is one of the most exclusive resorts in the Caribbean."

"You know very well we could never pay for the cost of a campaign relying solely on money received from Political Action Committees and individuals. There just is not enough to cover the money we spend on these elections. I suggest you leave the financing arrangements to me and John and just keep doing the fine job you do as campaign manager. I feel very comfortable about our winning a new term, and maybe one after that."

Francesco left the mayor's office with serious anxieties about the direction his job had taken. In the initial campaign, it was all about doing right for the people of the city. The Mayor now was in the last year of his second four-year term, and although they did struggle with the cost of the first campaign, they were in compliance with every law dealing with elected officials. Every required form about every aspect of the campaign was properly submitted. They adhered not only to the letter of the regulation but to the spirit of the rules as well.

It was during the second campaign that Francesco Basso noticed that funds were more readily available. Now as he was preparing himself for this third campaign, he questioned whether he was putting his professional career in jeopardy by being associated with a mayor who took direct contributions from a man reputed to be heavily involved in drug trafficking. He found little comfort in the law stating a campaign manager is not answerable for wrongdoings with campaign finances; only the candidate and the campaign treasurer are held accountable in law for any financial malfeasance.

To get some guidance on the matter, he visited his brother at his home one evening. "Gianni, I want to talk to you off the record as a brother and not as a police officer. I am very concerned about the legality of the funds being contributed to Bixby's campaign. I know the police are ambitiously trying to solve the drug problem in this city, and their prime person of interest is Diego Santiago. I have seen where our campaign received a huge donation directly from Santiago's company, and as you know, the campaign treasurer is Santiago's CFO. I guess I am looking for advice on what position you think I should take."

"Francesco, that is startling news, but then again, not totally surprising to me. I want you to know we are investigating two murders that could have direct association to Santiago. If you are telling me he is bribing the mayor of our city, and you are working actively to get him elected again, then you are on very dangerous grounds both legally and morally. That is a slippery slope to be on. This campaign manager business is a sideline for you. You have a good regular job with the city that could be impacted if knowledge of this became public. So, my advice to you is, you need to divorce yourself from Bixby, because if Santiago goes down, more than likely all the people on his unofficial payroll will probably go down. Whether or not you come forward with the information you have is your business. But if you continue in your campaign role, I can almost guarantee it will lead to disaster."

Francesco was in a difficult position. He knew his job was a direct result of the mayor's actions based on the work he did for the campaigns. Not only that, if Santiago was as dangerous as people said he was, he had more to worry about than simply losing his job.

Basso had an amusing thought that some people would not see as funny. His older brother Francesco was in a position to implicate Santiago in bribery of a public official, his younger brother Alberto was on the verge of charging Santiago with tax evasion, and he was trying to link him to two murder cases that could bring down his drug empire. "Looks like the name Basso will be removed from his Christmas card list," he joked, although he knew full well none of these issues was a joking matter, particularly when it came to the well-being of his brothers.

The day after Francesco Basso challenged Bixby over the questionable campaign contributions, Bixby scheduled a meeting and drove to Santiago's prestigious home. He and his limousine driver were immediately recognized by the security guards, who had been given prior notification to expect him. He was admitted without hesitation.

Bixby was a short, portly man in his early sixties with thinning hair and a Southern drawl he was not able to lose despite having lived in the North for over forty years. The Virginia native attended Dickinson College in Carlisle,

Pennsylvania on a scholarship, where he earned a degree in Social Services. After graduation, he took a civil service job in Harrisburg with the Pennsylvania Department of Conservation and Natural Resources. He involved himself with the local governmental scene, working as a volunteer for various state senators while he learned the workings of the powerful political machine that controlled the state.

Eventually, he ran for public office as a district magistrate, which did not require him to be an attorney. From there, he parlayed his persuasive speaking skills into other elected offices, and eventually he gained a seat in the lower house of Pennsylvania's legislative branch. Seven years ago, his popularity gained him a place on the ballot for mayor of Harrisburg, which he won in a contested race against a formidable opponent. His Democratic party challenged the original election results, and a recount proved Bixby the winner. Now in his second term as mayor and looking forward to his third, he no longer worried about losing; he had gained the full support of the people who mattered in politics.

"What brings you out here, Bill? Do you think it is wise considering all that is going on around me?"

"I would not have come if I didn't think it was important, and I could not discuss it over the telephone. I know you are under pressure from Gene Basso over this double murder thing, but now his brother Francesco, my campaign manager, has been snooping around the records of campaign contributions. He knows all about the money you provided through your company for my second term as well as the current contributions for the upcoming election. I am worried about this, Diego, although I did not let on to him that I had any concerns. He is throwing words around like 'illegal' and 'violation of law', and to make matters worse, he questioned the source of funds for those wonderful trips you offer me to Evergreen Cay. And God forbid he learns somehow about the millions John has transferred to that offshore account of mine. He already thinks your CFO is culpable in this whole thing because of his role with your firm."

"It must run in the family. His other brother is challenging my federal income tax return filings. What exactly do you want me to do? And why are you talking about all these supposed dealings and money exchanges? Are you wearing a wire? Did you make a deal with the Basso family?" Santiago moved aggressively toward Bixby in a manner that struck instant fear in the mayor's heart.

"No, no please understand my concern is for both of us. I would never try such a ridiculous trick, and I am not suggesting anything nefarious. But I did think you ought to know that this is out there, and it could come back to bite us hard if he were to go public." Bixby was shaking and stammering like a frightened child who knew all too well what the consequences of such a stupid act of wearing a wire would be.

Santiago sensed Bixby's genuine and palpable fear, which reassured him since Bixby – to avoid implicating himself – would be motivated to remain complicit and take steps to resolve the Francesco Basso problem. Santiago backed away but only slightly while still retaining control of the situation and of Bixby. "Bill, right now, I have more on my plate than you can imagine, and although this could potentially be calamitous, the other issues that are hounding me are as important as or even more important than this. I don't think silencing him would be a solution, although it would be easy to do. But more than likely he discussed this with his wife or his brothers, so if anything were to happen to him, it would compound the issue rather than resolve it. I suggest you handle your own people and have another talk with him. Get him to back off. If you still want me to get involved, I can, but it will have to wait until these murder cases are resolved."

Bixby left the compound dejected and concerned. But before he reached the front door, the ever-cautious Santiago alerted his guard to pat him down just to be sure. Bixby decided he would have another talk with his campaign manager to convince him it was in everyone's best interest for him to let this issue slide.

CHAPTER 35: THE P.I.

For the last several months, Eszter Curto was struggling to comprehend what was happening to her marriage. She understood the role a police officer's wife had to play, but this situation was not about his job and its demanding hours. His late-night habit seemed to be more prevalent; he was difficult to reach during the day, and impossible to reach on the nights when he worked late. When he was home, the passion they had once known in the marriage was gone. He was respectful to her and loving to the boys, but it just wasn't the same. After searching her conscience for confirmation that her intended actions were justified, she concluded she needed help to confirm or deny her suspicions. She wondered, *"Was it possible he was involved with another woman?"*

Eszter contacted Matt Inovaca, a private investigator specializing in domestic cases, whose office was in a strip-mall on the outskirts of the city. She found his name on the internet. Eszter asked their regular baby sitter to come over for the afternoon. She went to his office to discuss how this thing worked, having never gotten involved in this type of business arrangement. His office was not at all the professional style she expected. It was in a seedy part of town, and it fit right in with its surroundings.

Inovaca told her he charged a daily fee and could incur some receipt-supported out-of-pocket expenses, which she would be responsible for paying. On the day she was sitting in Inovaca's office hearing the ins and outs of his investigative process, her cell phone rang. Eszter had never ignored a phone call from her husband before, but when she saw it was Julius, she chose to disregard it. She was hit with a sudden sense of panic, as though by some mystic power, he would know where she was and what she was doing.

Eszter relayed her suspicions to Inovaca, being a bit reticent to divulge some of the private answers to his probing questions. But she knew she had to be truthful with him if she expected results. She gave him a check for $500 as a deposit and told him about her husband's job and its location, and she provided a picture to assist in identification. Inovaca said he would take over from there, and he promised to have some information to her in a week or so.

Inovaca followed Curto for over a week while assuring himself he was eluding detection. He was told he was good at his job. In the entire time he was spying, Curto was never seen with a woman in a social situation. He did keep very late hours in his investigative position, but in no instance was

Inovaca able to catch him in any compromising situation. Eszter was overly relieved with this report, but she wasn't at all convinced. She asked Inovaca to continue his work for another two weeks, even though it was getting very expensive. He watched every move Curto made but came to the same conclusion. In the three weeks on the job, he was never seen with another woman. Inovaca maintained the surveillance usually until around midnight. There were a couple of evenings when for some unknown reason, he lost Curto after tailing him to a restaurant, but he thought nothing of it. *"Nothing ever comes of these late nights, anyway,"* he muttered to himself.

Eszter Curto came away from this experience gratified with the conclusion but dissatisfied that she still had no answer to Curto's change in behavior.

Eszter decided it was necessary to confront him with her feelings of being neglected. Building up her courage one evening, she asked him directly, "Julius, you are a very different man lately and not your usual self. We no longer make love, you work long hours, and when at home you are distant. What is going on? Even the boys made a comment about not seeing you laugh as you used to do."

"I assure you Eszter nothing is going on. I am really stressed out about the Ambrose killing and the Aspect killing. We are under a lot of pressure from the police brass, the district attorney's office, and the press to resolve these murders and put someone behind bars. That is all there is to it. I just am overworked, and I guess it is showing at home."

Curto sat alone in his living room thinking about what Eszter said. The boys were in their room playing, and she was in the kitchen. He also began thinking about the man he knew was following him for the last couple of weeks. He did not know the man and was sure he did not work for Santiago, but Curto did not give off any signal that he was on to the surveillance. On more than one occasion, he gave the man the slip late at night, as well as on the evening he spent with Barbara DeRiso. This amused him as would a cat and mouse game. His military training and undercover work obviously provided him with more skills in this situation than his pursuer. "If this guy wasn't a Santiago goon, who was he?" On one occasion, he doubled back and snapped a photo of him using his cell phone. Deciding to act on that photograph, he told Eszter he was going out for an hour. During that time, he talked with several informants who often provided him with tips for a fee. It was not long before he learned the man was a private investigator. A $20 bill was all it took.

Back home, he pondered how he was going to approach Eszter on this. "What did he tell her? What does she know?" He was determined to get the answers.

CHAPTER 35: THE P.I.

The next morning, Curto made the trip across town to the office of Matt Inovaca. He walked into his office with his gun holster showing, causing Inovaca to shudder in fear. No one else was there. Being confronted by the subject of his investigation face to face was a frightening thing. Inovaca was a middle-aged man who was overweight, balding, and out of shape. He made his living on the suspicions and misery of others, although never had he earned enough to get out of credit card debt.

"Why were you following me for three weeks? Who hired you?

"You know I can't tell you my client. That information is confidential."

Without hesitation, Curto slammed his fist into Inovaca's face, breaking his nose and causing blood to squirt all over his desk. He tried to defend himself, but Curto grabbed him by his lapels, pushed him up against the wall, and said one more time, "Who hired you?"

Cringing in fear, the private detective admitted "It, it, it was your wife."

"I want to see the report you gave her."

"There is no report. I told her orally that I never saw you with another woman. That is what she wanted to know. I swear, that is all I told her."

"How much did she pay you? Hand it over."

Inovaca reached in his desk drawer that held a handgun, but Curto anticipated his action and slammed the door on his hand, breaking a finger. "Next time you try something like that, you will be dead."

Whimpering profusely, Inovaca blurted, "I, I, I was reaching for her two checks. I didn't deposit them yet."

Curto ripped up both checks while Inovaca remained motionless as blood dripped from his nose and hand. He dared not move.

"You better get into another profession. I spotted you as soon as you were on the job."

Curto continued to wrestle with how he was going to handle this with Eszter. The more he thought about it, the more he realized she was not at fault. Obviously, his behavior drove her to this, and he conceded his actions gave her the reason to do this. He decided not to bring the subject up just now. "She'll know something is up eventually when the checks never clear the bank."

CHAPTER 36: THE WEEKEND

The pressure on Basso to solve the two murders was really getting to him. Through all his career, he realized great success in a short period of time with every assignment handed to him. This one was a stickler. He rolled all the facts around in his brain, but nothing jumped out at him. Raphael Pino, Gregory Ambrose, Diego Santiago, Damian DeRiso, Roberto Santiago, John Halbrook, the Garcia brothers, Tomás Rojas, plus all the other men in his gang were all names on his list of potential perpetrators. Even Susan Aspect couldn't be fully dismissed, but that was the most improbable of his suppositions. Motive, of course, was not always evident with many of these names. To take his mind off work, he invited Gerri Allen to take a trip with him to Lancaster, Pennsylvania, about 40 miles southeast of Harrisburg. The area is famous for its Amish food, which typically is served plentifully family-style in many of the area restaurants. They went to an authentic Amish restaurant for dinner where they ordered the traditional dishes of scrapple, sauerbraten, and pepper cabbage, and for desert shoofly pie. Locally produced Amish wine was also on the menu, although many Amish people choose not to drink alcohol themselves. Much of Amish food is home-grown and homemade.

The Amish religion is a traditionalist Christian faith with origins dating back to the 16th century in Switzerland. They were known and still are characterized by a simple form of living that eschews modern conveniences, preferring for example, horse and buggy transportation over automobiles, hand tools over electric, and manual processes over modern technology in their agrarian lifestyle. They settled in Pennsylvania in the early 18th century when a large mass fled religious persecution and the religious wars prevalent in Europe. Historically, families were large, typically consisting of six or seven children who would join the family in their daily chores. The people have steadfastly preserved their culture and way of life, giving most visitors to the city a look back in history to a bygone era.

Basso enjoyed his occasional visits to Pennsylvania Dutch country, as the region is commonly called. It was far enough from his office to ensure his privacy yet close enough for either a one-day or overnight trip. This time, they chose to stay overnight at the popular Host Resort and drive back on Sunday.

Allen went to browse in the gift shop while he went to the front desk to inquire on room availability. Basso was surprised when the registering desk clerk recognized him. "Mr. Basso, so nice to see you again."

Basso racked his brain and was proud of himself when he remembered the man had worked in a restaurant close to the precinct where the police frequently ate. He recovered from the unnoticed embarrassment nicely and greeted the gentleman politely.

"This is a coincidence. I moved from Harrisburg and have worked here at the resort for a month or so, but right after I started, I was pleased to greet your partner right here as well. I don't get to see any of your old crowd anymore. I enjoyed serving all the men and women from your precinct."

"Really, he never mentioned he was here."

"Yes, he checked in with a beautiful blond woman who he introduced as his wife."

Basso let the comment drop, and he and Gerri made their way to the room. He repeated what he was just told. "Gerri, what the desk clerk said to me is very strange. We know Eszter has long black hair. What do you make of it? I want to know more about this."

Basso returned to the front desk and in a pleasant tone, asked the man if he could look in his records for the date Mr. Curto and his wife were here, providing a flimsy but believable excuse for asking. The trusting desk clerk looked in his records and wrote down the date on a piece of hotel stationery. "I remember him telling me they were not interested in Amish food, and I recommended the Ristorante Tuscano right next door. It has excellent Italian food, but I am afraid it is a bit pricy. They asked me to make an early reservation. The place gets very crowded later in the evening."

Basso went back to the room and started talking to Allen about Curto's private life. He had never known him to cheat on Eszter, so he was at a loss to guess what could possibly be the explanation here. Allen, being a very intuitive woman, looked Basso directly in the eyes and said, "Gene, could the woman in our wildest imagination be Jennifer Ambrose? She certainly was a blond, and a natural one at that."

"Gerri, that doesn't make any sense to me. There are thousands of blonds in the city. Why would he cheat on such a beautiful wife, and why would he be involved with someone who works for Santiago? Besides, we have pretty much concluded from what we pieced together of her lifestyle that if she were seeing the person who killed her, it most likely was someone associated with her job with Santiago."

"Gene, I simply suggested the possibility because of the blond hair comment, and because Curto was entrenched in the Santiago organization when undercover."

And in an instant, Basso shuddered at the thought that entered his mind. Not really wanting to go where his logical mind was taking him, he asked Allen hesitantly, "Gerri, the desk clerk told me the date Curto was here. It was the date Ambrose was killed. What if he really never left the Santiago organization? What if after we extracted his alias Stefano Grassi from his undercover role, he continued to work for Santiago? What if he really was playing a triple role. He worked as a policeman. He went undercover to spy on Santiago for the police. What if he changed sides and really became a mole in the police department for Santiago instead of being a mole for us? What if he was leading three lives instead of two? Gerri, you remember the conversation between Ambrose and Santiago on the surveillance tape – what if they were talking about Julius?"

"Gene, there is one simple way to prove I am way off base. You have in your bag a picture of Jennifer Ambrose taken before she died – I don't mean the morgue shot. Let's take that picture to this Italian restaurant and talk with all the wait staff and the manager. We can also demand a copy of the credit card receipt. We know from the records Ambrose charged nothing that day.

Basso was too shaken to respond immediately. He sunk in his chair and started visualizing all the stray pieces of the case. He recalled Curto's push to pin the crime on Raphael Pino, and then Pino was killed in the drug raid that we

273

learned about through an anonymous tip. "Could he possibly have wanted Pino out of the way to push his theory further? That would mean he would have to double cross Santiago."

They left the room and walked to the Ristorante Toscano. The restaurant was reasonably crowded but not bustling, so they were able to confront the manager with the question, displaying their police badges as identification. "Do you recognize this woman?"

"No, I do not, but I see hundreds of people each night."

"We have reason to suspect she was here about a month ago. I have the date. Please pull your credit card receipts to see if a man named Julius Curto paid the bill."

The manager took Basso and Allen into his office and booted his computer. "This might take a moment or so."

In a short time, the manager showed Basso the computer screen for the charges made on the night in question. Basso put his finger on the screen and scanned down until he found a charge for $450 paid by credit card in the name of Julius Curto. "Who was the waiter or waitress assigned to his table? I want to speak with him or her."

The manager announced that Giuseppe Condoro was the waiter for that table and called him into his office. "Mr. Condoro, this is Detective Basso and his associate Ms. Allen from the Harrisburg Police Department. They want to ask you a few questions."

Basso hoped and prayed that this man did not recognize the picture. "Mr. Condoro. Do you recognize this woman? You waited on a table for two about a month ago. Per the credit card records here, the gentleman was Julius Curto. I can get a picture here of him quickly if you do not recognize the woman; that might refresh your memory."

"That won't be necessary," he replied in a heavy Italian accent. "You notice the credit card has a substantial tip posted. I always remember customers who are good tippers. They ordered our exquisite Italian special that night along with a lovely bottle of a 2010 Gaja Barbaresco. If I did not remember him from the tip, I certainly would remember him from the wine, which is one of our most expensive. Yes, that is the woman who accompanied him. I am certain. One does not forget a lovely wine, a beautiful woman, or a good tipper."

"Thank you very much, Mr. Condoro. We are most appreciative."

Allen secured the business card of the waiter for future reference, and they walked back to their room.

"Gerri, I am stunned. I was just socked in the gut by a monster of a punch. I am still not grasping the reality of what we just learned. If Curto was with Ambrose on that night, and that appears to be the case, then he was more than likely the last person to see her alive. The implications of this are too far-reaching for me to digest at this moment, not to mention the triple role he could have been playing. If there is truth to any of this, what could possibly be the motive. And to cloud the issue even more, it doesn't explain the Susan Aspect murder.

The next morning after checkout, they stopped for a traditional Amish breakfast casserole at another authentic Lancaster restaurant. The trip back was troublesome for Basso. He and Allen discussed all the case specifics and tried to plan a course of action.

"How am I going to approach him on this?" Going to Lancaster was simply a lucky break, but his heavy heart made him wish they had never made the trip. "First thing tomorrow morning, have McIntyre match a DNA sample from the unborn child to what he has on file for Curto. And get his report on those threads found on her dress. No, wait a minute. Don't do that. I don't want anyone having the suspicions we have until we are absolutely sure. But check the files for Curto's blood type. If it is AB positive…, oh hell, Gerri, what will we do?" Basso was too distraught to go on.

CHAPTER 37: THE DEDUCTION

It did not take long for the news of the Minnie Robinson death to reach Bogota. Alejandro Moreno was furious. He pondered what course of action against Santiago he should take. Two unsolved murders of his employees, a killing by the police of another employee, another killing of an employee found in the river, and now this attempt on his life that triggers a huge race riot getting headlines all over the country and even reaching out to Europe and South America. He contemplated what his next step should be. Moreno had threatened Santiago by giving him one last chance, but he was not sure he wanted to follow through with the threat just yet. He no longer was making shipments to Santiago, so there was no inventory at risk. Terminating the business was not a good alternative; he had put years into building it into the most lucrative operation he ever managed. Killing Santiago would not solve anything either, since there was no true leader standing in the wings to replace him. That Santiago had maneuvered himself into this protective position irritated him. He decided to bide his time and not rush into action if the result would hurt his business. If the police could solve the crimes soon, it would influence how he proceeded.

But the next morning, Moreno had second thoughts about letting the situation with Santiago slide. If he made an exception to his policies, it could have disastrous consequences. He had given him a warning, and if he did nothing now, it would be a great show of weakness on his part. News would get out, and he risked losing control of the entire operation. "Better to stick to my word. I can't be viewed as getting soft."

Moreno decided he would not assassinate him, but he would make a definitive statement to let him know he does not tolerate mistakes. The risk was simply too high. He decided he would send two of his most trusted men to the States to show Santiago he was serious. They were to use a medium amount of force but were not to kill him. The plan was for Hernando Gomez and Michele Sanchez to board a plane for New York and rent a car to drive to Harrisburg. They were to stay in their hotel in Harrisburg until he contacted them to give them specific instructions. No contact was to be made with Santiago or any of his men until Moreno gave them the word.

The next morning, Santiago called Rojas into his office to get a status report on the botched drug drop and the anonymous call. He was still reeling from the personal visit by Moreno, and he needed to get to the bottom of it. Telling Moreno he had it under control was stretching the truth more than a little, so the pressure was mounting on him. There had not been another shipment since the Philadelphia raid. Moreno was waiting for him to come up with an alternative plan, since the use of planted crewmen on ocean vessels was no longer safe. But he wondered what the reaction would be if Moreno learned of the attempt on his life. Remembering the warning and not wanting to take any chances, he asked Rojas to assign two men to him as bodyguards. Being cautious was one of his most consistent traits. But his immediate tasks were to resolve the Philadelphia fiasco and come up with a new arrangement for receiving shipments going forward.

He thought about his airstrip in the Bahamas. The resort for which the land was officially purposed was now fully developed and operating at a profit under the name Evergreen Cay. He visited it often for a quick get-away, as did Barbara, Damian, and Roberto. His son's partner had a different face each time. Santiago also offered it as a luxurious bribe to city officials, giving them all-expense paid time at this island paradise. It was one of the most lavish resorts in the Caribbean. Ultra-rich customers flew their own jets onto the airstrip that was expanded to accommodate larger planes. It boasted a dozen beautifully decorated villas with multiple bedrooms facing a pristine beach, fully equipped kitchens, a championship golf course, an infinity pool overlooking the ocean, a three-star Michelin restaurant, a world-class wine cellar, state of the art health spa with trainers, a staff that typically outnumbered the paying guests, and all the other amenities the rich expect when they pay thousands of dollars a night for accommodations. Plus, it offered assurance of exclusivity and privacy.

Santiago had not used the airstrip for a drug run since the successful maneuver several years ago when he outwitted the police. He knew who tipped off the authorities on the drop, so that was not a problem, but he preferred to use the ship route as being less cumbersome. He also wanted the island's development to progress without being at risk from the Bahamian government if something went wrong.

Rojas came into the office, fearful as always of any encounter with Santiago. He always felt he was on the hot seat. Santiago was not hostile on this occasion. He politely asked, "Where do you stand on finding out how the police learned of our drop location in Philadelphia?"

Rojas had spent over a week going into extensive analysis of all the possibilities. He then, one by one, brought in each of his direct reports and conducted an interrogation that made the men think the police were sissies in comparison. Rojas did not get to be the right-hand man of Santiago by being a softy. His threats were taken seriously, and he used a certain amount of brutality to ascertain if they were speaking the truth. Every member of his gang sat through this ritual, and soon after the first was over, the word was out. He would tolerate nothing other than the truth. Visual signs of bruising frequently appeared on the men exiting their meeting with Rojas.

Not all his men were involved in the planned drug drop, but he grilled all of them in the identical manner just the same. When he was finished, he concluded that none of his people was the traitor. His interrogation style was too forceful for any of them even to think of deceiving him.

"Diego, the only people who knew the details of that drop were Pino, Martinez, Rodriguez, Lopez, and the Garcia brothers, and of course the Colombian crewmen, but I put the screws to all of my staff, even the couple newcomers. I can look you straight in the eye and put my reputation on the line when I tell you none of them was the snitch. I have my ways of determining a lie from the truth, so you have to trust me on this."

Santiago listened to what Rojas said and went into deep concentration of the entire process. He emerged from this trance-like state saying, "We are forgetting about one person. Julius Curto."

In the first year Curto was underground as the mole Stefano Grassi within the Santiago organization, he became comfortable with the lifestyle his double standard afforded him. He provided information to the police in bits and pieces on Santiago's illegal activities but was cautious not to overdo it for fear of exposure. His position was not secure enough to leak a major operation. But at one point, he realized that working for a cop's salary was not the way to go. He took a brave step after a year on the job and approached Santiago in a private meeting.

Closing the door to Santiago's office, Curto said, "Diego, I want to talk with you about a very serious matter. My name is not Stefano Grassi, it is Julius Curto. I have been working with the police for about a year as an undercover agent. Now, before you pull that gun from your desk drawer, hear me out. I would like to make an arrangement with you. I would like to continue my work as Stefano Grassi but actually be fully under your employ. I will have to, on occasion, tip them off to some deal you have going down, but you will be fully aware of my intended action in advance. But the real benefit to you is that you will have a mole in the police department, a luxury few men in your position enjoy. In return, I expect to be compensated appropriately."

Santiago's first reaction was to have the man killed immediately, but the more he thought of it, the more the idea made sense to him. "How do I know I can trust you? You seem to know how to work both sides against the middle."

Curto had assessed the risk of his bold move and replied, "Well, I guess your best assurance is my life, which is on the line. If I cross you, I'm a dead man. So, the way I see it, you have nothing to lose. It is a solution where everyone benefits. If you kill me now, you will be missing an opportunity of a lifetime."

Santiago was not quick to decide. He told Curto he would get back to him in a day or so. Until then, it was business as usual as far as he was concerned.

The only person with whom Santiago discussed this proposition was Rojas, a man he had found trustworthy the entire time he knew him.

The two men evaluated the pros and cons of the proposal. It was decided to take Curto up on his offer, but the only people who were to know about it were the two of them. Nobody else in the company was to know the true identity of Stefano Grassi.

Curto was advised of the decision and told he and Rojas were the only people privileged with this information. They agreed to a compensation figure, and monthly, money was wired to an offshore account in the Bahamas that Curto controlled in another name.

Over the next three years, Santiago realized he had made a good deal. He learned more about police operations than he ever dreamed of knowing and fed Grassi/Curto the small crumbs necessary to keep his cover in the police department safe. The big deals never were given to the police, but Curto gave enough smaller tips to keep the brass happy.

After three years, Curto told Santiago he wanted out. His family life was suffering, and he felt he could be just as much help to him working inside the force as in undercover. He told Santiago he had already spoken to his lieutenant, and a plan was hatched for him to give information on the next major drug run and finally bring down the Santiago organization. Grassi was to be killed during the raid, but of course, Santiago would change the plans and not be caught. Curto told the police of the drugs coming from Bogota to the Bahamas, of the switch to seaplane and drop in Florida, of the transporting of the goods up the coast, and of the drop location at the abandoned warehouse. What he did not tell the police was that Santiago changed the plan by unloading the goods in Maryland and moving them to a different location using other trucks for unloading in Scranton instead of Harrisburg. Nobody in Rojas's group knew about the switch except for Rojas, so it worked to perfection. Grassi was killed in the raid, Rojas made sure he was able to escape unharmed, the drugs were safely delivered elsewhere, and Curto was reborn as a mole within the police force instead of within Santiago's organization.

The scheme worked well for Santiago over the next years, and he avoided all attempts to bring down his organization through having previous knowledge of all police plans. He reminded Rojas that besides his men, Curto was plugged into all the operations as a safeguard against any police action being planned. So, Curto was fully aware of the Philadelphia drop timing and location.

"But why would he turn on us now, Diego? He has been faithful to you all this time."

"I don't know the answer to that, but I suspect his relationship with Ambrose and her death might have something to do with it. What, I don't know, but it must be related. I told her she should put an end to it, and now she is dead. It really does not matter why. If he sabotaged the drug drop, then he must pay the consequences. Curto should have alerted us to what was going down, but he did not. I must confront him personally to ask why. No one is ever going to cross me and get away with it. See if you can come up with a pretense to have him meet us somewhere – maybe the Wilson Park bridge, which should be a safe place to go unnoticed."

CHAPTER 38: THE ANALYSIS

B asso and Allen sat in his office, trying to decide a course of action on how to approach the Curto situation. Curto had scheduled the day off for personal reasons, so they had time to plan their strategy.

"Gerri, I think I should visit with Jeff at his lab and talk to him personally. Maybe I should bring him into my confidence and tell him what we suspect."

Basso drove the short distance to the medical examiner's office that adjoined the morgue. McIntyre was studying results from the autopsy of Minnie Robinson to ensure accuracy when he testified at the hearing required of every killing involving police personnel. "What brings you over here, Gene?"

"Jeff, I need your promise that what I am about to discuss with you will go no further than this office for now. I have uncovered some very disturbing evidence that could impact the Ambrose case."

"Of course, Gene, anything we discuss will be strictly confidential."

"First Jeff, I would like to know if you have completed the DNA analysis on Ambrose's unborn child?"

"Yes, I have the results back from the analytical staff. Why do you ask?"

"I want you to go into your archives where you keep the DNA results for all personnel on the police force. When I volunteered my sample, I thought the only time it would ever be used would be to identify my body if some tragic accident happened. Now, I see another use for those records. Here is where the confidential part comes into play. I want you to pull the records of Julius Curto and compare them to Ambrose's unborn child."

McIntyre showed a stunned look on his face, but seeing the seriousness of Basso's tone, he did not question him. "I will make it a top priority. That would typically take a couple of days, but if I oversee it myself, I should have something for you within 24 hours. We have known each other for many years, so I know you must have good reason to make this time-consuming request."

"I do, Jeff. You simply must trust me on this. I also want to know about the threads you pulled that did not match the

Saks dress she was wearing. Could they have come from a suit coat, the type of inexpensive suit we all wear on the job?

McIntyre referred to his records and answered, "Yes, they are consistent with a man's suit fabric, but of course, I would need to test the actual garment against the evidence. These threads are polyester, the most popular man-made synthetic fabric because it is durable, light weight, and won't attract moths. But they easily snag, and she could have grabbed at him during the assault. It is preferred by people in your line of work because of its durability. The type of coat you are wearing is of similar material, but my sample threads are dark blue. Get me a sample for comparison."

"That could be a little tricky to get, Jeff, but I might be able to handle it. I will get back to you on that one. I may not need it, but just for the record. You told me she had sex before she was murdered. Do you have enough of a sample to make a positive identification if you have the comparative evidence?"

"Yes, we made sure we collected that evidence. It's available if you need it."

"One last request. I want you to pull the records on the blood sample from the belt fragment that fell from Ambrose's waist presumably while she was being dragged down the slope under the Wilson Park bridge. This one should be easier. Compare it to the records you have for Julius. I know from Gerri's research both are AB positive. Even though that is a rarer type, I am looking for something more conclusive. If all these tests come out like I am guessing they will, I am going to be one disappointed and angry person. How long will it take?"

'I'll have everything for you late tomorrow. Gene, I am shocked by this revelation, but you have my word you will be the only one who will know these results until you tell me differently."

Basso drove back to his office still perplexed by all the circumstantial evidence. He asked Gerri, "Being a woman, you are very observant of men's dress. Like most men, I can't tell you what you wore the last time we saw each other. How many suits have you seen Julius wear and what type are they? I know neither of us has an extensive wardrobe."

"Well, let's see. He wears either a black, dark blue, or dark brown suit which are a polyester fabric just like all you men wear on the job. Gene, we know they were out of town that night, and he might not have been wearing a work suit while on a short holiday."

"You are right, Gerri. The only way that thread will come into evidence is if we get a court order to search his home, and I am not ready to do that. Probably don't have enough to get a warrant anyway. Talk with Nancy Kowalski and get her opinion on what is necessary to convince a judge to issue a warrant."

Gerri went to Assistant District Attorney Nancy Kowalski's office in the adjoining building and asked a general question on the matter without giving any specific details. Kowalski said that any positive results from the medical examiner would be sufficient to get a warrant. Kowalski was still very upset at having her case against Jose Caderas dismissed, so she was hopeful something would be breaking on the murders soon. Of course, she assumed improperly that Allen had evidence that would implicate Santiago, and Allen was careful not to undermine that assumption.

Back at the precinct, Allen briefed Basso. "Gene, we can get a warrant if any of the tests you have Jeff doing come back positive. Looks like we are going to have to wait at least until tomorrow to proceed on this angle."

Basso began thinking about the blood on the belt fragment while Gerri was gone. If the blood proved to be Curto's, that would mean he had an injured hand. To draw blood, a bite must be very forceful. And then a spark of light hit Basso. His deductive reasoning ability allowed him to recall the events the day after her murder. He was playing squash with Curto and the match was halted almost at the start because he hit Curto with his racket and his hand bled.

"What if that was a ruse? What if Curto already had bite marks that caused bleeding, and he needed a cover to explain why his hand was injured?" He was getting overwhelmed with circumstantial evidence all pointing in the same direction.

CHAPTER 39: THE ENCOUNTER

Santiago made numerous attempts to contact Curto. They had a special code system for setting up meetings, but Curto was not responding. Curto had taken a personal day off work to sort out the mess he made of his family life. He reflected on how he slid into this position in the first place. Although he was perfectly satisfied with the sex life he enjoyed with Eszter, he was not immune to the flirtations of Jennifer Ambrose. Under attorney/client privilege, Santiago previously told her Curto was Stefano Grassi and was still working for him. Santiago thought it best his general counsel know this, since it might be necessary to use this against the police someday. Ambrose had seen Grassi with the Rojas gang and always felt attracted to him, but being married at the time, she would never get involved in any extracurricular intracompany activities out of respect for her husband and for fear of exposure.

But one night recently by sheer accident, she spotted Curto in a local restaurant. Although he looked unrecognizable as Grassi without the beard, hair and eye color changed, and a general, more dignified demeanor, knowing who he actually was allowed her to make the association with Grassi easily. He was with his wife, who Ambrose thought was beautiful with her long flowing black hair and piercing eyes. Curto's two sons were also at the table. Both were very good-looking boys, causing Ambrose to think there really is something to this gene pool thing. He recognized her and tried to avoid contact, but Ambrose excused herself from the two women having dinner with her and approached Curto's table to introduce herself as the attorney for Diego Santiago, with whom Curto's department was well familiar. She gave off clues, however, with her sly phrasing that she knew he was Grassi, and the astute Curto caught the signals, guessing correctly Santiago confided in her. There was a slight flirtation, but it was subtle enough to elude the unsuspecting Eszter, who was trying to be polite while scolding the boys for misbehaving.

While he was undercover, Ambrose was still married to her husband Gregory, and no inkling of misconduct had ever been associated with her. She was simply the no-nonsense professional attorney. So, it was a surprise to him when a few days after the accidental encounter in the restaurant, she phoned him while he was driving home. Curto pulled over, and a long conversation ensued that left no doubt that Ambrose was a free woman and he was not off limits. They decided on a first rendezvous out of town in Pittsburgh where Ambrose had a business meeting with other attorneys helping her on a trademark case. She was staying at a lovely hotel atop Mt. Washington, the previously all-ethnic, now gentrified area overlooking downtown Pittsburgh where the Allegheny and Monongahela Rivers meet to form the Ohio River. In 1754 at the start of the French and Indian War, Fort Duquesne was built on that site by the French, who four years later defeated the British in the Battle of Fort Duquesne.

Ambrose and Curto had cocktails and dinner, admiring the scenic view from a prime window seat, and from there, the relationship started to grow. Curto had no idea what to expect when he agreed to meet her, but it became evident quite quickly that Ambrose was a lustful woman. She invited him back to her hotel room on the 20th floor where the view was even more dramatic, but they did not go there for the scenery. Within minutes, they were ripping each other's clothes off and getting more passionate by the second. Although Curto had always used his good looks to charm women into assisting him in his work, he never was unfaithful to Eszter until now. When lust overcomes one, however, any semblance of conscience soon dissipates.

When finally the exhausted couple fell asleep, it was 4 a.m. After only a few hours of sleep, Curto showered, dressed, and left for Harrisburg. Ambrose still had business in Pittsburgh, so he kissed her gently in her drowsy state and quietly exited his first extra-marital affair. Such things can be a strong intoxicant to men despite their professing they are happily married, and Curto was no exception.

From there, the illicit romance flourished, albeit sporadically due to the difficulty Curto had in getting away. They always met in out of the way places, and the sex routine remained consistent with the first night in Pittsburgh.

But something seemed to be changing with Ambrose. Instead of the affair being a ritual between two consenting adults, she, for the first time in her life, was feeling more than the pleasure to her body. She saw solid character and personality traits in Curto, traits she greatly admired. She felt listless waiting for the next time they could get away. Certainly, the physical needs of her body drove her, but when that extra something set in to take it a level or two above the sex threshold, she came to the realization that for the first time in her life, she was falling in love. It was an odd feeling, a bit painful at times, but a pleasant pain. The time between meetings seemed to drag on for her, and when at last they were together again, she was in ecstasy. How this feeling had eluded her during her life puzzled her, but it was here now.

To her dismay, she did not see the same thing happening to Curto. During their romantic times together, he was gentle, kind, considerate, and satisfying, but she did not see in him the same emotional need she was feeling. Rather than upset the situation, she decided to give it time to see if mutual true love would ensue. She was overjoyed when he called and suggested their making a trip to Lancaster for the weekend. He had told his wife he had out-of-town business his boss required him to handle. Curto met her at an indoor lot where she parked her car, and the two made the trip to the Pennsylvania Dutch country.

When they checked in at the Host Resort, Curto was caught off-guard by the desk clerk who recognized him, but since he remembered it was a work-related acquaintance, he was not bothered. Ambrose was introduced as his wife, and they retired to their room. It was mid-day, so they spent the afternoon again engaging in what they did best – satisfying each other. Ambrose had made up her mind she was going to confront Curto about their relationship, so she decided this evening after dinner was the best time to do so.

Although early for them to have dinner, they went to the front desk and asked for a recommendation other than Amish food. The Ristorante Toscana next door was suggested as having excellent food and a great wine list. Both were very pleased with the selection. The place was not yet crowded, so they enjoyed a casual dinner with a very expensive bottle of wine. Curto's family roots were from the southern part of Italy, but he had fallen in love with northern Italian wines, and the Barbaresco from the Piedmont region of the northwest, known as the queen of Italian wines, was his favorite. Both the Barolo, known as the king of Italian wines, and the Barbaresco come from the same Nebbiolo grape, but the soil where Barbaresco is produced is richer in nutrients, causing it to be less tannic.

Their waiter Giuseppe Condoro was particularly pleasant and knowledgeable on wines, which encouraged Curto to be overly generous with his tip. It was turning out to be a wonderful weekend for the two of them. What Curto admired most about Ambrose was that after the passion subsided, the two could hold an intelligent conversation.

They returned to the room. Ambrose decided it was the proper time and place to confront him. They had a wonderful day together, and she concluded the vibrations were right for her to proceed. To lead off, she confessed without hesitation she was in love with him. His reaction was surprise, and her reaction to his surprise was astonishment and annoyance.

"Jennifer, you have met my wife and two sons. You knew going into this thing I was married. How could you let that happen? I thought it was supposed to be all fun and games with no strings attached."

That struck a nerve in Ambrose. Here she was bearing her heart and soul to a man, and he reacts not only indifferently but arrogantly. "I thought you were beginning to love me and would eventually leave your wife for me. Was I just imagining things? Did I not read that in your actions more and more with each date we had?"

"Jennifer, if I ever gave you reason to think that this was anything other than a casual affair, I apologize. I never had any intention of leaving my wife, nor did I ever think you expected that of me."

At this moment, she dropped a bombshell. "I'm pregnant, and there is no question you are the father. I may have had other affairs since my divorce, but I was always extremely careful. I was not that way with you, as you well know."

Curto was stunned. His first kneejerk reaction was to tell her she had to get rid of the child. "We will have to find a doctor and take care of this. You weren't thinking of keeping it, were you?"

"Yes, I was. I thought it would be something to bind us together. I know you have been an excellent father to your sons, so I have no reason to believe you would not be the same to our child."

"Look, Jennifer. I am sorry if I misled you, and I am sorry you allowed yourself to get pregnant, but I repeat, I am not going to leave my wife and the boys over some sexual entanglement."

This blunt statement hit Jennifer like a lightning bolt. She was at once stunned, embarrassed, and angry. In a desperate move to turn the tide in her favor, she committed an unforgivable and fatal mistake. "Gene, if you do not leave your wife and marry me, I will expose our relationship to your wife, your boss, and the world, and I will expose you to the police as being a traitor still working for Santiago." The moment the words blurted out of her mouth, she realized she had gone too far. She was intelligent enough to realize you can't talk someone into loving you, nor can you blackmail them into it. She wished with all her heart she had never said it, but it was too late.

Curto began quietly fuming. He saw his marriage, his career, and his freedom crumbling before his eyes. He knew what happens to police who end up in prison, so he was not only fighting for his marriage and job, he was fighting for his life. Curto was in a state of rage, but his military training taught him to control his emotions. "I think it best we check out and drive back to Harrisburg. We are both too upset to salvage the rest of the time here."

While she packed, he went on-line and settled the hotel bill, and the two exited through the rear doors into the parking lot. Before they left the room, he neatly cut off part of the thick coarse cord used for drawing the heavy drapes covering the large sliding glass doors and slipped it into his pocket. In the car, she apologized for what she said and sobbed, "I would never do anything to hurt you. I said that in a fit of anger, but I did not mean it. What I do mean is I love you."

"Jennifer, I can't take the chance of your being overcome with that thought again." Knowing everything he had worked for his whole life was on the line if she followed through with her threat, he pulled the rough drapery cord from his pocket, pulled her toward him as though to kiss her, and looped the cord twice around her neck. Ambrose began gasping for breath and attempted to scratch at him, but he kept her at bay as he pulled harder and harder. Not being able to fend him off, she twisted her long neck and reached for his hand with her mouth. She bit down as hard as she could on his index finger to a point there was blood in her mouth, but Curto stoically endured the pain without loosening his grip. Slowly he watched the life drain from her body. Although death was common to him in his job and in the military, he had never seen a person die right in front of his eyes. He had mixed feelings at this point, realizing how lovely she was, but there was no turning back. Again, his military training helped him silently eliminate this perceived enemy, even though he was in obvious pain from the bite.

After confirming she was dead, he took his handkerchief from his pocket to wipe the blood off his finger. He did not notice he inadvertently touched her belt with his bloody finger.

He made the trip home on back roads. Ambrose was propped up as though sleeping with her head against the car window, so nothing looked out of the ordinary. He could have left the body along the route home, but he decided that Wilson Park would be a good cover. The surrounding neighborhood was noted for its criminal element, so he surmised the murderer would be presumed to have come from that area.

He drove into the park and stopped the car on the one-lane dirt road opposite the stone bridge. Then he spun the car around to allow for an easy exit from the trail. It was a clear night, and he cautiously scanned the surrounding area to assure himself he was alone. Curto carefully lifted her body from the car. He grabbed her ankles, and walking backwards, pulled her down the grade to under the bridge. In his rush to dispose of the body, he made a few mistakes, such as not removing her jewelry to suggest robbery. Being careful to touch only the fabric, he threw her handbag in the nearby bushes and hurriedly left. He also was unaware of Officer Josh Brady's walking beat around the park, but luckily, he had already disposed of the body and was leaving the park when he saw his flashlight circling the area. Curto left without turning on his lights and drove home to his wife. She was surprised to see him, and he explained he finished his work and did not want to be away from her longer than necessary. In the morning with very little sleep, he dressed for work as usual.

CHAPTER 40: THE SHOWDOWN

Hernando Gomez and Michele Sanchez arrived in New York from Bogota and rented a car for the trip to Pennsylvania as instructed by Moreno. They checked into a cheap Harrisburg motel, contacted Moreno to alert him of their arrival, and were told to wait for further orders. They prepared by doing their research on where Santiago's office and home were located. And they waited.

Prior to driving to Harrisburg, the two made a stop in uptown Manhattan on the instructions of Moreno. The address they were given was a delicatessen, which was crowded with mid-morning customers. They entered and asked for Bonito, the code name they were advised to use. The proprietor took them to a back room and pulled open a wall of shelves holding canned goods to reveal an arsenal of weapons. There appeared to be enough munitions to start a small war. From the cache of arms they were shown, they selected two AG-043 Soviet-made fully automatic assault rifles plus the appropriate ammunition. Moreno knew they needed to be armed, but there was no way to transport these types of weapons on a plane or through customs. After selecting their weapons, Gomez handed the proprietor an unmarked sealed envelope, and the two then proceeded on their way to Harrisburg.

Santiago, meantime, decided to lure Curto to the warehouse rather than Wilson Park, feeling he had more of a turf advantage there. Rojas was finally able to contact Curto through their code process of making a call to his cell phone but confessing he had the wrong number, saying, "Terribly sorry. I thought I was calling the dry cleaners." The dry cleaners meant Curto was to go to the warehouse. If Rojas had said the drug store, it meant to meet on the bridge at Wilson Park. Grocery store meant a third location, etc. If the caller led off by saying "Terribly Sorry," it meant at midnight. Other lead-ins meant other times.

Curto was still in a state of disarray over the way his life was changing. Not knowing what Santiago could want, he prepared for the trip mentally. To cover his absence from home at that hour, he told Eszter he was being called out on an emergency. As always when on assignment, he strapped on his shoulder holster to secure his Glock 22.

Curto made the drive out to Central Penn Warehousing and entered through a rear door as usual. He went to aisle 26A, which was the designated location pursuant to the coding system. The warehouse was deserted at that time of night, but the lights were always kept on as a deterrent to break-ins. Curto was about ten minutes late, but nobody seemed to be around. Santiago was delayed. He was on the phone with Moreno in Bogota, who called ostensibly to inquire on progress on the Philadelphia bust. Santiago told him he was at the warehouse at that moment and had set up a meeting with the one he suspected of being the anonymous caller who alerted the police. Moreno thanked him for the update and hung up. Santiago was relieved he did not bring up the failed attempt on his life. *"Maybe he does not know,"* he mused.

The recent turn of events was starting to affect Santiago's confidence. Curto double crossing him, Basso hounding him, his legal staff decimated by two murders, his high-ranking associates abandoning him after the fiasco at his father's funeral, Bixby's panic over contributions, and the IRS auditing him were all extremely troubling. But these things paled when compared to the problems Moreno could cause. Money and muscle could fix most of his problems, but this issue with Moreno touched much deeper. At stake was his life.

After hanging up from Santiago, Moreno immediately phoned Sanchez and Gomez at the motel and told them to proceed to the warehouse and get this job done. They arrived at the rear of the warehouse just as Curto was entering. Both quietly edged their way in and took up tactical positions to cover the entire floor area.

Meanwhile, Curto was getting nervous. It was not like Santiago to be late to a meeting he called. He checked his watch again, and another 20 minutes had gone by. Curto then heard footsteps and saw Santiago descending the metal stairs from his second-floor perimeter office. He walked slowly to aisle 26A where Curto was waiting.

"Diego, I received a coded message from Rojas to meet you tonight. What's up?"

Santiago started off slowly. "Julius, you and I have been working together for many years, and I admit, you have been a great help to my organization. Of course, you became wealthy in the process, but that is only fair given the amount of advance information you provided in keeping my operation secure. "

"Yes, it certainly has been a win-win situation."

"But one thing bothers me about our arrangement. You have notified me in every case when the police had a raid scheduled, no matter where it was to happen or how big or small. Of course, to protect you, we had to allow some of them to proceed on schedule, but knowing in advance allowed me to minimize my losses."

Curto became belligerent. "Yes, what you say is true. But where is this conversation leading?"

"I do not understand why you did not tell me about the Philadelphia raid? And who could possibly have alerted the police to it. You and Rojas's men were the only ones who knew it was going down, and we have eliminated all his people from suspicion. So that leaves you. Why didn't you tell me about it? Were you the anonymous phone caller?"

Curto was not prepared for this. He never anticipated being suspected of sabotaging the operation. "Diego, you're wrong. Why would I do a thing like that?"

"I'm thinking it had something to do with the Ambrose murder. I knew about your relationship with her. Raphael Pino was the prime suspect in her murder, and he was killed during the raid. Was that what you wanted to happen all along? Pino dead, case closed. Did you kill Ambrose?"

As a normal reflex reaction to danger, Curto reached for his gun. Before he could pull it out, a shot rang out, and Santiago fell to the ground, blood oozing from his right knee. Curto ran for cover in another aisle and tried to assess the situation, asking himself, "*Who just shot Santiago? They apparently did not want to kill him, since the bullet was obviously directed at a non-fatal area.*"

As soon as Santiago fell, Rojas emerged from out of the shadows and hovered over his boss. "Diego, we have the place in lock-down. Whoever did this is still in the building."

Within seconds, more gunshots rang out, and a raging battle ensued. Gomez and Sanchez were well positioned on opposite sides of the warehouse floor, while Rojas had Lucas Lopez, Joaquin Gonzalez, and the Garcia brothers stationed in strategic spots - two on the second-floor balcony and two on opposite sides of the warehouse floor. The intruders had entered the warehouse undetected by the local gang, but now after the first shot, they were exposed.

The fully automatic weapons of Gomez and Sanchez fired continuously. Rojas and his men were equipped with semi-automatic weapons that fire a single shot with each pull of the trigger, putting them at a slight disadvantage against the rapid-firing type. After seeing that Santiago did not have a life-threatening wound, he tried to take cover from his exposed position but was hit in his left shoulder before scurrying behind a rack. The entire warehouse became a battlefield, with shots fired from every direction. Sanchez concentrated on the balcony area and was successful in taking Juan Garcia out with a spray of bullets. His body tumbled over the railing down to the floor. Gomez fought against Lopez and Gonzalez on the warehouse level. The men traded fire for several minutes, with Lopez being the next to be hit and die. However, Gonzalez made a decoy move to catch

Sanchez off guard; his bullets hit Sanchez directly in the forehead. After witnessing his brother's death, Jose Garcia made a bold move by jumping from the balcony onto the top of a high warehouse rack. Before he could descend to the ground to attack his assailant, Gomez riddled his body with bullets, and he toppled to the concrete floor. Gomez spun around to see Gonzalez charging him; he held his finger on the trigger to riddle Gonzalez with a dozen bullets. In obvious pain from his shoulder wound but forever faithful to his role as protector, Rojas staggered forward and fired at Gomez as he paused to load another clip. Gomez died with his finger still on the trigger, and bullets cascaded aimlessly toward the ceiling.

And just as quickly as it began, the shooting stopped. Rojas was bleeding profusely while mumbling to himself, *"Why didn't I assemble a larger force? This was supposed to be an easy set-up to entrap Curto. What went wrong?"*

While the shooting was going on, Curto remained out of the line of fire. Crouching down, he played a waiting game. He was thinking he was out of harm's way until he felt a gun barrel forcibly poking his back.

"Don't move, Julius." Basso had put officers on duty around the clock to watch every move Curto made. They called Basso immediately when he left the house and alerted Basso of his destination as it became obvious he was going to the warehouse. Luckily, Santiago was late for the meeting, so Basso was able to sneak in before the lockdown. He heard the entire conversation between Santiago and Curto.

Curto was again caught off guard. "What are you doing here, Gene?"

"Tailing you. I was in Lancaster and learned all about your trip there with a blond who we both know was Jennifer Ambrose. We followed the leads to the Italian restaurant, and the whole thing started to add up. The affair, the baby, the blood on her belt, the dark blue thread on her dress – I even deduced your trick with the cut on you hand. That was very clever, allowing me to smash my racket into your hand to cover up the bite injury."

Curto, being younger and stronger than Basso, used all his military training to good advantage. When he saw Basso pause in his explanation, he spun with such a sudden forceful movement, it caused Basso's gun to fly out of his hand and slide under a bin as he fell to the ground. Standing over the fallen Basso, Curto pulled his Glock from his holster and pointed it directly at his head.

"Gene, I have to hand it to you. You are a smart detective, but in this case, you outsmarted yourself."

Trying to stall the inevitable, Basso started talking fast. "Julius, why did you do it? Having an affair is one thing, but killing that person is another. Does it have anything to do with your still being a Santiago goon? Yes, I figured that out as well, and you and Santiago just confirmed that. Was she going to reveal your duplicity. You might be stronger than I am, but you are not as smart. I plan on having the lab match the DNA of the unborn child to yours, the blood on the belt to yours, the threads to your dark blue suit."

"Well, you are not going to live long enough to tell anyone all that."

"Julius, before you kill me, I must know something. I can see why you felt you had to get Ambrose out of the picture if she threatened to expose you. But I do not for the life of me understand why you killed Aspect. Yes, I know you killed Susan Aspect. That is an obvious conclusion. Again, you screwed up. You used the same weapon on both."

Curto opened up, feeling there was no harm in explaining his reasoning. "Remember, I was trying to pin the blame on Raphael Pino, so it had to be the same weapon and method."

"But why kill her?"

"Don't you see. If I could divert the emphasis from the Ambrose killing, it would create confusion in your investigation. Her killing was simply a ruse to throw you off track, and it certainly did just that. You could not connect the dots to the two murders. Maybe it would suggest a serial killer, maybe put more suspicion on Pino or even Santiago. She was nothing more than a diversionary tactic. As a Navy SEAL veteran, you should understand the necessity for a move like that. I also tried to discredit Aspect's defense tactics of Pino simply to establish motive for the Ambrose murder. Actually, she did nothing improper as defense counsel. The sting on him was by the book, and she could not claim entrapment. By the way, how did you find me tonight."

"I've had a tail on you ever since I returned from Lancaster. A phone call from the stakeout cops was all it took. You don't think I came here alone, do you?"

"Forget about it, Gene. There is nobody back here except the two of us, and it sounds as though there is nobody left standing out there either. He cocked his weapon, pointed it directly at Basso's forehead, and a shot rang out. Santiago had painfully crawled on one side, leaving a trail of blood as he inched himself forward to the aisle where Curto stood ready to fire at Basso. Santiago was quicker and lodged a bullet into the center of Curto's back. Basso grabbed Curto's gun as he was falling and fired at the prone Santiago, hitting the drug lord in the head. He died instantly.

Thinking he was out of danger, Basso rose to retrieve his own gun from under the shelving. As he was bending down, he saw Rojas standing over Santiago's body. In keeping with his long-standing loyalty to Santiago, he aimed his gun at Basso just as three police officers shot him simultaneously. Basso was not lying to Curto about having called for backup. As soon as the first shots rang out, the police department's tactical group of ten men complete with bullet proof vests were authorized to break down the door and invade the premises. One stray bullet did hit a member of the tactical group in the arm, but no overt action was taken. They witnessed the gun fight, but they held their fire as the two opposing groups eliminated each other.

"Are you all right, Detective?"

Those were the sweetest words Basso ever heard.

CHAPTER 41: THE AFTERMATH

The tactical unit closed off the warehouse perimeter to deny access to all, posted guards all around, and called it a night. Central Penn Warehousing would not be open tomorrow for business as usual. Employees arriving at work would be told to return home until further notice. No details were to be given to any of them.

Basso was helped to his car by one of the force and headed away from the devastating site that saw eight men die. It was now after 2 a.m., so there was no way he was going to his office in the morning at his normal starting time. Besides, he still had one other job to complete before he could rest.

Basso drove to Camp Hill to the home of Julius Curto, knowing that his ringing a doorbell at that time of night would set panic into the heart of his wife. Eszter answered the door in her robe after identifying Basso through the peep hole. She took one look at him and began crying profusely. Basso took her in his arms and tried his best to comfort her, but it was no use. She was wailing in agony, and he had not yet told her what happened. As all police officers' spouses instinctively know, calls at that hour from his or her partner can mean only one thing.

When she regained some of her composure, he told her Julius had been shot in a gun battle with some drug hoodlums, but he decided tonight was not the time to mention her husband was a double murderer and a traitor to his job, to her, to his partner, to the city, and to himself. That would have to wait. For now, the fact that he was dead was more than she could handle, so he saw no need to destroy her completely tonight with the rest of it. He did not die in the line of duty, making it even more difficult for Basso. The police administration would never allow a coverup, given the gravity of the crimes.

They talked quietly for twenty minutes, then Basso suggested she get some rest. She could come down to the precinct in the morning to learn all about it and handle all the administrative tasks that go with the death of a police officer. Through all her sorrow and pain, Eszter kept saying over and over, "What am I going to say to Robert and Ronald." She had a bitter task to face, and she was all alone in doing it.

Basso left when he felt she was as calm as she could be in these circumstances, promising he would be there for her tomorrow and anytime thereafter. Before going to sleep, he texted Gerri Allen to let her know he was fine and promised to brief her in the morning. Then he collapsed into his bed. But sleep would not come. His mind kept spinning through all the events of the last few days. Realizing he was inches away from death from a gunshot from either Curto, Santiago, or Rojas weighed heavily on him. He asked his mind question after question, but no answers came. Finally, he fell asleep, but his human chronometer still set off an alarm in his brain at 7 a.m. Forcing himself to ignore it, he struggled to get back to sleep. Deciding it was hopeless, he showered, dressed, and drove to the precinct.

Captain Ralph O'Brian was waiting for him in his office. Wanting a full briefing on the night's happenings, Basso went through the entire scenario of how he pieced together the clues to the Ambrose murder, had an around-the-clock tail put on Curto, was alerted by his stakeout officers that Curto was on the move, called out the tactical force as backup, learned the motive of the Aspect killing, and was nearly killed three times. He explained the deaths of Curto and Santiago, plus the deaths of Tomás Rojas, several of his henchmen, and two others of whom he had no idea as to their identity. The bullet wound to one of the tactical force was superficial.

O'Brian told him the other two arrived in the country on falsified passports very recently, and their actual identity had not been learned. They were working on it, but he doubted they would be able to trace these men back to the people who sent them.

"Ralph, Eszter will be coming in sometime this morning. We must decide what we tell her. There certainly won't be any 21-gun salute, so we need to be brutally honest with her. It will be one of the hardest things I have ever had to do."

That morning, droves of policemen descended on the warehouse. The financial records were commandeered, all known bank accounts of Santiago and the company were frozen, and the FBI undertook a thorough audit of the financial records they confiscated. The DEA was also on hand searching for evidence that drugs were stored at the warehouse. They needed a court order, since the property in the warehouse was not the property of Central Penn Warehousing. Title to goods stored in a commercial warehouse does not transfer but remains with the warehouse's client. This caused a huge uproar from the legitimate companies storing their goods there, but a judge granted the request, and the DEA went on a hunt through an enormous amount of merchandise. It payed off; Santiago had stored his illegal inventory of drugs from Moreno in 55-gallon drums in a separate area apart from that of the paying customers. The DEA also found the drug processing room used by Rojas's crew to cut, process, and package the product before distribution.

To their dismay, none of the contraband could be linked back to the source. They had put one czar out of business, but they had not been able to identify where the drugs originated. Alejandro Moreno was not linked to any of Santiago's dealings.

From a financial side, the FBI auditors in the ensuing days found the first link in the money laundering in the Bahamas, but from there, the trail ended. They were, however, able to find the account in the Bahamas used to pay Curto under an assumed name. It contained over $2 million dollars, all of which was confiscated by the federal government through negotiations with the Bahamian government.

Chief Financial Officer John Caravacca, as well as the controller, and the treasurer of Central Penn Warehousing were arrested, tried, and convicted of charges for money laundering, drug conspiracy, and wire fraud, plus numerous other SEC violations. The government had to prove the money originated from a specific criminal activity, and finding the drugs in drums at the warehouse and the cutting room gave them the proof they needed. All three men currently are serving ten years each in a federal prison for white collar criminals, and they were fined $100,000 each.

Over the days of the audit, the FBI also uncovered records of very large payments made by Santiago to Mayor

Bill Bixby, a city councilman, a judge, and a high-ranking member of the prison parole board. After being confronted with the evidence, they admitted accepting bribes to look the other way from Santiago's illegal activities. George Ziegler refused to allow them to plead to a lesser charge of accepting campaign contributions in violation of the rules, particularly after the offshore accounts were found. Bixby had the impudence to rationalize his actions by claiming the people Santiago's drug business targeted were not worth protecting, a position that contradicted the very oath of office he swore to uphold. The four men pled guilty and were sentenced to six to ten years in federal prison. These convictions for corruption in office were all upheld by the appeals court, forcing them to begin serving their time.

Fortunately for Basso's brother Francesco, he was not implicated in any of the scandal. He was overjoyed that the FBI found the bribery evidence before he was forced to go public with the information he intended to disclose. He realized taking his brother's advice was the only way to go. What he did not realize is how close he came to becoming a victim in a conspiracy to silence him.

Further impacting the Santiago estate was the completion of the IRS net worth audit by Alberto Basso and his team. The government claimed that unreported income over the scope of their three-year audit period resulted in unpaid taxes of over 150 million dollars, excluding interest and penalties that applied. Lawyers for the estate negotiated with the IRS, since the evaluation process was not precise and explicitly documentable in a new worth determination. The final settlement found the estate of Diego Santiago paying 85 million dollars to the government.

It took about a year for the legal aspects of the Santiago holdings, the SEC audit of the warehouse, and the IRS personal tax audit to be settled. Trading price of its shares plummeted after Santiago's death. Santiago was the majority stockholder in the company, and his daughter Barbara inherited his shares. Her husband Damian DeRiso was appointed president of Central Penn Warehousing, Inc., and he was successful in building the business back to its former level of operation by regaining the confidence of the previous legitimate customers while expanding the customer base. DeRiso hired back most of the hourly staff, but all the professionals, including the lawyers, found employment elsewhere. Disheartened and embittered, a grieving Grace Fuller retired but remained in constant denial of the allegations against her employer. Her pension was protected by the Pension Benefit Guarantee Corporation, a federal government agency created by the Employee Retirement Income Security Act of 1974 and could not be expropriated.

The rehabilitation program with the State Board of Probation and Parole was cancelled. The few parolees who remained alive after the death of Santiago and Rojas were required to find suitable work in 60 days or be forced to serve out the remaining time of their original sentences. Since their warehouse jobs were a cover for the covert work they did as drug enforcers, their employment at Central Penn Warehousing was terminated. None returned to prison nor were any deported.

The attendance at the funeral of Diego Santiago was far smaller than realized at his father's. Missing were most of the celebrities and notables who chose not to be linked to the man despite their willingness to accept his generosity while he was alive. Prominence is a fleeting mistress.

Roberto Santiago did not return to the company but chose instead to continue his life as a playboy enjoying the money his father had bequeathed him not touchable by the government. Evergreen Cay in the Bahamas was immune to confiscation, enabling Barbara Santiago DeRiso and Roberto Santiago to inherit it free of any debt.

CHAPTER 42: THE RIGHT THING

The day after the shoot-out at the warehouse, Gianni Basso and Gerri Allen were finally able to find some free time to talk privately, but not before he, the chief of police, and the mayor took the podium in front of a room full of reporters and cameras. The day had been hectic, what with the media having a feeding frenzy over the revelations Basso and O'Brian announced at the scheduled news conference. Newspaper, TV, and radio reporters packed the police conference room to hear the heroics of Gianni Basso and the defamation of Julius Curto. Adding to their plethora of newsworthy events was the death of Diego Santiago, the most notable crime boss on the East Coast. For Joan McCabe of the Harrisburg Tribune, it was the biggest story she ever covered.

Basso was praised during the press briefing not only for his intuitive detective work in solving the murders, but for his bravery in risking his life in the line of duty and almost being killed. Humbly, Basso told the reporters the police tactical unit, who were called in as backup, were the real heroes.

"They are the ones who made sure the gangsters were controlled, and they are the ones who saved my life."

All the media coverage was not positive. Although they did play up the solving of the murders and the elimination of one drug lord, they were brutal in their attack on the police hiring practices. The Tribune was particularly acrid on this point, calling out the mayor and the chief of police for allowing a mole to flourish within the department for so many years.

"Why weren't Mr. Curto's activities with the Santiago drug empire discovered earlier?" McCabe demanded.

Ralph O'Brian tried his best to respond, saying, "the police attempt to screen psychologically all new applicants, but most times that type of behavior is latent and without reliable indicators predicting its potential to surface."

After the press conference, Basso and Allen met with Eszter Curto to tell her the full story even though it was just as hard for them to say it as it was for Eszter to hear. She confessed she had suspicions of another woman and had hired a private investigator to learn more, but it came to no avail. Basso told her the P.I. could not have uncovered anything, since Julius' partner in his affair was already dead before the investigator was hired. For her own peace of mind, she wanted to know everything, so Allen and Basso painfully filled her in on the events from start to finish. It has been said the truth hurts, and in this case, it hurt the speaker and the listener.

"Are you going to stay in the area, Eszter?"

"My sons were born in this town. I would never go back to Iraq, so yes, we are going to pick up the pieces and get on with our lives. Julius was the most wonderful human being I ever met or would ever hope to meet, but I will pull through this and survive. Plus, I still have our incredible two sons, and soon our daughter, who will be an eternal reminder to me of their father. I have plans to bring their grandparents to America soon."

"Do you plan to get a job?"

"Yes, my first love is biochemistry, which I worked at in Iraq. There will be plenty of opportunities for me here."

"No doubt. With your educational level and experience, you will have no problem."

Within a few days, all the furor died down, and the story was no longer front-page news. That is, until the trials of the public officials and the finance group from the warehouse started the excitement all over again.

Basso and Allen began tackling the backlog of cases that had piled up during the Curto/Santiago case, as it became known. After about a month, Allen said to Basso, "You know,

Gene, I could perform the same case research work I do now from home as a private citizen. There really isn't any reason for me to stay on this job any longer."

"Gerri, are you proposing to me?"

"I think you could say that is what I am doing."

Gianni Basso and Gerri Allen were married a month later. She was required to resign her post with the police department, which was fine with them. They honeymooned for three weeks in the Caribbean's Lower Grenadines, chartering a 60-foot sailing vessel to island-hop starting in Grenada, then making stops in Petit St. Vincent, Palm Island, Tobago Cays, St. Lucia, and a few other dots on the map before leaving the boat in St. Vincent for a flight back home. Bareboating, the term used for chartering a yacht and doing the navigating and crewing oneself without hiring a captain or staff, was a favorite pastime of Basso. After his six years in the Navy, he could never get the love of the ocean out of his system.

A young rising star with the police bureau was assigned to Basso as his new partner. He was certainly well qualified for the job and had an excellent record of accomplishment in the vice squad from where he transferred. Developing the trust factor with a new man, however, proved difficult for Basso. It was not an easy adjustment to make after having allowed himself to get comfortable, probably too comfortable, with Curto over their years together. The Curto/Santiago case continued to haunt Basso despite the passage of time because of the betrayal he experienced from a man he not only called his partner but his friend.

"You know, Gerri, it is really ironic. Julius Curto's first assignment on the force was to infiltrate the Santiago empire and attempt to bring it down, and it looks like he was successful in accomplishing that goal through his death."

EPILOGUE

With the death of Diego Santiago, the supply of drugs to Greenfield residents was provisionally halted. The police make a concerted effort to ensure there was not an immediate resurgence of the situation that had plagued the city for so many years. With a change in city government administration and without the powerful influential interference of Santiago and his money, law enforcement was better able to deal with the problem and do its job. Drug pushers were arrested and prosecuted, although the problem would have died a natural death without the supply chain of Santiago's empire available to them. No heir apparent surfaced to assume his notorious throne. The city introduced a program to assist those who fell victim to the greed of the people who profited from the misery of others. Support groups emerged, and immunity from prosecution was granted to anyone who voluntarily entered the rehabilitation program. It proved to be very successful.

The benefits from these efforts were felt throughout the city, but nowhere more than at Wilson Park. Over time, people returned to the park knowing the police had greatly enhanced security. The pool reopened, the ballfield again was used by a softball league sponsored by local business owners, joggers were regularly seen circling the perimeter, and the grounds were kept manicured for picnickers and sun bathers. And once again, the historic landmark of the park - its stone bridge - became its focal point.

ABOUT THE AUTHOR

Frank Rubolino has been a writer and photographer for decades, having published over 2,000 feature articles, photo essays, and reviews of live and recorded music in both hard copy and on-line magazines. He also has published interviews of noted musicians and has written liner notes featured with the recordings of prominent performers. He is a native of Pittsburgh but currently lives in Houston, Texas. This is his first publication in the field of fiction.

CPSIA information can be obtained
at www.ICGtesting.com
Printed in the USA
BVHW072021060320
574261BV00001B/2